sinner

sinner

maggie stiefvater

SCHOLASTIC INC.

Copyright © 2014 by Maggie Stiefvater

This book was originally published in hardcover by Scholastic Press in 2014.

All rights reserved. Published by Scholastic Inc. *Publishers since 1920.* SCHOLASTIC and associated logos are trademarks and/or registered trademarks of Scholastic Inc.

The publisher does not have any control over and does not assume any responsibility for author or third-party websites or their content.

No part of this publication may be reproduced, stored in a retrieval system, or transmitted in any form or by any means, electronic, mechanical, photocopying, recording, or otherwise, without written permission of the publisher. For information regarding permission, write to Scholastic Inc., Attention: Permissions Department, 557 Broadway, New York, NY 10012.

This book is a work of fiction. Names, characters, places, and incidents are either the product of the author's imagination or are used fictitiously, and any resemblance to actual persons, living or dead, business establishments, events, or locales is entirely coincidental.

ISBN 978-0-545-65459-3

12 11 10 9 8 7 6 5 4 3 2   17 18 19 20/0

Printed in the U.S.A.   40
First printing 2015

The text type was set in Adobe Garamond Pro.
Book design by Christopher Stengel

This one's for the readers who are always there. You know who you are.

"Down, down, down. Would the fall never come to an end?"
— Lewis Carroll, *Alice's Adventures in Wonderland*

"Where you used to be, there is a hole in the world, which I find myself constantly walking around in the daytime, and falling in at night. I miss you like hell."
— Edna St. Vincent Millay, *Letters*

Not the End, but Right Before

I am a werewolf in L.A.

You asked why I did it.
Did what?
— *The whole thing, Cole. The everything.*
You, hyperbolic you, don't really mean *the everything*. You mean the last five weeks. You mean me burning down your place of work. Getting kicked out of the only sushi restaurant you liked. Stretching your favorite leggings and then tearing them running from the cops.

You mean why I came back here.

That is not the everything, even if it feels like it now.
— *I know why you did it.*
Yeah?
— *You just did it so you could say "I am a werewolf in L.A."*
You're always telling me I only ever do things because they will make good TV, or say things because I know they'll make good lyrics later, or do things because I like the way I look doing them. You say it like I have a choice. Things come in my eyes

and ears and through my pores, and my receptors begin to pulse restlessly and my neurons fire like cannons, and by the time everything gets into my brain and comes out the other side, it's all transformed into a different species, pixels or channels, glossy or matte. I can't change the way I'm made. I'm a performer, a singer, a werewolf, a sinner.

Just because I'm singing it for a crowd doesn't make it untrue.

If we make it through this alive, I'm going to tell you the truth of why. And this time you had better believe me.

I came back for you, Isabel.

CHAPTER ONE

· COLE ·

F♮ LIVE: *Today on the wire we have young Cole St. Clair, lead singer of NARKOTIKA, giving his first interview in — well, a long time. Two years ago he went facedown during a concert, and right after that, he went missing. Totally off the radar. Cops were dredging rivers. Fangirls wept and built shrines. Six months later, news came out that he was in rehab. And then he was just gone. But it looks like soon we'll be hearing some new music from America's favorite rock prodigy. He's just signed a deal with Baby North.*

"Are you a dog person or a puppy person, Larry?" I asked, craning my head to look out the deeply tinted window. View out the left: blinding-white cars. View out the right: fossil-fuel-black cars. Mostly Mercedes with a chance of Audis. Sun glittered and dazzled off their hoods. Palm trees sprouted from the landscape at irregular intervals. I was here. Finally here.

I had an East Coaster's love of the West Coast. It was simple and pure and unadulterated by anything as obscene as the truth.

My driver looked at me in the rearview mirror. His eyelids

were halfhearted tents pitched over his red eyes. He was a dismal inhabitant of a suit unhappy to house him. "Leon."

My cell phone was an insubstantial sun against my ear. "*Leon* is not a possible answer to that question."

"That's my name," he said.

"Of course it is," I said warmly. I hadn't thought he looked like a Larry, now that I thought about it. Not with that watch. Not with that mouth. Leon was not from L.A., I decided. Leon was probably from Wisconsin. Or Illinois. "Dogs. Puppies."

His mouth deflated as he considered it. "I suppose puppies."

Everyone always said puppies. "Why puppies?"

Larry — no, Leon! — stumbled over his words, as if he hadn't considered the idea before. "They're more interesting to watch, I guess. Always moving."

I couldn't blame him. I would've said puppies myself.

"Why do you think they get slow, Leon?" I asked. My phone was very hot against my ear. "Dogs, I mean?"

Leon didn't hesitate with this answer. "Life wears them down."

F♮ LIVE: *Cole? Are you still there?*

COLE ST. CLAIR: *I sort of took a mental vacation during your intro. I was just asking my driver if he preferred dogs or puppies.*

F♮ LIVE: *It was a long intro. Does he have a preference?*

COLE ST. CLAIR: *Do you?*

F♮ LIVE: *Puppies, I guess.*

COLE ST. CLAIR: *Ha! Double ha. Larry — Leon — sides with you. Why did you choose puppies?*

F♮ LIVE: *I suppose they're cuter.*

I held the phone away from my mouth. "Martin from *F Natural Live* chose puppies, too. Cuter."

This knowledge didn't seem to cheer Leon very much.

COLE ST. CLAIR: *Leon finds them more entertaining. More energetic.*

F♮ LIVE: *That's exhausting, though, isn't it? I guess if it's someone else's puppy. Then you can watch it and the mess is someone else's problem. Do you have a dog?*

I *was* a dog. Back in Minnesota, I both tenanted and belonged to a pack of temperature-sensitive werewolves. Some days, that fact seemed more important than others. It was one of those secrets that meant more to other people.

COLE ST. CLAIR: *No. No, no, no.*

F♮ LIVE: *Four nos. This is an exclusive for our show, guys. Cole St. Clair definitely doesn't have a dog. But he might have an album soon. Let's put this in perspective. Remember when this was big, guys?*

On his end of the line, the opening chords of one of our last singles, "Wait/Don't Wait," sang out, pure and acidic. It had been played so often that it had lost every bit of its original emotional resonance for me; it was a song about me, written by someone else. It was a great song by someone else, though. Whoever came up with that bass riff knew what he was doing.

"You can talk," I told Leon. "I'm sort of on hold. They're playing one of my songs."

"I didn't say anything," Leon replied.

Of course he hadn't. He was suffering in silence, our man Leon, behind the wheel of this fancy L.A. limo.

"I thought you were telling me why you were driving this car."

It poured out of him, his life story. It began in Cincinnati, too young to drive. And ended here in a hired Cadillac, too old to do anything else. It lasted thirty seconds.

"Do you have a dog?" I asked him.

"It died."

Of course it had died. Behind us, someone honked. A black car or a white car, and almost certainly a Mercedes or an Audi. I had been in Los Angeles for thirty-eight minutes, and eleven of those had been in traffic. I've been told there are parts of L.A. where the cliché of continuous traffic is not true, but I'm guessing that's because no one else wants to frequent them. I was not excellent at sitting still.

I swiveled to look out the back window. There, in a sea of monochrome, a yellow Lamborghini idled, bright as a child's toy, a knot of palm trees as backdrop. And on the other side of it was a swimming-pool-colored Volkswagen bus driven by a woman with dreadlocks. As I turned back around, sliding down the leather seat, I saw the sun glance off warehouse roofs, off terra-cotta tile, off forty million pairs of huge sunglasses. Oh, this place. *This place.* I felt another surge of joy.

"Are you famous?" Leon asked as we crept forward. My song still played in my ear, tinny.

"If I was famous, would you have to ask me?"

The truth was that fame was an inconsistent friend, never there when you needed it, ever-present when you needed some time away from it. The truth was that I was nothing to Leon, and, statistically, everything to at least one person within a five-mile radius.

In the car beside us, a guy in Wayfarers caught me gazing at California and gave me a thumbs-up. I returned it.

"Is this interview on the radio right now?" Leon asked.

"That's what they tell me."

Leon ran through the stations. He blew right by "Wait/ Don't Wait." I shook his seat a little until he backtracked.

"This one?" He looked dubious. My voice crooned through the speakers, coaxing listeners to remove at least one item of clothing and promising them — *promising* them — it would be worth it in the morning.

"Doesn't it sound like me?"

Leon looked at my face in the rearview mirror, as if looking at me would give him his answer. His eyes were so very red. This, I thought, was a man who felt things deeply. It was hard to imagine being as sad as he was in a place like this, but I guessed I had been sad here once, too.

That felt like a long time ago, though.

"I suppose it does."

On the radio, the song drew to a close.

F♮ LIVE: *So there we are, people. Remember now? Oh, the summers of rocking out to NARKOTIKA. Okay, Cole. Are you there, or are you conducting another study on dogs?*

COLE ST. CLAIR: *We were musing on fame. Leon has not heard of me.*

LEON: *It's not your fault. I just don't listen to much else but talk radio, or sometimes jazz.*

F♮ LIVE: *Is that Leon? What's he saying?*

COLE ST. CLAIR: *He's more of a jazz guy. You'd know it if you saw him, Martin. Leon's very jazzy.*

I jazzed my hands for the rearview mirror. Leon's hooded eyes regarded me for a sad moment. Then one of his hands crept off the gearshift to do 50 percent of jazz hands.

F♮ LIVE: *I believe you. Which album of yours are you going to tell him to start with?*

COLE ST. CLAIR: *Probably just that cover of "Spacebar" that we did with Magdalene. It's jazzy.*

F♮ LIVE: *Is it?*

COLE ST. CLAIR: *It's got a saxophone in it.*

F♮ LIVE: *I'm blown away by your knowledge of musical genres. Say, let's talk about that deal with Baby North. Have you worked with her before?*

COLE ST. CLAIR: *I had alw —*

F♮ LIVE: *I wonder if everybody knows who Baby is?*

COLE ST. CLAIR: *Martin, it's very rude to interrupt.*

F♮ LIVE: *Sorry, man.*

LEON: *I know who she is.*

COLE ST. CLAIR: *Really? Her and not me? Leon knows who she is.*

F♮ LIVE: *He is jazzy. Does he want to sum it up for the listeners at home? I mean, if he's not in danger of crashing?*

I offered my phone to Leon.

"This is a hands-free state," Leon said.

"I'll hold it for you," I offered, expecting him to refuse. But he shrugged, agreeable.

Sliding behind his seat, I held my phone to his ear. He had one of those haircuts with a very defined ear shape carved into the side of it.

LEON: *She's that lady with the web TV shows. The crazy one. It's Sharp Teeth Dot Com, but she spells it strange. With numbers, I think? Sharp t-three-three-t-h dot com? I don't know. It might be ones instead of ts.*

F♮ LIVE: *Do you watch any of her shows?*

LEON: *Sometimes in between pickups, I watch on my phone. She had that one last year. That drug lady with the baby?*

F♮ LIVE: *Kristin Bank. That's the one that put sharpt33th .com on the radar for most people. Who knew serialized rehab pregnancy could be such a draw? Did you like it?*

LEON: *I don't know if they are shows that you like or don't like. You just watch them.*

F♮ LIVE: *I know exactly what you mean. Okay, let's have Cole again. You might be wondering why she's interested in putting him on an original web TV program. Why do you think that would be, Cole?*

I was not an idiot. Baby North was interested in me because I came with a built-in audience. She was interested in me because I had a pretty face and knew how to do my hair better than most guys. She was interested in me because I overdosed on the stage of Club Josephine, and then vanished.

COLE ST. CLAIR: *Oh, my great music, probably. Also, I'm super charming. I'm sure that's it.*

Leon offered a limp smile. In front of us, the cars sluggishly shuffled like playing cards. The sun rippled thickly off mirrors and reflectors. The palms lining the highway were lanes and lanes away. I couldn't believe I was here in California, looking right at it, and yet couldn't touch it yet. The interior of this car still felt at least two states away.

F♮ LIVE: *That sounds true. She's known for her taste in music.*
COLE ST. CLAIR: *I get that. That's a joke.*
F♮ LIVE: *You are a quick one.*
COLE ST. CLAIR: *I've never actually heard that before.*
F♮ LIVE: *Oh! I get that. That's a joke.*

Both Leon and I laughed out loud.

I'd met Martin. Though he had an eternally youthful voice, he'd been in music journalism for longer than I'd been alive. The first interview I'd done with him had been twenty minutes of tastelessly conveyed sexcapades, and then I'd met him in person and discovered he was old enough to be my father. Questions,

questions: How dare he sound twenty and be sixty? Did they make cosmetic surgery for your vocal cords? And just how badly had I offended him? But it turned out that Martin was one of those not-dirty older men who were amused by us still-dirty younger men.

F♮ LIVE: *How long are you taking to write and record this album? It's not long, right?*
COLE ST. CLAIR: *I think it's six weeks.*
F♮ LIVE: *That seems ambitious.*

If you looked up *ambition* on Wikipedia, my photo was the first thing that came up. I did have some material that I'd written while sitting alone at camp in Minnesota, but it had been strange to try to complete anything in a vacuum. No band. No listeners.

They'd come together in the studio.

COLE ST. CLAIR: *I've got a vision.*
F♮ LIVE: *Do you think you'll stay in L.A.?*

I wasn't particularly gifted at *staying* anywhere. But L.A. was where Isabel Culpeper was. Thinking her name was a dangerous, obsessive thought-road. I would not let myself call her until I had gotten to the house. I would not call her until I had thought of a theatrical way to tell her I was in California.

I would not call her until I was sure she would be happy I was here.

If she wasn't happy I was here, then . . .

With one move, I slapped shut the air-conditioning vents. I felt too close to a wolf for the first time in a long time. I felt that churn in my stomach that meant the shift was close.

COLE ST. CLAIR: *That depends. On if L.A. wants me.*
F♮ LIVE: *Everyone wants you.*

Leon held up his phone so that I could see the screen. He had just purchased "Spacebar" by NARKOTIKA (feat. Magdalene). He seemed happier than when I'd first met him, back when he was Larry. Outside, the heat tantalized. The asphalt shuddered in the exhaust. In a minute, we hadn't moved an inch. I was looking at L.A. through a TV screen.

And now I'd let myself think Isabel's name and there wasn't room for anything else. This car, this interview, this everything else — Isabel was the real thing. She was the song.

COLE ST. CLAIR: *You know what, Martin and Leon, I'm going to get out of the car now. Walk the rest of the way.*

Leon raised an eyebrow. "This isn't a walking road. I think it's illegal to walk on the shoulder. Do you see anyone else getting out of their cars and walking?"

No, I didn't. But I very rarely saw anybody else doing anything I was doing. And if I did, it usually meant it was time for me to stop.

Isabel —

F♮ LIVE: *Wait, what's Leon saying? Where are you?*

I'd already left the interview behind. It took every bit of my willpower to drag my attention back to Martin's questions.

COLE ST. CLAIR: *He's advising against my plan. We're on the 405. It's okay. I'm in good shape. You wouldn't believe the muscles we pick up in rehab. Leon, are you coming with me?*

I had already unbuckled my seat belt. I dragged my back-pack — the only thing I'd brought from Minnesota — to my side of the car. Leon's eyes opened wide. He couldn't tell if I was serious, which was ridiculous, because I was always serious.

Isabel. Only a few miles away.

My heart was starting to tumble inside me. I knew I should contain it, because I still had a long way to go. But I couldn't quite pull it off. This day had been so many weeks of planning and dreaming in the making.

F♮ LIVE: *Are you trying to get Leon to abandon a car on the interstate?*

COLE ST. CLAIR: *I'm trying to save his life before it's too late. Come with me, Leon. We shall walk away from this car, you and I. We shall find fro-yo and make the world better.*

Leon held up a helpless hand. Only moments before it had been a jazz hand. How he was letting me down.

LEON: *I can't. You shouldn't. Traffic is bad now, but in a few minutes, it'll be over. Just wait —*

I clapped my hand on his shoulder.

COLE ST. CLAIR: *Okay, I'm out. Thanks for having me on the show, Martin.*

F♮ LIVE: *Is Leon coming with you?*

COLE ST. CLAIR: *It doesn't look that way. Next time, though. Leon, enjoy the track. The account's all settled, right? Good.*

F♮ LIVE: *Cole St. Clair, former frontman of NARKOTIKA. A pleasure, as always.*

COLE ST. CLAIR: *Now, that I've heard before.*

F♮ LIVE: *The world's glad to have you back, Cole.*

COLE ST. CLAIR: *The world says that now. Okay. Gotta go.*

Hanging up, I opened the door. The car behind us let out the softest of honks as I climbed out. The heat — oh, the heat. It was an emotion. It owned me. The air smelled of forty million cars and forty million flowers. I felt a spasm of pure adrenaline, memory of everything I'd ever done in California and anticipation of everything that could be done.

Leon was staring out plaintively, so I leaned in swiftly. "It's never too late to change," I told him.

"I can't change," he replied. It crushed him.

I said, "Stab it and steer, Leon."

I slung my backpack over my shoulder, walked in front of an idling black Mercedes, and headed toward the closest exit.

Someone shouted, "NARKOTIKA forever!"

I blew him a kiss and then I jumped over the concrete barrier. When I landed, I was in California.

Chapter Two

· ISABEL ·

There was always room for more monsters in L.A.

"Isabel, beautiful. Time to work," said Sierra.

I *had* been working, watering Sierra's ridiculous plants. .blush., the tiny, concrete-floored outlet for Sierra (no.last. name's) clothing line, always contained more plants than clothing. Sierra loved the look of the ferns and palms and orchids, but she never wanted to put in the effort to make them flourish. Her talent rested more with the torture of dead things and inanimate objects. Things that you could stick a needle in without it getting angry. Things you could hang on a rack without violating human rights.

"I *am* working," I said, stabbing a fertilizer spike into potting soil. "I'm keeping your plants alive."

Sierra inserted two dried palm fronds into her updo, which was several shades closer to white than my blond hair. The addition worked for her; most things worked for someone who looked like her. She was a former supermodel. *Former* meaning *last year*. That's seven years in dog years or L.A. time.

"Plants live on sunshine, gorgeous."

"Sierra," I said, "did your parents ever explain photosynthesis to you? It's like this: When a plant and the sun love each other very much —"

"Christina is on her way," Sierra interrupted. "Please, Isabel. Endless smooches. Thanks."

Ah, Christina. *The* Christina. She was a very good spender when she was in the mood, and she liked to be waited on. Well, really she liked to know that she could be waited on if she wanted it. She did not want to be hovered over. She did not want to be patronized. She didn't want someone to hold a pair of leggings for her. She didn't want to be asked if she wanted to see it in champagne. She wanted a selection of attendants to be present so she could make a point of not asking them for anything.

So Sierra sent us all out to lean on the five pieces of furniture and examine our nails and text our boyfriends. All of us blond little monsters. Bangs sliced jagged and frosty, eyes lined kohl-black-sinister, lips bubblegum or cherry, all of us kissable as a plane crash.

Although I had only been here a few weeks, I was very good at this job. It wasn't that Sierra's other monsters were bad at elegantly folding tunics or boredly adjusting tanks on hangers. It was that they didn't know that the secret to selling Sierra's clothing was to lounge on the stool near the front, not giving a damn, demonstrating to every potential customer exactly what the clothing would look like if they were to buy it and not give a damn.

The other monsters weren't good at this because they gave a damn.

I was mostly focused on opening my eyes in the morning and moving my legs and eating enough food to keep my eyes opening and my legs moving. That was enough. If I added anything else to my emotional workload, I got angry, and when I got angry, I broke perfectly nice things.

Christina arrived. Her hair was crimped this time.

"Is this a new plant?" she asked Sierra.

"Yes," Sierra replied. "Isn't it the lushest of lush?"

Christina touched a leaf with a manicured nail. "What is it?"

Sierra touched it, too, but in a way that told me she was thinking of how it would look in her hair. "Lovely."

While Christina browsed around the store, I stretched over the stool on my belly, typing the names of famous neurosurgeons into Google image search on my phone. I wore two of Sierra's low, see-through tanks and a low-slung sisal belt and my favorite pair of leggings. Metallic and shimmery-rainbow-beautiful until you looked close and saw all the skulls. They were not Sierra's design. Not quite her thing in general. The leggings were a little ugly, once you got over how pretty they were.

I stopped looking at surgeons and typed in *define friendliness.* My mother, who had no friends, kept telling me that I had no friends other than my cousin Sofia and Grace, who lived in Minnesota. She was not wrong. My friendlessness was for a variety of reasons. For starters, I had only been at the school here for the last five months of my senior year. And second, it turned out that it was a lot harder to meet people once you'd graduated. Third, most of the girls at .blush. were older than I was and had twenty-something lives and problems and gave a damn when I did not.

And finally, I wasn't friendly.

"Everything she's wearing," Christina said.

Her voice was very close, but I didn't look up. I suspected, however, that *she* referred to me because of the way she had said it. It was like when there were two Isabels in my class growing up. They called us Isabel C. and Isabel D., but I knew which Isabel they meant before they got to the final initial.

I glanced up just long enough to see that Christina was staring at me in a mistrustful way. The others slithered and crawled to get her the tanks and the belt, unaware that in order to really get my look, you had to accessorize with death in the family and generalized heartbreak. The bass of the music overhead pulsed and whispered. I began to close windows on my phone. So many neurosurgeons were weird-looking. Cause or effect?

"Isabel," Sierra said. "Christina wants your leggings."

I didn't look up from the screen. "I'm not interested."

"Isabel, precious. She would like to buy them."

I flicked my eyes up to where *the* Christina stood. Some celebrities don't really look that famous in person. They're a little dustier or shorter when the camera's not looking. But Christina was not one of them. You'd know she was someone even if you didn't recognize her face. Because she looked *on purpose*.

It can be incredibly intimidating, even in this town.

It was clear from her expression that she was very used to this being the case.

But I looked from my waiting boss to beautiful Christina and I thought, *I have kissed more famous lips than yours.*

I shrugged and looked back at my phone. I typed in *frontal lobatomy*. It autocorrected. Turns out you can't spell *lobotomy* without *ooo*.

"Isabel."

I didn't look up. "The Artemis leggings in charcoal sort of do the same thing." When nobody moved, I lifted a limp hand and jerked it in the direction of the Artemis collection.

Fifteen minutes later, Christina had bought two tanks, a sisal belt, and two pairs of Artemis leggings, all for the price of a cut-rate tonsillectomy.

After she'd gone, Sierra told me, "You are such a bitch." She slapped my butt fondly.

I didn't really like people to touch me.

I shoved off the stool and headed toward the back. "I'm going to go sit with the orchids now."

"You've earned it."

What I had earned was a trophy for generalized disinterest. It felt as if it had taken all of my energy to be so limply disengaged.

As I pulled aside the linen curtain to the back room, I heard the front door open again. If it was Christina returning to make a second effort at my leggings, I was going to be forced to get loud, and I didn't like getting loud.

But it wasn't Christina I heard at the front of the store.

Instead, a very familiar voice said, "No, no, I'm looking for something very particular. Oh, wait, I just saw it."

I turned around.

Cole St. Clair smiled lazily at me.

CHAPTER THREE

· ISABEL ·

I gave so many damns at once that it actually hurt.

It was impossible to understand the truth of the moment. For starters, because Cole St. Clair was like *the* Christina, in that he generally appeared famous and not true and not really present in any given moment. There was always a dissonance between him and his surroundings, as if he were being smoothly and handsomely projected from a distant location.

And second: Cole was a wolf.

I didn't know if I was glad to see him or scared to see him. I had seen him laid out on the floor with a needle in his arm; I'd seen him shift into a wolf right in front of me; I'd seen him begging me to help him die.

And third: He had seen me cry. I didn't know if I could live with that.

Why are you here? Are you here for me?

"Heya," he said. He was still smiling that slow, easy smile at me. He had the best smile in the world, and lots of people had told him about it. His awareness of the smile's charms should have diminished its power, but that casual arrogance was part of its glory.

But I had been inoculated several months before, and since then, I'd been building up resistance. I was now immune.

We stood two feet apart. There was a buffer of history between us, and everything else pulling us together.

"You could have called," I said stupidly.

He grinned wider. He gestured grandly at himself, narrowly avoiding knocking over a rack of filmy shirts. "That would've ruined *this*."

The entire store looked different with him standing there. Like he'd pulled the afternoon sun in the door with him.

"What is *this*?" I asked.

"Ta-da." He was trying really hard to keep his Cole St. Clair smile on instead of his real one. Every time the real one came close to breaking through, my heart crashed.

I was aware that we had an audience. Not full-on staring — they were trying to be polite about it — but soft-focus curiosity. I wanted to take this out onto the sidewalk, or into the back, or at least look at my hands to make sure they weren't shaking like they felt they were, but I couldn't quite put it all together.

Here was the thing: I was in love with Cole.

Or had been. Or was going to be. I couldn't tell the difference.

I didn't know if he was here for me, though, and I couldn't take it if he wasn't. There was no way, actually, that he'd come all this way from Minnesota for me. Probably he just stopped by to say hi after moving here for something else. That was why he hadn't called first.

"Come on," I snapped. "Out back. You have time?"

He idled after me as if time was all he had. On the way through the opening into the back room, he raised his eyebrow at Sierra as if he was used to my tone.

Was this really happening?

I led him through the back room, which was cluttered with neonatal leggings and aborted tunics in every shade of khaki. Then we were out in the blue-washed alley. There was a trash bin, but it didn't smell — it was full of cardboard and dead plants. There was Sierra's old Beetle, but it didn't run — it was also full of cardboard and dead plants.

As I led him out beside the car, I talked myself down, explaining to myself all of the ways that his being here changed nothing, meant nothing, was nothing. Nothing, nothing.

I turned around, my mouth open to say something else scathing about him not calling me before showing up in my state, in my work, in my life.

But then he wrapped his arms around me.

My breath stopped as if he'd slapped a hand over my mouth. I didn't hug him back right away, because I didn't have enough information to know how to hug him back.

He smelled like strange airport hand soap and felt like a hole to fall into.

Cole stepped back. I couldn't tell from his face what was going on.

"Why did you do that?" I asked.

"Hello, too," he replied.

"*Hello* is what you say when you first call someone."

He was completely unoffended. "You don't call someone before *ta-da*."

"Maybe I don't like *ta-das*."

Honestly, I had no idea what I liked. I only knew that my heart was galloping so fast that my fingers were numb. Logically, I knew it was just from surprise, but I didn't know if it was like *Surprise, here is a cake* or *Surprise, you've had a stroke*.

In front of me, Cole's smile had emptied. His eyes were going blank, which was what happened to Cole when you hurt him. The real Cole vacated the situation and left his body standing by itself.

Cruelly, I was grateful for it, as grateful as I'd been for the brief glimpse of his true smile earlier. Because this reaction was real. It meant he really cared how I felt about this reunion. A smile I couldn't trust, but pain — I knew what the genuine article looked like.

"Look," I said. "You can't just show up and expect me to scream and giggle, because I'm not that person. So don't look all hurt because I'm not doing that."

His expression poured back into his face. This new one was hungry and restless. "Come somewhere with me. Let's go somewhere. Where is there to go around here? Let's go there."

"I have to work until six." Six? Seven? I couldn't even remember when my workday ended at the moment. Where were we? The alley behind .blush. The ocean breeze finding my skin, the starling overhead singing dreamily on a telephone wire, a dry palm leaf drifting down to rest on the concrete. This was real. This was happening.

He jumped from foot to foot — I had almost forgotten how he only stopped moving when things went badly for him. "What's the next meal? Lunch? Dinner? Yes. Have dinner with me."

"Dinner?" To this point, my evening plan had involved battling my way back to Glendale to the House of Divorce and Separation for an evening of estrogen and laughs that were the same as tears and vice versa. "Then what?"

He grabbed one of my hands. "Dessert. Sex. Life." He kissed my palm — not a sweet kiss. A kiss that made my skin twist with sudden, furious desire. His *mouth*.

Now I thought I *was* having a stroke. "Cole, stop, wait."

Stopping and waiting were not strong concepts for him.

"Cole," I said. I thought I might drown in this blue alley. "What?"

I started to say *stop* again, but that wasn't what I meant. I said, "Give me a second. God!"

He let me have my hand back. I stared at him. This was Cole St. Clair: sharp-edged jaw, brilliant green eyes, tussled and spiked dark brown hair. His smile would have been famous even without NARKOTIKA. I could tell he liked me staring at him. I could tell that he liked everything about this moment. Everything about it had been designed to catch me off guard, to make me react.

Hope and terror rose in me in equal measure.

I asked, "Why are you here?"

"You."

It was the perfect answer said in an imperfect way. He'd answered so fast. Just like that: *You.* It was so easy to say just one word. I wanted him to say it again, so that the second time around, I'd have a chance to *feel* something.

You.

Me.

"Okay," I said. I could feel a smile trying to happen. I hid it, fast. No way did he get a smile without calling me first. "Dinner. Are you picking me up?"

Cole laughed, a sound utterly unattainable in its pure joy. "I just did."

Chapter Four

· COLE ·

According to the clock in the taxi, I was incredibly late for my appointment with Baby North. Tardiness is not one of my multiple vices, and normally this would have bothered me. But nothing could knock me at the moment. I buzzed with the pleasant anxiety spurred by the razor line of Isabel's mouth.

When we had met, I had just saved my life by becoming a werewolf, and her brother had just died trying to stop being one. Isabel had been the only thing in Mercy Falls sharper than I was.

She was the only one who knew me.

Above me, the sun glowed in the sky, one thousand times more brilliant than the sun over Minnesota. Everything in this place was concrete and invented grass and palm spikes.

"What's the street again?" asked the cab driver. He wore a hat that was from a country that was not L.A., and he looked tired.

"Ocean Front Walk," I said. "Venice. If there are two. Probably not. But in the case of duplication."

"That's not a driving street," he replied. "It is on the beach. I will have to let you out. You will have to walk."

I didn't know if it was because I hadn't been to the West Coast for a long time, or because I hadn't been anywhere but Minnesota for a long time, but I kept being surprised by the fact of California. As we grew closer to Baby North's home, everything seemed familiar and dreamy, seen before on tour or in a dream or movie. The names of the streets — Mulholland Drive and Wilshire Boulevard — and the names painted on the signs — Hollywood, Cheviot, Beverly Hills — called up thoughts of blond hair, red cars, palm trees, endless summer.

Isabel —

Los Angeles. The first time I was here, a Yankee usurper, a bumbling almost-there, I snapped a photo of a Hollywood Boulevard street sign and sent it to my mother with a text: **guess what i'm famous**.

Now I actually was famous, though I didn't text my mother anymore.

I'm back.

It felt good. It was like when you had been unhappy and didn't know it until you weren't anymore. I had thought I was fine in Minnesota. Bored, lonely, fine.

California, California, California.

I could still feel the realness of Isabel in my arms. It was like the sun on my eyelids and the ocean scent in my mouth as I sucked the air in over my teeth. I'd been here before.

This time was going to be different.

I called my friend Sam back in Minnesota. He surprised me by answering immediately — he hated talking on the phone because he couldn't see the other person's face during the conversation.

"I'm here," I told him, picking at the taxi company decal on the interior of the car window. In the front seat, my driver had a hushed and intense phone conversation in another language. "My face is relaxed and content. My lips are curved upward."

Sam did not laugh, because he was immune to my charms. "Have you been to the place you're staying yet? Is it okay?"

"I'm fine, Mother," I replied. "I haven't been yet. I'm going to go see Baby now."

"I had the worst nightmare about you last night," Sam mused. "You went around Los Angeles and bit about twenty people so you could have a pack of wolves there, too."

There is that old chestnut that when someone tells you not to think about a specific image, you cannot *not* think of it. Sam had in effect forced me to consider the idea of multiple werewolves in Los Angeles, which should have occurred to me before now, but hadn't. It was not an entirely unromantic vision. Wolves galloping down Sunset Boulevard at dusk.

"Twenty," I scoffed. "I would never bite an even number of people."

"When I told you that it was a terrible idea, you told me you didn't want to be alone."

That did sound like me, but there was no way I'd go around biting myself new friends. While I dazzled into wolf form for only a few minutes at a time, most people had to wear their lupine bodies for months on end. Which was exactly what had happened back in Minnesota. That left me with only Sam and Grace, and they'd both decided to go to *college*, of all places. Summer school. In Duluth. Who did that?

"The worst part," Sam went on, "was that the clock was set to radio and when I woke up, your stupid song 'Villain' was playing."

"What a great station you must have had it set to." The taxi was slowing. I said, "I have to go. The future is here, decked in flowers and fruit."

"Wait —" Sam said. "Have you seen Isabel yet?"

My fingers still felt the shape of her. "Da. We embraced. Angels sang, Sam. Those fat ones. Cherubs. Cherubim. I must go."

"Don't bite people."

I hung up. The taxi driver put the car in park. "Now you walk."

I opened the car door. As I handed him some cash, I asked, "Want to come with me?"

He stared at me.

I got out. As I shouldered my bag on the sidewalk, a posse of young skater kids zoomed by. One of them shouted at me, "We're skateboarding!"

The others behind him keened joyfully.

My lips still tasted like Isabel's perfume.

The sun beamed overhead. My shadow was tiny under my feet. I didn't know how I could stand to be in my own head until dinner.

Baby North lived in a Venice Beach house that looked like it had been built by a caffeinated toddler. It was a collection of brightly colored blocks of different sizes stacked on one another and next to one another and joined by concrete stairs and metal balconies. It faced the endless tourist-dotted beach and the touchable blue ocean. It was a more mirthful establishment than I had expected.

People were afraid of Baby North. This was because she was a home wrecker, I thought, in the sense that she had destroyed the lives of the last seven people she'd put on television. It was sort of her brand. Get a train wreck, put it on television, wait for the explosions, toss a fluttering paycheck over the scene of the wreckage.

Everyone who signed a contract with her thought they would be the one to escape unscathed with their dignity and sanity, and they were all wrong.

None of them had seemed to know it was just a performance.

I climbed the concrete stairs. When I knocked on the door, it fell open. There was no point calling for her. The music inside was so loud that nothing was for sure except the purest of the trebles in the vocals and the ugliest of the bass from the drums. It was the sort of track sung by a girl who might possibly have been discovered on the Disney Channel.

When I stepped in, the air-conditioning hit me like a punch. I could feel every single one of my nerves tensing and considering their shape and species.

This was going to be a thing here.

It had been a very long time since I had been a wolf. And it had always taken a lot to convince my body to shift — a precipitous drop in temperature, an interesting chemical cocktail, a persuasive kick to my hypothalamus. The temperature difference now wasn't enough to do it, but it was enough to shock my body into the seductive memory of shifting.

Werewolf, werewolf.

That would be a good song.

Inside, the ceiling soared up above the concrete floor, all the way up to the exposed ductwork. There were four pieces of furniture. In the middle of them, Baby North stood bent over an iPad. I recognized her more from gossip blogs than our brief meeting years before. Her brown hair was cut in a heavy fringe over her deep-set eyes like a '70s model. She wore scrunchy leggings and some kind of smocky-tunic thing made out of canvas or linen or something monklike. She was short and pretty in a disconcerting way — a way to look at, not to touch. I had no idea how old she was.

I pointed toward one of the speakers overhead. The singer was chirruping something about how we should all call her and do something before it was too late. It was relentlessly catchy. "You know this stuff will make you go blind, right?"

When Baby turned to me, her smile was huge and genuine and world-eating. She tapped something on the iPad, and the music died instantly.

"Cole St. Clair," she said.

Though I was sure that she wouldn't break me, I felt a twinge. It was the way she said my name. Like it was a triumph that I was standing here.

"Sorry I'm late."

She clasped her hands to her chest, enraptured. "God, your *voice*."

A review of NARKOTIKA's last album had summed it up like so:

> The title track of Either One/Or the Other begins with twenty seconds of spoken words. The boys of NARKOTIKA are well aware that even without Victor Baranova's insistent drums and Jeremy Shutt's inspired bass guitar riffs, Cole St. Clair's voice would lure listeners to an ecstatic death.

Baby said, "This is the best idea I ever had."

My heart stuttered hard, just once, like an engine turning over. It had been a long time since I'd been on tour. Since I'd been out in public as a musician. Now, with my pulse faster, I couldn't believe that I'd thought I might give it up for good. It felt intentional, powerful, purposeful. I'd been in stasis for a year and now I was back on solid ground.

I was not a disaster.

Isabel was going to dinner with me.

I had been taken apart and put back together again, and this version of me was unbreakable.

Baby set her iPad on one of the four pieces of furniture — a birch ottoman or house pet or something — and circled me, hands still curled up on her breastbone. I had seen this posture before. It was a guy circling a car on the auction block. She had acquired me with a not-insignificant amount of effort, and she wanted to know if it was worth it.

I waited until she'd circled once.

"Happy?" I asked.

"I just can't believe you're real. You were dead."

I grinned at her. Not my real smile. My NARKOTIKA smile. One sly side of my mouth working wider than the other.

It was coming back to me.

"That *smile*," Baby said. She repeated, "This is the best idea I've ever had. Have you been to the house yet?"

Of course I had not. I had been haunting Isabel in Santa Monica.

"Well, you'll see it soon enough," she said. "The rest of the band moves in tomorrow. You want something to drink?"

I wanted to ask her about the band she'd assembled for me, but I thought it would sound like I was nervous. Instead, I asked, "You got a Coke?"

The kitchen was big and spare. Nothing looked particularly residential or even human. The cabinets were all thin slats of pale wood, and the walls were covered with exposed PVC pipes headed to the upstairs. The fridge looked like a surprise, like it ought to have been a vat of some commercial fluid instead. I needed no one to tell me Baby lived alone.

She handed me a Coke. One of those glass bottles, satisfyingly cold in your hand before you even cracked the cap. Baby watched me tip my head back to drink before she put hers to her lips. She was still appraising me. Looking at my throat and my hands.

She thought she knew me.

"Oh, I have —" She used just her pinky to pull open a drawer, and she withdrew a notepad. One of those tiny ones, palm-sized, that urged you to be brief. "This is what you wanted?"

I was pleased she remembered, but I just nodded coolly as I accepted the pad. I slid it into my back pocket.

"Look, kid," she said, "this is going to be hard."

My eyebrows twitched at "kid."

"I want you to know that I'm here whenever you need me. If the pressure gets to be too much, I'm just a phone call away. Or if you want to come over, that's fine, too. The house is only a mile from here." Her concern looked genuine, which surprised me. From her body of work, I'd expected an infant-devouring monster.

"Right," I said. "You told me. See, I already have your number programmed."

I flipped my phone around so that she could see her number and above it, in the name field, *Nervous Breakdown/Death*.

Baby laughed out loud, absolutely delighted.

"But I am serious. You'd be surprised how the cameras can get to you," she added. "I mean, they won't be on you all the time, of course. Mostly just for the episodes. A little bit in the house, you and the band. You pretty much tell them where and when you need them. But, you know, the viewers can be pretty cruel. And with your background . . ."

I just flashed my NARKOTIKA smile at her again. I've seen it, this smile of mine. In magazines and on blogs and in liner notes and in the ever-fond gaze of the mirror. I've heard it takes more muscles to frown than smile, and I'm sure it's true when it comes to this particular expression. It's just a twitch of the lips, really, just a narrowing of the eyes. Without a single word, it tells the other person that not only have I got them figured out, but I also have *it* figured out, where *it* stands for the world.

I mostly use it when I can't think of anything clever to say.

"It's been a bit much for others," Baby admitted, as if we didn't both know the fate of her previous television subjects. "Especially if they have a history of . . . well, substance problems."

I kept smiling. I swallowed the rest of my Coke and handed her the bottle.

"Let's see the house," I told her.

She smashed the Coke into a recycling bin the color of the sky. "What's the hurry? You East Coasters are always in a rush."

I was about to tell her I had dinner plans, and then realized I didn't want to tell her who I had them with. "I'm excited to see this future you've planned for me."

CHAPTER FIVE

· ISABEL ·

"I made sandwiches," my cousin Sofia said as soon as I walked in the door to the House of Dismay and Ruin that evening. She said it so fast that I knew that she had been waiting for me to walk in the door so that she could say it to me. Also, I knew that even though she said *sandwiches*, what she meant was *please look at this culmination of a culinary process involving more than four hours of preparation.*

I asked, "In the kitchen?"

Sofia blinked huge brown eyes at me. Her father — one of the numerous males who had been jettisoned from our collective lives — had aptly named her after the drop-dead gorgeous actress Sophia Loren. "And a little in the dining room."

Great. A sandwich that filled two rooms.

But there was no way I couldn't accept one, even if I was meeting Cole for dinner. Sofia was my cousin on my mom's side. She was a year younger than me and lived in breathless fear of failure, time passing, and her mother falling out of love with her. She also adored me for no reason I could discern. There were plenty of other people more worthy of her adulation.

"They wouldn't all fit in the kitchen?" I kicked off my slouchy boots at the front door, where they landed on a pair of my mother's slouchy boots. The empty coat rack rocked, tapping against the sidelights before righting itself. God, this place was soul-sucking. Although I'd been here for twenty-one Tuesdays, I still wasn't used to it. The McMansion was sterile enough to actually remove pieces of my identity every time I returned to it, insidiously replacing them with wall-to-wall white carpet and blond hardwood floors.

"I didn't want to be in anyone's way if they wanted to make something else," Sofia replied. "You look pretty today."

I waved a dismissive hand at her and walked into the dining room. Inside, I discovered that Sofia had spent the afternoon preparing a long, color-coordinated buffet bar of homemade sandwich toppings. She'd carved flower-shaped tomatoes, roasted a turkey, shaved a cow's butt. Conjured four different flavored vinaigrettes and aiolis. Baked two different kinds of bread in two different shapes.

It was arranged in a spiral with the vegetables in the very center. Her phone and huge camera lay at the end of the table, which meant she'd already put it on one of her four blogs.

"Is it all right?" Sofia asked anxiously. She crumpled a napkin in her lily white hands.

This was usually the part where people assumed Sofia suffered from heavy parental expectation. But the only thing I could tell that my aunt Lauren expected of Sofia was for her to be as stressed out as she was, and Sofia seemed to be doing that admirably. She was a finely tuned instrument that hummed in emotional resonance with whomever she was standing closest to.

"It's a gross overachievement as usual," I said. Sofia sighed in relief. I circled the table, examining it. "Did you vacuum the entire upstairs, too?"

Sofia said, "I didn't get the stairs."

"God, Sofia, I was joking. Did you really vacuum?"

Sofia peered at me with giant, luminescing eyeballs. She was such an imaginary animal. "I had time!"

I attacked a piece of bread with a serrated knife. Goal: sandwich. Side effect: mutilation. When Sofia saw my struggle, she hurried around the table to help me. Like a slow-motion murder scene, I wrestled the knife out of her hand and cut two uneven slices on my own. Aunt Lauren had no problem with her being so goddamn subservient, but it bothered the hell out of me.

"What about that book you were reading?"

"I finished it."

I selected roast beef and shaved Parmesan. "I thought you had that collage-sculpture-thing."

Sofia carefully watched me select a very green mayonnaise. "The first part is drying."

"What is this? Arugula? When is your erhu lesson?" I wasn't sure how I felt about Sofia as the whitest girl in the world taking erhu lessons. I couldn't decide if they counted as cultural appropriation or not. But Sofia seemed to enjoy them, and she was good at it, like she was good at all things, and no one on her erhu blog ever seemed to complain, so I kept my mouth shut.

"Watercress. It's not until tonight. I already practiced this morning."

"How about a nap? Normal people nap."

Sofia looked at me very heavily. What she wanted was for me to take it back and tell her that no, she was actually normal, everything was fine, she did not have to take deep breaths because this was not an emergency, this was life, and this was how it looked for everyone.

Instead, I returned her heavy gaze with a long blink, and then I took a bite of the sandwich. I couldn't believe Sofia had spent yet another afternoon with condiments as friends.

"You should get a life," I told her, swallowing my bite. "This is delicious and it offends me."

Sofia looked cowed. Whatever small creature that was my guilt was pricked. And now I was thinking about how my mother kept saying the same thing to me. Getting a life, I mean. I kept telling her I would get a life just as soon as I found people worth hanging out with. It was possible Sofia just hadn't found anyone worth her time yet.

I said, "Look, let's go out tonight. You can put on something red."

"*Out?*" she echoed, just as I remembered that I was supposed to be going out with Cole. I couldn't believe I'd forgotten, but on the other hand, I could. Because it was like having a good dream and forgetting it by the time you got downstairs for breakfast.

I felt a not entirely great sensation in my stomach, like someone was opening an umbrella inside it. It was like I was afraid of Cole, but it wasn't that. I was afraid that I wouldn't be who he thought I was. He'd been so charmed by the idea of me in California, like the state and I would be good for each other.

I wondered what I was walking into.

"Damn," I said. "Not tonight. I have dinner out. But tomorrow night. Red. You and I."

"*Dinner?*" she echoed.

"If you keep saying everything I say, it's canceled." I took another bite of the sandwich. It really was an exceptional sandwich. "Where's your mother?"

I never knew how to refer to my aunt Lauren. When I said *Lauren* to Sofia, it sounded like I was being snotty. When I said *your mother*, it sounded like I was being cold. And I could not say *your mom*, because I never said the word *mom* if I could help it. Probably because I was snotty and cold.

"At a closing," Sofia replied. "She said she'd be home before Teresa."

Teresa was my mother. When Sofia said it, she sounded neither snotty nor cold. She sounded respectful and fond. What ferocious magic that was.

The doorbell rang. Sofia looked martyred. "I'll get it."

She did not want to get it. Getting it meant she might have to speak to whoever was behind the door, and if she spoke to them, they might judge her clothing or hair or face or skills and find any of these things wanting.

"Oh, stop," I said. "Seriously. I'll get it."

Only it was a celebrity at the door. Before my brother died, he used to say that things came in threes. Three celebrities in one day. Not bad, even for the greater Los Angeles area. This one was a petite woman with a heavy brunette fringe half covering her sleepy green eyes. She was beautiful in a casual, vintage way that looked so effortless that it must have taken a long time to achieve. She was not a woman. She was a picture of a woman. It took me a moment to place her, because she was one of those third-tier celebrities who got featured in interior tabloid pages and on slow-news days on gossip blogs. Her name was something strange, I remembered. It was —

"Hi, I'm Baby North," she said. "Are you Isabel?"

She clearly thought I would be shocked into something by hearing my name, but I made it a point of pride to not be shocked by anything. Especially after my sense of surprise had pretty much been broken by the appearance of Cole St. Clair earlier in the day. I could *feel* Sofia behind me, though, and I could just tell that her mouth was ever so slightly open.

"Sofia," I said, stepping out onto the too-bright front stair, "would you go check the oven? I think I left it on."

There was a pause, and then Sofia vanished. She was not stupid.

"What's this about?" I asked. I didn't realize it wasn't polite until it came out of my mouth.

"An opportunity. If you'd give me a moment, I can introduce myself, tell you who I am, what I do —"

"I know who you are," I said. She was a very pretty vulture who reanimated corpses for web TV, but I didn't add that part, since I figured she already knew. I had an uncomfortable feeling inside me, a sense of why she was here, and some part of me knew I wasn't going to like it.

"Good!" she said, and she smiled hugely. I didn't trust that smile, because it was so great. It was wide and dimpled and symmetrical, a pinup girl from the past. "Can I come in?"

I surveyed her. She surveyed me. Her car sat on the curb behind my SUV. It was very chrome-y.

"No," I said.

Her mouth changed and became something much more real. "Well, okay."

Now manners were starting to catch up, so I added, with as much icy congeniality as I could manage, "It's not my house. I wouldn't want to compromise their privacy. And like I said, I know who you are."

"Clever," Baby said, like she really thought so. "Well, I'll make this quick, then: Are you dating Cole St. Clair?"

I tried to keep my face blank, but surprise robbed me of my secrecy. I knew my expression had given me away for half a second. "I don't think *dating* is a word I would use," I said.

"Right," she replied. "I'd like to ask you if you'd like to be on a show with him. Cool, right? It wouldn't take a lot of your time, and it can open up a lot of opportunities. 'Specially for a beautiful girl like you."

The uncomfortable feeling inside me grew and solidified. I held the doorknob. "What sort of show?"

"We're just doing a quick little show following him and his band around while they record their next album."

    Quick

        little

            show

I *knew* he wasn't here for me. I had known from the beginning.

But my foolish heart hadn't. It had wanted so badly to believe him. Now it was crushed up against my ribs by the growing terrible feeling inside me.

"I'm not interested," I said. "Like I said, we're not really dating."

"But even as a friend —"

"We're not even really friends," I said. I needed to shut this door *right* now, so that I could go scream or cry or smash something. "I just knew him for a while."

She studied my face, looking for the true answer, but I had gotten ahold of myself now, and I just gazed dead-eyed out at her from behind my eyeliner.

"If you change your mind," she said, and flicked out a card from the pocket of her linen smock.

I didn't change my expression, but I took it. I needed something to burn.

"It would be cool," Baby said. "The sort of thing you'd always remember. Just think about it."

She retreated down the sidewalk. I retreated back into the House of Dismay and Ruin. As I shut the door behind me, the house took another piece of my soul and transformed it into a piece of semi-custom cabinetry. My brain was exploding.

Sofia stood at the door to the living room. "Was that really —"

"Yes." I snatched my phone out. Punched in a number.

"What did she —"

I clawed my hand through the air and pointed at the phone. I heard a little tap as someone picked up on the other end.

"I thought you said you were here for me," I snarled.

"Hello," Cole replied. "I was just putting pants on. Unless you'd prefer me to leave them off."

"Act like you heard what I said."

"But I didn't."

"You said you were here for me. You lied."

There was a pause. The thing about a phone call is that you can't tell what is happening in the pause. I couldn't tell if it was a find-a-way-to-make-this-better pause or an I-am-genuinely-confused pause.

"What?" he asked finally.

"You're recording an album? You're going to be on television. Those things are not me."

Another pause.

"Say something."

"Something."

"Oh, ha. Well, listen. The problem is that you made me feel as if you came here just for me, and actually you came here to be on TV. You didn't come for me. You came here to be Cole St. Clair."

Exasperated, he replied, "That is backward."

"Funny how you didn't mention it before," I snapped. "Forget about dinner. Forget about it all."

"It's no —"

"Don't talk. In fact," I said, "drop dead."

I hung up.

Chapter Six

· COLE ·

When I was a wolf, I didn't remember anything about being me. I was reduced to my very basic self, solved for x. I was nothing more or less extraordinary than an animal.

It was what every other drug I had ever used was trying to be.

All I could think about after Isabel called was how if I was a wolf, this feeling would go away, at least for a little bit.

Instead I stood on the wire-strung balcony of the Venice house and looked out at the nighttime glitter of the city. The moon was a huge, round Hollywood set piece at the end of Abbot Kinney. Palm trees were exotic silhouettes against its face — movie-perfect, L.A.-perfect. This place: Were movies Hollywood-perfect because this place was, or had they built this place to perfection because of the movies?

Standing on the balcony, a silhouette myself against the purple sky, my depression was just another glamorous thing.

What should I have told her?

I was aware of the tiny camera pointed at my back. It was attached to the roofline and was one of several positioned throughout the compound — *compound* was really not the right word for it. My studio apartment, bright and wide-eyed and sky-lighted, occupied the second floor of a concrete block house. The first-floor apartment was slated for another band member. A wide deck led to a third apartment in a flat stucco house on the other side of the block. In between was a tiny yard full of plants that looked unrealistic to my foreign eyes.

Six weeks suddenly spooled out. I didn't understand how I'd ever thought that forty-two days was a short time.

I rocked my weight against the edge of the balcony. I wished for a beer; I wished for a needle to push into my skin.

No, those weren't me anymore. I was straight, clean, brand-new. Baby had hired me to fail, but I wasn't going to fail.

Isabel hadn't even given me a chance.

I thought about how quickly I could be a wolf. How completely it would empty my mind. Just for a few minutes. And unlike any of my other chemical salves, it left no marks and demanded nothing more from me. It wasn't an addiction.

But I didn't move.

Crossing my arms on the balcony, I laid my head on them, my chest slowly filling with black. My face was buried into the place where track marks had been before the wolf in me had erased them.

What was the *point* of being here, if not for her? What was the point of anything if I couldn't even work out this one thing. It was just dinner. It was just —

Isabel —

In the alley behind my apartment, I heard a car pull up and

stop. A car door opened and closed. A trunk opened and closed. The gate to the courtyard rattled.

I flicked my gaze up to an indistinct figure with a light-colored hat struggling at the gate. He/she/it spotted me. A female voice, probably, called, "A little help, man?"

I didn't move. I watched her/him/it work at the lock for another minute until the lockbox was persuaded to give up its key.

This had all seemed like such a fun game earlier when I'd been standing in Baby's house. But now? *Drop dead.*

It felt like I'd never stopped arguing with Isabel, way back in Minnesota.

It was impossible how fast everything had gone to shit in my heart.

Down below, the figure entered the courtyard. She had a bag. It didn't seem to have wheels but she dragged it anyway. Pushing past an intrusive fig tree, she stood directly beneath me, her lanky shadow diffuse and multiheaded from the street-lights and porch lights and moon. I could see now that what I'd thought was a hat were actually massive blond dreadlocks. Tipping her head back, she said, "Thanks for that, man."

When I still didn't reply, she dragged the bag a few more feet. Then she dropped beside the house and lit up a cigarette or a joint.

Slowly, I dragged myself into performer mode. Cole St. Clair mode. It was a thing to wear, a familiar shirt, but it took a moment to get on.

I clomped down the stairs. In the dark, the faint glow at the end of her joint illuminated the smoke around her. Her face was very long and very thin and a lot like Ichabod Crane, if Ichabod had blond dreadlocks, which he might have. The eighteenth century was a bad time for hair.

"Hi, why are you here?" I asked.

"I'm your drummer," she replied.

There were no fireworks or parades or signs raining from the heavens to announce her, the first of the musicians assembled around the musical feet of Cole St. Clair, ex-frontman of NARKOTIKA.

This girl was not my band. My band was one-third Buddhist and one-third dead.

I said, "That isn't a fancy way of saying you're a hooker, is it? Because I'm really not in the mood."

She blew smoke out at me. In a slow, nasal voice that seemed like it had to be cultivated, she said, "Don't harsh my buzz, man."

She closed her eyes. She looked utterly at peace with the entire world. Marijuana had never had that effect on me. I got super funny, and then I got sad. The entire process had only ever been a good time for onlookers.

"I wouldn't dream of it. I thought you were coming tomorrow. If you aren't familiar, that's the day after today."

Girl Ichabod opened her eyes. Her dreadlocks were massive. They needed a zip code. I had seen some great dreads in my time, but these looked like they had been made with the ruins of abandoned third-world villages. "Buzz. Harshing."

"Sorry. I'm Cole."

"Leyla." She offered me her joint.

"I'm straight," I said, although once upon a time I had

considered pot the most minor of an array of sins available to me. It was the first time I had said *I'm straight* out loud, and the words had a glorious nobility to them.

"Might want to take the edge off," she told me. "Before the rest of them get here."

"The rest of them?"

As if on cue, lights flooded the backyard. I threw a hand up to shield my eyes. Four people walked through the gate, easy as you please, all dark and ghoulish at the yard's edge. Two of them carried cameras. The other two carried instrument cases. The former was pointed at the latter, but when they caught a whiff of Leyla and me, the lenses instantly swung to us.

I felt like I'd been thrown onstage without a set list. *This is the show,* I told myself. *It starts now.*

"Like I said," Leyla said, indifferent.

"Cole, hey," said the camera guy. I could see half of his face, and it reminded me strikingly of Baby. The same heavy lids, the same brown fringe of hair, the same feeling that he'd stepped out of a vintage '70s photograph. "I thought you'd be sleeping. Sorry for the surprise. Everyone got in early and we thought we'd shoot a couple minutes of them walking in." He stuck out his hand at me, camera still in his other hand. He was wearing about four hundred hemp bracelets. I instantly made at least three judgment calls about him based upon the bracelets alone. "I'm Tee. Just the letter."

"Which letter?"

"*T.* My name. Just T."

I made another judgment call, and then I shook his hand. "You have Baby's face."

"Ha, I know. I'm her twin brother."

"Kinky."

"Yeah, I know, right? I'm going to be one of the camera crew." I could tell right off that he was one of those pliable guys who just liked being around celebrities of all sorts. Not a fan of anyone specific, just a fanboy of anyone who'd ever been anyone in general. Still, I immediately liked him better than Baby. He was more straightforward. "Joan's the other one you'll see all the time. That's her." He pointed. "So if you see us around, you won't freak out."

Part of my attention was on him, but the better part of my mind was working over how his parents had collectively named their children *Baby T*.

"Anyway, we'll just, like, get a quick shot of them walking into the house, and then we'll get out of your way," T said. "We'll try to be as, you know, unobtrusive as possible."

"Do what you gotta do," I said.

T and Joan backed up, pointing cameras hither and thither, looking for the best possible lighting. Joan nearly stepped on Leyla, who reclined in the grass. I caught a glimpse of the scene through Joan's viewfinder and it looked like one of those lion documentaries after dark. All that was missing was the fender of a Land Rover and the half-eaten corpse of a wildebeest.

I focused on the two musicians at the same time that Joan's camera did.

"Why are there two of them?" I asked.

T, eager and amiable, immediately stopped what he was doing and turned to me. "Two of what? Cameras? Differ —"

"No, them."

"It's your band, man," T said. He wore the same wide smile as Baby. "Guitarist and bassist."

"Which one is the guitarist?"

T looked at the two guys with their two similar instrument cases. He didn't have half a clue. One of the musicians lifted his hand.

I said, "You can go."

T's sleepy eyes got unsleepier. "Hey, wait a second."

"The door's over there," I told the guitarist, who was staring at me with an expression I'd forgotten — disbelief mingled with indignation. "Nice to meet you, *da svidaniya*, etc., etc." I turned to the bassist, who swallowed. "And y —"

"Hey, wait," T interrupted. He was still smiling, but his eyes looked a little alarmed. "Baby handpicked these guys. I don't think she'll be so happy if you just send one packing before we eve —"

"I didn't ask for a guitarist," I said. "Why would I need a guitarist? This isn't the Beatles." I pointed. "Bassist. Drummer. Me. Done."

T clearly wanted to keep the peace. "Why don't you just keep him to see how it goes? Then you're happy, Baby's happy, Chip's happy."

I presumed Chip was the guitarist I was going to have to forcibly eject from my life. The most annoying thing about all of this was that I was certain Baby hadn't forgotten that I didn't want a guitarist. Someone who remembered a notepad didn't misremember an extra band member.

"If he wants to sit around, whatever," I replied. "But that thing's not coming out of the case. I don't write for guitar. He can keep the plants company."

T held my gaze, waiting for it to waver. But it wasn't going to. If nothing else in the world went right, I was going to at least keep this: I was recording the album my way.

Finally, T said, "Chip, why don't you wait in the car?"

Leyla blew a puff of smoke into the lion-documentary lights.

Chip pushed his way out of the yard.

"Well," said T.

I turned to the bassist. He was a tall, lanky kid with long hair. He had fingers like insect legs. I said, "Are you any good? Let's hear you."

The bassist's mouth opened, but no sound came out.

T was no fool. He saw the writing on the wall from a million miles away. "Right now? I thought we'd jus —"

I interrupted, "No time like the present, T. We're not getting any younger, and youth, they tell me, is where it's at. Pop that sucker out, dude. Let's hear what you're made of."

The bassist, realizing immediately that I, and not T, was in charge, scrambled to retrieve his bass. "It's, uh, better, amplified."

"I'll use my imagination."

"What should I play?" he asked.

"You tell me."

Jeremy, NARKOTIKA's bassist, hadn't been the greatest player in the world, but he'd had a sort of relentless energy about him. He'd have to study each song for days before he worked out even the most basic riff, but when that riff appeared — oh, man, hold on to something or sit down. It hadn't ever mattered that it took him so much time to get there. All that mattered was that he got there in the end.

Now the long-haired bassist played a riff from one of our songs. I couldn't remember the name of it. Damn, I felt old all of a sudden. Pimpled kid adoringly playing an old riff of Jeremy's from a song I couldn't recall.

"Not that one," I said. "Something I haven't heard."

He played something else. It was funky and very acceptably skilled and like nothing I ever wanted to hear in one of my songs, ever. I didn't even really want it in the room with me. It might get some of its funk on me.

"Thanks, Charlie, but no," I told him. I couldn't believe how this night had gone. I should've been out with Isabel right now.

"My name's not —"

"He can go sit in the car, too," I said. "Have a good night, all. I'm out." I left them there. As I climbed up the deck stairs, I wondered if I should call Isabel. Maybe I should send her something. Not flowers. That was boring. She'd never be convinced by flowers. A midget jumping out of a card or something.

"What a dick," said the bassist, loud enough for me to hear. He didn't know my reputation at all if he thought that was anywhere near enough to offend me.

"Cole, come on," T called up. "What am I going to tell Baby?"

"It bothers me that you call your sister *baby*," I told him. "Tell her that auditions start tomorrow. I'll do it myself. Bring your camera and a clean pair of shorts."

The other cameraperson — Jane? Joan? — spoke for the first time. She asked peevishly, "Are you going to fire Leyla, too?"

I glanced back at where she sat, still smoking contentedly. I wanted my band. I didn't want all of these jokers.

"Not yet."

In the bathroom, I double-checked for cameras, turned on the shower for white noise, and then I took out the things I needed to become a wolf for five or seven or nine minutes.

It was a small sin in the relative scheme of things. At the height of NARKOTIKA's fame, I had been known for my chemical fearlessness — there was no drug I wouldn't try at least once. Some of them had incredibly gross and complicated side effects, but I hadn't been very interested in my body at that point. Really what I had wanted was to get out of life entirely, but I was too much of a coward.

I set my stuff on the edge of the sink and stripped. My mad-scientist father, an ardent fan of the scientific process, would have been proud of the steps that had brought me to this moment. Several months of self-experimentation had brought me to my proprietary blend for stress-free werewolfing: epinephrine to start the process, a vasodilator to make the process more streamlined, a beta-blocker to keep my head from actually exploding, and an aspirin to keep my head from feeling like it was actually exploding.

It was so much tidier than any substance I'd ever done. It

was no messier than getting a beer from the fridge. No, cleaner than even that. Because there was no hangover.

So there was nothing to feel guilty about.

But I did, a little. Probably because of association. I'd only become a werewolf because every other drug's purported kicks had ceased to kick and I needed something that wouldn't let me down. Because I'd hit the absolute bottom. Because I just wanted out and was a coward, always a coward.

But that wasn't the point tonight.

Tonight it was no different than a beer. Just something to restart my brain, convince me to sleep, tide me over until L.A.'s sun could heal me. Five or seven or nine minutes.

I injected, swallowed, waited. I looked at the little things they had put into this bathroom that had nothing to do with bathrooms: the orchid on the windowsill, the fake street sign hanging above the mirror, the concrete statue of a giraffe in the corner. It had been weeks since I'd shifted. Sometimes shifting a lot seemed to make me more likely to turn, and I hadn't wanted any surprises in the Minneapolis airport.

The shower hissed on the small pebbly tiles. I could smell the iron in the water, like the blood in my veins. I heard my pulse in my ears. I couldn't believe that Baby had hired me a guitarist and *that* bass player. I couldn't believe that if everything hadn't gone to absolute crap, my dinner date would have started an hour ago.

Isabel —

My pulse suddenly surged through my body's crumpling infrastructure.

My thoughts vanished with my human skin.

CHAPTER SEVEN

· ISABEL ·

That night I lay in my soulless bedroom with my laptop on my stomach and I watched early videos of Cole performing with NARKOTIKA. In these, he looked young and bright and on fire with something so volatile that it ignited everyone in the audience. His smile was the most brilliant thing in the place.

As the videos got newer, Cole changed. His eyes deadened. It was a model of Cole, thrown up onto the stage, propped behind the keyboard, a rock-star-shaped sack of meat. Sometimes you could actually see him shaking with the ferocity of whatever he'd taken before the show. Destroying himself like he'd destroyed the crowd in those early shows, all the fire turned inside.

I knew this was what Baby North wanted out of him. She knew how to pick them, the sure bets, the certain losers.

Aunt Lauren's cat jumped on the end of my bed. I hissed at her. She jumped down, but she didn't look upset. She'd been here long enough that all of her feelings had been replaced with high-end linoleum. As I let her out of my room and started to shut the door, I heard the front door open: my mother back from her shift. She had just enough time for a little HBO and maybe some brief weeping over her dead son and estranged husband.

Here's a secret, though: Crying doesn't bring back the dead or the missing.

I quickly closed my bedroom door.

I sank back onto the bed and found videos of Cole's last show as NARKOTIKA. The one where he fell down and didn't get back up. A thousand unblinking camera phones had captured the wail of his synthesizer as he grabbed for it and missed on his way down. No one was close enough to catch him. In the end, the only thing that stopped his fall was the ground.

He was terrible to look at in this video. Not in a chic, slick way. In a sweaty, singed, rotting way. I kept playing it over and over again, every time I thought about how much I wanted to call him.

He wasn't here for just me. And this was who he had been. This was who he might be again. But I didn't know if that mattered. Enough to stop me, that is.

I hated crying.

I hit PLAY again. This time I watched his bandmates, hovering at the edges of the video screen. Jeremy, mouth parted in concern. Victor, withering.

Like, *not again.*

Through my thin bedroom wall, I heard my mother fighting with my father on the telephone.

MY MOTHER, OVERHEARD: *My permission? You want my permission to come see me? If you had really wanted to see me, you'd already be here. Don't play games.*

MY FATHER, ASSUMED: Teresa, games are for children. We are not children. We are educated professionals. We both attended decades of schooling to ensure we never had to play games again.

MY MOTHER, OVERHEARD: *It is my work, Tom. I can't change my schedule. You could at least move clients.*

MY FATHER, ASSUMED: Moving clients sounds a lot like a game, and you and I both know my feelings on that, Teresa, as I just said them.

MY MOTHER, OVERHEARD: *Act like you heard what I just said.*

MY FATHER, ASSUMED: Act like you heard what *I* just said.

MY MOTHER, OVERHEARD: *This is what I heard: "LaLaLa The Tom Culpeper Life Story Is About Him." Do you think you're the only one with feelings?*

MY FATHER, ASSUMED: Don't be ridiculous. I don't have feelings. Feelings are for wimmin and children.

MY MOTHER, OVERHEARD: *You're such an asshole.*

MY FATHER, ASSUMED: Are you crying again? God, I thought they sold out of tears at Crate & Barrel. Are you ordering them online again? We're not made of money.

MY MOTHER, OVERHEARD: *This was the best decision I ever made.*

She hung up.

This place. What a hole. I could feel it tugging at the edges of my soul, trying to worry a piece free.

I pressed PLAY on the video of Cole passing out on the stage of Club Josephine.

Then I called him.

At once he picked up. "Da?"

My cruel and hating heart beat faster. On my laptop, Cole's eyes vacated. The music faltered, but you could only really tell that after you'd watched it forty times.

"Are you still on Minnesota time?" I asked.

"I am on whatever time makes this call last longer," he said.

"What's the next meal from now?"

Cole in the video grabbed for the keyboard. His fingers slid from the keys.

"Breakfast, I think. That's the first one, right? The morning one?"

In the video, his face hit the ground. He was utterly still.

I was so tired of the missing and the dead.

I wouldn't get in too deep. I wasn't going to fall in love with him again. I could always walk away again.

"Let's do that one."

CHAPTER EIGHT

· COLE ·

Everything was all right after Isabel called.

I ordered delivery falafel and sat in the apartment and watched music videos in my underwear. Someone had once asked me after a show, "Don't you think music videos are dead?" There is no way for music videos to die. As long as there is a song and a person left alive, someone will sing it, and as long as there is a song and two people left alive, one person will sing it and the other will film it.

The music video will die when we all go blind, and music will never die, because even when you can't hear it, you can feel it.

Now that I was alone and washed out with relief and a far way away from anything like home, it felt like the only thing that could fill me back up was music. I started with bands I knew, and then I let comments and referrals and Wikipedia pages guide me down endless sonic wormholes. I listened to Swedish folk rock and Elvis and Austropop and Krautrock and dubstep and things they hadn't invented names for.

Back before I was anyone, back when I was just a kid with a keyboard and a strange last name, this had been my drug.

I was a shapeshifter.

I lay back in my bed with my headphones on and the window open, and as the moon rose and striped over my eyes and car lights made a metronome pattern on the ceiling and the California smells washed over my remade wolf nostrils, I fell into song after song. The chords buoyed and buffered me. Down below was the crappy world full of insubstantial people, but here in this sound was nothing but perfection.

Later, I woke up and I was wide-awake and my headphones were hot on my ears and I was tired of sleeping and it was too early to get up.

The music that had carried me only hours before now felt too sluggish. I sat there for a few minutes, listening to it anyway. Part of me knew that if I stayed still long enough, the music would work its sleepy magic on me again.

But the rest of me was awake and gnawing.

I stood up. The closeness of the apartment, the domesticity of it, the four walls of it, pinched like a shoe.

I went outside.

In the cool night air, I was sharply alive, my heartbeat a guillotine.

The stucco house opposite was dark and still as I let myself out of the gate. In the alley behind the house, I stood on the concrete pad and grimaced at the car Baby had secured for me. In the dim streetlight, I couldn't tell what it was until I walked around it and stared at the badge, and even then, the fact of its brand meant nothing to me. It was an invisible car from the early 2000s. I unlocked the door and opened it. Inside, the seats were made of cloth the color of orphans' rags.

I stood outside it, the door hanging open, and dialed my phone. After a long space, Baby's voice answered, sounding sharper than it had in person. "St. Clair?" Then she corrected: "Cole."

"This car isn't going to do," I said. "No one wants to watch a show about a rock star who drives around in a — what is this? Saturn. You know, I have seen Saturn, and it is much more impressive than this car. Also, Saturn is yellow, and this car is more like . . . menstrual."

"Cole, it's three twenty-three."

"Twenty-four," I corrected warmly. "How those minutes fly as we age. I want my Mustang."

I hadn't, actually, until I got to the end of the sentence. But now I wanted it in an all-consuming way that was going to ruin easy sleep for days.

"I'm not getting you a Mustang," Baby said. "I don't have the budget for that."

"Don't be silly. I already *have* one. It's in Phoenix, New York."

In my parents' garage, next to my old bicycle, covered in dust. Paid for with my advance, driven by no one. "People would watch a show about a rock star in a black Mustang."

"Three twenty-five," Baby said.

The image of that car was worming its way into my brain: a solution to all of the problems that unending nights presented. I wondered if I was willing to call my parents in order to get it.

No. I was not willing.

"I don't see how I can continue without it, the more I think about it."

"Three twenty-six."

"Six twenty-six in Phoenix," I replied. "And that Mustang looks good in the morning light. Think about it."

I clicked END. The Saturn was still there. I was still awake. It was still three twenty-six, although that seemed impossible.

I stood there, trying to think of my next course of action. Before, I probably would've driven to Crenshaw or something to score, not for now, saving it for later, just for something to do, something to stop my insides from gnawing away at me. But now, I'd just been a wolf; I'd just spoken to Isabel; I'd just slept.

I was relieved to feel like it was only a dull muscle ache. A memory. It was okay. I was okay. *History of substance abuse.* Key word: *history.*

And Isabel —

I considered calling her, but I was enjoying the fact of her taking my calls too much to risk ruining it with an early morning phone call.

Still three twenty-six. It was never going to be morning.

I dialed another number and waited.

This reply was wary but polite. "Hello?"

"*Leon,*" I said broadly. "Did I wake you?" I knew I hadn't. Leon wasn't sleeping nights. He wasn't sleeping days. He was too sad for sleeping. "This is Cole St. Clair. I'm one of the rock stars you were driving around yesterday. Do you remember? I was the most charming of them. With the saxophone track."

"I — I remember. What can I do for you?"

"I'd like to get food, I think. Nothing heavy. Popcorn. Ice cream. Sardines. Something like that. More like the idea of food than anything else."

Leon took a long time to answer. "And you need car service?"

I picked a fleck of anemic red paint from the fender of the Saturn. "Oh, no, no. I have a car. I thought you might want to come with me."

An even longer pause. "Mr. St. Clair, is this some sort of prank?"

"Leon," I replied sternly, "I am always serious. I'm going out to get something. I'm awake. You're awake. It seems like good sense to be companionable. Follow up and see how you're liking that track. No pressure. Also, it's Cole. There's no Mr. at three twenty-eight A.M. Night is the great equalizer."

"And this is for real. Not for your show."

"I hadn't even considered it. What a thought! But no. Even the cameramen lie sleeping now, Leon."

I heard a rustling sound, but he didn't answer. I was depressed by the knowledge that if Leon didn't agree to go out, I would have to go out by myself. With nothing but the Saturn to remind me of my humanity, I'd surely make poor decisions.

Leon said, "It'll take twenty minutes for me to get to Venice."

CHAPTER NINE

· COLE ·

It turned out that Leon, in his spare time, didn't drive a black Cadillac, but instead a rather pristine and stately Ford Five Hundred. He permitted me to twiddle with the radio knobs as we drove up and down Abbott Kinney looking for something that was open late and wasn't a bar. A bar would be fine, except I'd be recognized, and seeing people drinking would remind me of how glorious and friendly I got when I drank, and it would all be over.

No, in retrospect, a bar would not be fine.

Leon drove us both a total of two miles to the beachfront.

Climbing out of the car, he said, "Not far now." He sounded kind, puzzled, bewildered. He wore black slacks and a blue dress shirt, neither of them rumpled. A tasteful watch. He was the sort of man people trusted without thinking about it. He was the sort of man people didn't think about, period.

I let my gaze eat the world. My wolf-sharpened sense of smell caught the scent of ice-cream cones, of asphalt, of churning ocean, of swirling beer, of first kisses and last kisses. The diagonal street parking was full of rust-free cars that had never existed outside summer. The girls were all legs, and the boys were all teeth. That moon was closer than before. The empty shops were still bright with aqua and pink and yellow paint. I tripped on the curb, my eyes on a pair of guys flying a kite on the night beach, its tail rippling silver in the moonlight. My chest felt full with the images.

There was no place for a wolf to hide here.

"You aren't from here," Leon said, and I knew he was watching me watch everything else. I knew he knew I liked it, but I didn't mind.

This whitewashed place sang my name to me, over and over.

"New York," I replied. And added, "State."

I couldn't remember when I'd first clarified *state, not city*, but I remembered the distinction had felt a lot more important then. Where was I from now? Not here.

"You aren't from here, either," I reminded him. "Cincinnati."

"I can't believe you remember that."

He had brought us to a café that reminded me of the restaurants in Italy — a small, dark interior, most of the dining space underneath an open-air awning. Although I hadn't expressed any concern over being recognized, Leon stood in front of me, blocking my face from the hostess, and said, "Two, please. By the sidewalk, maybe?"

I felt intensely validated. I'd judged him right. Decent was decent.

The hostess sat us at a tiny table. Across the sidewalk was the beach, and beyond it, the black ocean. I felt dreamy and drunk.

We nearly knocked heads as we sat, and I thought about writing some lyrics down in my tiny notebook (*Like lovers or lawyers/biting and smiling*). Instead I watched some skateboarders sail by us. "Do you like it here?"

There was too long of a pause, and when I looked at Leon, he smiled ruefully and cut his eyes down to the table. He gently unfolded his napkin. He had sturdy hands, blunt and sure.

"I've been here a long time."

"Did you like it when you first came?"

Leon said, "What is it you see when you look at it?"

"Magic," I replied.

He pushed the menu toward me. "If you tell me what you want, I'll order for you. While you enjoy the ocean."

He meant so that I wouldn't have to talk to the waitress with my famous voice, or look at her with my famous face. Now I really looked at him. He must've been a handsome bastard when he was my age. He'd still be handsome, now, if he squared his shoulders and acted like he had some testicles. "You drive around a lot of famous people?"

"A few."

"You didn't even know who I was when I got into your car, and now you're protecting me from waitresses?"

Leon said, "I Googled you after you got out."

It was warming to hear I still had some currency on the Internet.

He continued, "The news stories about when you disappeared were . . . . Do you mind me mentioning it?"

I shrugged. Everything was cool as long as he didn't say Victor's name. As long as he didn't ask me where Victor was.

"Well, it caused a big fuss."

"I'm really not that famous," I said, although I was a little all that famous. "Most people can't recognize me on sight. And if they do, they either think I'm just someone who looks like me, or they don't have the guts to talk to me, or they don't care that it's me."

Really, it wasn't exhausting to be recognized. It was exhausting to feel alone in a crowd.

Leon studied me pensively. I could tell that he, in any case, did not like being recognized as Leon the driver. He dreaded the supermarket line chitchat. He waited until the postal service lady had knocked on the door, left the package, and gotten in her vehicle to open his door. His dog dying had been bad, I could tell, but the worst part for him had been trying to figure out how to handle the pity of the vet assistants.

"I know what you're saying," I told Leon, and by *you*, I meant *your face*. "You hate small talk. It makes everything seem irrelevant. I agree. It's ridiculous. We should only talk about big things, you and I."

"I'm not good at small talk." Leon downgraded *hate* to something slightly kinder, but didn't disagree. "Do I have big things to talk about?"

"You told me your life story in the car. That's big."

"You *asked* me for that."

"Did I? That doesn't sound like me."

The waitress returned. I ordered a BLT without incident. Leon ordered a milk shake without incident. When his shake arrived, he cradled it in his hands, savoring it. He seemed to regard it as a guilty indulgence, something only permitted in the middle of the night with a stranger.

He looked glum, which wasn't the point of this exercise, so I asked, "So, Leon. I know you're not a fan of this city, but where would you tell me to go, as a tourist?"

"Haven't you been here before?"

I had been here before. "I was on tour."

"No time to explore?"

There had been time to explore. I'd explored a few streets in Koreatown and one in Echo Park and another in Long Beach, and then I'd explored a Rite Aid for some syringes, and then I'd explored my hotel balcony and my hotel floor and, finally, the tile of the hotel bathroom. Then Victor had come got me out of my own puke and cleaned me up for the show.

I'd been in Los Angeles before, but it hadn't mattered. Really, I'd never left my own head.

"The Pier, I guess," Leon said, but dubiously, like he was repeating advice he'd heard from someone else. "That's supposed to be nice at sundown. Malibu? That's about forty-five minutes up the coast."

"Malibu is not L.A., Leon," I said sternly. I looked out at the purple-skinned beach. I imagined running on that sand with paws instead of feet. It would be just as good on my own feet, I thought. "I think you should visit your own city."

"Maybe I will," Leon said, in a kind way that meant that he wouldn't. Our food arrived. Leon accepted the tomato from my BLT.

"Seems strange to order a lettuce and bacon sandwich. But she would've held the tomato if you'd asked." He shook salt on the slice. He looked as happy as he ever had as he put it in his mouth.

"I forgot I didn't like them," I replied. "They're a member of the deadly nightshade family, did you know? Slightly poisonous to dogs."

And wolves. Just enough to give me a stomachache.

"Chocolate, too," Leon said, looking at his milk shake, and I remembered that his dog had died. "Can I ask you a personal question?"

"All questions are personal."

"I . . ."

"That means, yes, Leon, ask it."

Just as long as it wasn't about Victor.

"Why did you come back?"

It felt like a trick question. My hard-won hermitage — begun by me, secured by Jeremy — was no small thing. It was a chance to be someone else, and how many of those do you get? And yet I'd left it behind.

I came back because I had to. Because there was nothing wrong in the world except that I was getting older in it. Because Sam and Grace had told me I should go if that was what I wanted.

What I wanted was:

I wanted.

Isabel —

I wanted to make something. At the beginning of all of this, I had just been a kid with a keyboard. It was less the game of it, and more those hours I spent falling from song to song.

"I want to make an album," I said. "I miss making music."

I could tell he approved of my answer. The waitress brought the check.

Leon said, "I liked that song."

"Which — oh? Yeah?"

"You were right. Jazzy." Leon made the subtlest jazz hands ever and I reflected them back at him, but bigger. "Did you ever do anything else with the lady who sang?"

Lady was not how I would have referred to Magdalene. I'd had the hardest crush on her back then. I said, "She's too famous for that now. You haven't heard of her? She's in the movies."

He shrugged. Probably not his sorts of movies. "I bought one of your albums, too."

"Which one?"

He considered. "It had a lady's undergarments on the front?"

He seemed uncomfortable, so I told him, "If it makes you feel any better, it was our bassist, Jeremy, wearing them."

Nostalgia chewed on me. No, not chewed. Nibbled. Just nibbled.

"Well," Leon said, eyes on our combined funds by the check, "I guess that's that. I better get you back."

I pointed at the ocean.

"Pacific," Leon said, with no smile, but a glint in his eyes.

"I think we should take off our shoes."

Leon frowned. "I'm not really that kind of person."

I knew that he wasn't. At least, I knew he wasn't the sort of person to abandon a car in the middle of the L.A. freeway. And that seemed to lead naturally to the sort of person who wouldn't roll up their pants and take their shoes off with an unfamiliar rock star at five A.M.

"Don't give me that look. I'm not asking you if you want to

get matching tattoos. I'm asking if you want to take a manly stroll on the beach. How long is it until sunrise?" I asked.

He looked at his tasteful watch. "Probably thirty minutes."

"What's thirty minutes more to see the sun rise over the ocean?"

"We're going to wait longer than that if you're hoping to see the sun rise over the Pacific."

"Don't be pedantic, Leon."

We faced off. He looked weary, tired, made soft by life, and I thought he was beyond my charms. But then he shook his head and bent to untie his shoes.

I triumphantly whipped off my sneakers. As Leon carefully untied his laces and cuffed the bottom of his slacks, I waltzed onto the cool sand. Up here, it was dry and soft and weightless. Beside me, Leon tipped his head back to watch a helicopter fly along the coast, north to south. The boys with the kite had disappeared, and it seemed like the beach was finally going to sleep, right when it was time to wake up.

I led Leon to the packed sand at the ocean's edge.

"Hot damn," I hissed. The water was freezing. I could feel every nerve inside me twitching and shaking and considering shifting into a wolf.

"Cold," remarked Leon.

Gritting my teeth, I hopped from one foot to the other until the nausea passed and my body remembered that it was human, only human.

"I remember reading that ocean temperature was sixty-four or sixty-five around here," Leon said. He experimentally stepped a little deeper into the briny deep. "Feels colder, doesn't it?"

Now that I was used to it, it wasn't that bad. I kicked my toes in the sand and felt something squirm away from the contact.

"We're not alone," I said. "Something's down there."

Leon knelt, careful to keep his slacks dry, and dug quickly. He made a few soft sounds of disappointment until he straightened with a handful of sand.

"Think one's in there," he remarked, holding it out to me.

I sorted through the sand until I found the creature: a white-backed insect or crustacean nearly the size of a quarter. It had a lot of legs. "It's an alien."

"Sand crab," Leon said. "It won't hurt you."

"It sure is ugly."

"Ugly never hurt a thing."

I scoffed. "Oh, ugly has hurt some things. It's just that pretty hurts more."

"Amen." Leon tossed the crab gently into the surf.

We walked in silence for a little bit, no sound but the ocean and the cars moving on the street. Above us, the sky grayed and then pinked. In a few hours, I could call Isabel, and then I would switch on that dusty keyboard and start to make something real. As a flock of pelicans soared by us in the half-light, I thought about how beautiful this place was and how lucky I was and how all I had to do was not screw things up in any way.

I eased my little notepad out of my back pocket. Leon was looking at me as I did, so I said, "What?"

"You're just something else, is all," Leon said. "Most people aren't. What did you write there?"

I turned it around so he could see what I'd written.

Lovers and lawyers
Lips and teeth
Tally that memory
Give it a price
Is that your dream?
Here's a check
Something clever here
Pelicans are clever

He was charmed. "Lyrics? You just wrote those now? Will those really become a song?"

"Maybe. That pelican stuff is some of my finest work."

Without any discussion, we both stopped and gazed out over the water. The sun rose behind us, but haze or smog filtered out most of the orange, making the ocean a slowly developing blue-and-purple portrait.

"You should take a photo," I told Leon. "Don't tell me you're not that kind of person. You can always delete it after you get home. I won't know."

Leon shot me a look, but he got his phone out. He told me, "Go on, then, pose."

"What? It's not supposed to be a photo of me. It's supposed to be a photo of this glorious morning. Or of you in this glorious morning. A memento."

He was amused. "I know what I look like. Go on."

I flipped amiable devil horns at him as he took the photo. I said, "I consider this day seized."

He checked his watch. "And it's only just started."

Chapter Ten

Cole had gotten a bag of stale powdered donuts for breakfast. Or possibly more than one bag. When I arrived at the house the next morning, I discovered a note taped to the gate. It said: *24-13-8. Follow the sugar, princess.*

And then there was, no shit, a trail of small, white donuts leading around the side of the concrete house.

Shaking my head, I entered the numbers into the combination lock. Then I followed the donuts. A sliding door to a house on the other side of the yard stood open, but the donuts didn't lead to it. A girl with blond dreads and dirty eco-cargo pants did yoga in the yard. She opened her eyes only long enough to give my outfit a brief gaze that managed to convey that she hated everything about my consumer lifestyle. The donuts didn't go anywhere near her, either.

As I got to the last donut, Cole manifested on the deck above me. He was beautifully shirtless, skin tinted light blue by my enormous sunglasses, and he wore the same pair of jeans I'd seen him in the day before. His hair was a mess. He was already a blur of motion, leaning hard on one side of the deck and then the other until he spotted me.

My heart lurched. I tried to call up that image of him collapsing behind the keyboard instead. The memory of him seizing beside a needle.

Not his face above me as he said, long ago, *That is how I would kiss you if I loved you.*

I wasn't going to get in too deep. That was the thing.

"Stairs," he told me, pointing. "I ran out of donuts."

I could tell that he was in brain-on-fire mode. "Is there anything better than donuts up there?"

Yoga girl's eyes continued to judge me — and now Cole as well.

If she didn't look away soon, I'd give her something really worth judging.

"Me," Cole said. He pointed to the corner of the roof. "Camera, camera, camera. PSA. Just saying. Camera. Also, camera." He craned his neck to look over the roofs. His back muscles stretched gloriously and distractingly. "Did you see anyone coming?"

I climbed the stairs. On the deck, the view all around was the flat roofs of California Avenue. "No. Is someone coming?"

"No. Probably not. I don't know. Come, come, come. Up, up, up."

"Nice of you to get dressed for the occasion."

Cole's eyes darted to himself; he plucked at the skin on his chest. "Am I not wearing — I'm wearing pants! In, in. Come into my lair."

The apartment was unexpected. It was a uniquely West Coast magic trick, I'd discovered: Take a building that looked like a small garage and turn the inside into a vast, airy living space.

I could tell at once that this streamlined studio had been furnished *for* Cole, not furnished *by* Cole. An artsy bookshelf studded with California knickknacks separated the bedroom from the living area. Framed vintage travel posters and fake vintage neon lights decorated the walls. In the living room, a rather fancy-looking keyboard sat on a stand, a thin layer of dust shimmering on the speaker beside it.

The keyboard was what made this moment real for me. This was really happening.

There were so many cameras. Several at knee height.

The only evidence of Cole's form of interior decorating was in the tiny kitchen area: The arm-length counter was spread with three half-drunk soda bottles, an open bag of chips, and the end of a hot dog lying on an exhausted bun.

"This is disgusting," I said.

I was as close to the trash can as he was, but I stood there until Cole made a little *mreh* noise and swept the lot of it into the bin.

"Was that breakfast? Should I have had the donuts outside?" I asked.

In response, Cole seized my arm. Rather dramatically, he dragged me into the bathroom and slammed the door shut behind us. My reflection appeared simultaneously in the mirror and the all-glass shower.

"Hey —"

Cole put a finger to his lips and shut the door behind us. "Cameras. Cameras, cameras, cameras."

"But not in here?" I spun. Like the rest of the apartment, the bathroom was light and airy. Plenty of room for a rock star and me. I inhaled, and could only smell air freshener and soap, no wolf scent. I had to admit that I was more relieved than I thought I would be.

"Well, that one," Cole said dismissively, gesturing at a camera lying in the basin of the chic sink. It was unplugged and half disassembled, an examined corpse.

"Where did it come from?"

He stepped into the shower without turning it on, slapping his bare feet against the tile inside. "Over the bed. I want to see how long it takes them to notice it's missing. Come in, child, and see the wonders that await."

"Are you being funny, or are you talking about the shower?"

Cole pressed himself back against the shower wall so that I could see that he had folded towels over the tiled seats inside it. A yellow plastic kitchen stool served as a tiny table. He made a grand gesture.

This was breakfast.

With a noisy sigh, I stepped into the shower and sat. Cole sat down opposite. The table held a bowl with a few donuts in it — these were the waxy chocolate sort, not the sort to lure girls into an apartment. A mug held two eggs and a single kiwi fruit. In the middle was an empty glass; Cole reached out and placed it one inch closer to me than him.

"This is fancy," I said. "Would you like to explain the dishes?"

Cole cracked his knuckles and pointed to the food in turn. "Here we have the glazed miniature chocolate bathroom cakes with a paraffin topping. These here are a duo of free-range eggs that are probably hard-boiled, or at least were wet for a long time. This here beside them is a furry, green egg. And this —"

He produced a two-liter Diet Coke from the edge of the shower and filled my glass. As it began to foam over the edge, he put his finger in it to stop the fizzing.

"No glass for you?" I asked.

Cole sucked his finger before taking a swig directly from the bottle. "I'll rough it."

"Noble."

It was hard to imagine a person on the planet managing to be uncharmed by this Cole.

He asked, "Can I peel an egg for you?"

"I don't know, can you?"

"*May* I?"

I waved a hand. He arduously peeled an egg and handed it to me. I nibbled the white while he worked on the other. I got to the middle, which was rather underdone, just as I noticed that Cole had pretty much swallowed his without chewing it.

"Chug chug chug," he told me.

I gave it to him instead. "Are they really filming everything you do?"

Cole swallowed the rest of my egg and handed me a donut instead. "It's supposed to be just an off-the-cuff documentary about me recording this album. But I'm sure they're hoping I mess up."

I held his gaze over the donut. Cole was in possession of so many different precedents for messing up that it was hard to know which one was the worst one to be caught on film.

"Could it happen?" I asked him.

His voice was careless. "Impossible."

It was like when he had answered so quickly before to say that he was here for me. I couldn't believe an answer given that easily. But maybe it was impossible. I didn't know the rules of shifting anymore. Once upon a time, it had seemed to be temperature-based. The colder it was, the more likely you were to be a wolf. But it had never seemed to work very reliably for Cole, who had studiously cooked his brain chemistry through a number of substances. When I'd left Minnesota, he had been conducting experiments on the shifting.

I suspected that now he could do it on purpose.

I didn't know how I felt about that. It was better than heroin, I guessed, but it wasn't heroin that had killed my brother.

He offered me another donut, which I accepted. The waxiness wasn't bad when you washed it down with enough Diet Coke.

I asked, "Does Sam know you're here?"

Sam was one of the members of the wolf pack back in Minnesota. Sort of. He was sort of cured. Sort of getting there. I probably should have called him to see how he was. Probably should have called Grace, too, to see if she was happily anticipating college. But like I said. I wasn't really friendly.

"Yeah."

"Did he think it was a good idea?"

Cole shrugged. "His concept of a good idea is majoring in obscure poetry. He wanted to know the pack was taken care of, and they are. I have it all set up. They'll be fine until winter. And, anyway, he knew I wanted to make some of my own money back again. Not that being a property owner isn't incredibly satisfying."

This was because Cole had bought the piece of land the wolves lived on now.

What about me?

"It didn't have to be California," he said. "It could have been New York. Nashville."

He didn't say anything else. I didn't want to ask him anything more about it, because I felt strangely emotional and unbalanced over just the few words he'd already said.

Instead, I asked, "What about your green egg?"

Cole picked up the kiwi fruit. "Do you peel it?"

"Not with your fingers," I said. I didn't really know. I'd only ever seen them as God intended: peeled and sliced. Sofia probably knew four ways to prepare one. "The skin is thick?"

He bit the fruit just enough to cut through the furry skin and worked at the edge with his fingers. It looked like he was taking the fruit's jacket off. After he'd revealed a precious inch of the interior, he offered it to me across the table. "First dibs?"

I leaned forward to take a bite. Juice welled on my lips, and before I could wipe it away, Cole pressed his thumb to my mouth. He swiped the juice away with his finger and then put it in his own mouth. Lingeringly, like he could taste my lips on his. I couldn't stop looking at his mouth.

Then we were kissing, hungry and hard and ceaseless, one bleeding into the next. I heard my glass tip and soda fizzle in the drain. The heel of his hand pressed my cheek; he still held the kiwi in his fingers. Everything smelled like paradise. My fingers grazed his collarbone, his ribs, his hipbones above his waistband.

It felt like it had been so long since I'd touched another person. He was so real, his skin so warm, all of him ribs and salt and sweat. It felt like so long since I'd seen him. It felt like this was the only thing I had wanted for so many months.

He restlessly shoved the wreck of the table out of the way and pulled me closer. The kiwi joined the diet soda by the drain. One of his palms was on my neck and the other gripped my thigh, half beneath my skirt. I couldn't catch my breath. This was bad. I wanted him too much to stop myself, and I needed to stop, or — or —

A phone began to shrill, urgent as a fire alarm.

Into my mouth, Cole said, very simply, "No."

But the phone kept ringing. I couldn't understand how it sounded so close until I realized there was a handset hanging beside the toilet.

Cole let out the most ragged breath imaginable.

I had thought I'd be relieved. I was not.

My fingers, which had been hooked on the top of his jeans, fell away as he stood up. He scrubbed a hand over his face before stepping out of the shower. With his foot, he kicked down the toilet lid and sat on it before taking the phone from the hook. His hair was still a mess, but now he somehow looked dressed.

"Da," he said, rather coolly. His expression had sharpened; it was twitchier than the person who had greeted me, or the person who had invited me into the shower, or the person who had been kissing me. He listened for a moment. "Right. E-mail it to me, then. Oh, this is my excited voice. You have no idea."

I started to pick up the things that had scattered across the shower. I turned the stool upside down and piled the bowls and eggshells in the cavity inside.

Then I stepped out and leaned against the sink as he stood in the middle of the bathroom, thumbing through his phone. My heart was still thudding. He leaned beside me, his shoulder against mine, still looking at the phone.

My thoughts were a movie screen with nothing projected on it.

After a moment, he tipped his phone to me so that I could see the e-mail on it. *From: Baby North. Subject line: AUDITIONS.*

T tells me you're doing auditions on the beach. I've touched base with people to make sure the world knew to come. When you're done with that, I've jotted some other ideas in the notebook. Let me know.

Cole pulled a small notebook from his back pocket. It looked brand-new, but when he flipped it open, the first page had slanted, excited handwriting:

Reveal your identity to fans in the music aisle of Target.
Run a block party.
Crash a wedding.
Steal a car.

You know. Be yourself.

"I thought this was a show about you recording an album?" I asked, but it wasn't really a question.

"Who would watch that?" he replied. He frowned at the list, but not like he was upset with it. More like it was a slightly perplexing shopping list, and he was contemplating the mechanics of fulfilling it.

"Are you really going to do all of those things?"

"Maybe," Cole said. "I can think of better ones."

"She wants you to be a disaster."

He tapped the notebook against his mouth. "She wants me to *look like* a disaster."

"Those are the same thing."

He was very disinterested in this line of questioning. "This is just performing. I know what they want."

"Who is 'they'? How did we get plural all of a sudden?"

"The masses. The people. Don't you watch TV?"

I did watch TV. I watched Baby's shows. I thought of those knee-high cameras. Perfect angle for catching a shot of someone on his way down.

I wanted to tell him to quit the show and stay here for me.

But that was the opposite of not getting in too deep.

Things were starting to get projected on the movie screen of my mind, and they were all things that might make me cry if they happened.

I pushed off the sink. "I have to go to work."

"*Work,*" echoed Cole, as if he had not heard the word before. "How can you work and help me destroy the hopes of a dozen hopeful bass players at the same time?"

"I can't. And I'm not going to be on your — your thing. I'm not part of the Cole St. Clair show."

"How boring that is." Cole's face was carefully expression-less, though, so I knew he meant *frustrating* or *upsetting* instead of *boring*.

"Well, that's how things run in the Isabel show. Call me next time you're off camera." For some reason, I was irritable now. It was as if every time my feelings were prodded into action, the first thing was always pins and needles.

I opened the bathroom door.

"Wow. Just like that?" Cole asked.

"Just like that," I replied. "Frosty."

I stepped back into the view of all the cameras. Cole, still out of their reach in the bathroom, held a pretend phone to his ear. He mouthed _____ *me*, only I didn't think the verb was *call*.

A smile flashed across my face despite myself. His own smirk bloomed so quickly in response to it that I knew he'd been waiting for me to do something forgivable.

Really, that made two of us.

CHAPTER ELEVEN

· COLE ·

After Isabel had gone, I felt charged and ready to be Cole St. Clair. I was so high that it made me think about how I used to replicate this feeling with drugs. Thinking about that feeling made me imagine how once upon a time, I would have gone looking for some now: not for right away, but for later, as a reward for good behavior. A private high in a harmless environment. Even through my thoughts of Isabel, I felt a surge of nerves and anticipation, some part of me already planning for the treasure hunt through L.A.

I shut it down, feeling dirty for even remembering it.

Thinking it is not doing it.

I thought of how I'd been a wolf just a few hours before. *Last time for even that, for a while,* I told myself. It wasn't a crime, but I didn't need it.

Then I got to work. I called Jeremy on my way to the beach, even though I knew what he'd say, because he'd been a part of NARKOTIKA, which meant he'd been a part of me.

He picked up on the fourth ring.

I peered at my reflection in shop windows as I walked down the sidewalk. "No chance you want to play bass for me again, right?"

"Hey, man," Jeremy replied, in his slow, easy way. He had the most glorious Southern accent you've ever heard on a guy from upstate New York. I'd known him long enough to remember him before he'd cultivated it. If he was shocked to hear from me after a year of silence, he didn't show it. "I thought you were underground."

It was at once comforting and suffocating to hear his voice. He was all tied up with my memories of NARKOTIKA, and they were all tied up with my memories of everything before becoming a wolf. It was all awful nostalgia.

"I have emerged like a wondrous butterfly," I told him. "And now I am going to be on the TV."

"Yup."

"I need a bassist. I —"

"*Shhh,*" Jeremy said, soft as a feather. "I'm Googling you."

I waited. There was no point hurrying Jeremy. It was like punching fog. I walked half a block in the brilliant sun while he researched my recent life.

"The only problem with you on a reality show," Jeremy said finally, "is that reality's never been your strong point."

I paused to look at a window full of sunglasses. A tiny, tinted version of me appeared in each lens. "They hired me the absolute worst bass player."

"Cole, I doubt that," he replied mildly. "They seem like

smart people. They used integers to represent the letters in their website name."

"There was nothing about the guy that was right. And she got me a guitarist, but that's another story."

"Guitars are the ones with six strings, right? Have I seen one before?"

I looked in another store window. This shop only sold belts in the color blue. It seemed unnecessarily specialized. "I *told* her no guitarist."

"I assume he's already gone."

"Oh, yeah, of course. So now I'm going to audition people on the beach, and the best thing would be for you to show up and be the best."

Jeremy said, "Oh, I don't know if I'm the best."

He would not brag, even in jest. This was the Buddhist in him or something. He'd become Buddhist around the same time he'd become Southern.

"You know what I mean. I'm auditioning for a Jeremy, and you'd be a Jeremy." I paused at another store window. It was impossible to tell what some of these shops sold.

"You know I'm playing with another band, right?" he asked.

I knew. He wasn't the only one with access to a search engine. I wasn't offended. I'd been theoretically missing for more than a year and then theoretically out of the music business for several more months than that. I'd have found another band, too. "They are not as cool as me."

Jeremy thought about this. "No. They aren't. But I like them, and I don't want to leave them in a tight spot."

"It's only six weeks. Then they can have you back. Undamaged. Entire. The only thing different about you will be that your mind will be blown by the time spent with me."

"I have no doubt of that. It wouldn't just be six weeks, though. You're touring for the album, right?"

I assumed so. That was what you did — make an album, play some shows, sell some records. There was a thrill to it, when it was going well. I was good at it, when it was going well.

It was just when things weren't going well that it got dangerous. Mostly to me, though. Not often to bystanders.

"So?"

He paused as if he were thinking about it. But like I said, I knew Jeremy. Back when we were in the band, we all knew one another better than we knew ourselves. That was the reason why we were *the band*. So I already knew what he was going to say. I just didn't know quite how he was going to say it.

"I don't think you and touring is a good idea," he said. "It's going backward."

I knew exactly what he was talking about, but I said, "Sideways. Backward is unnecessarily negative."

"Look, Cole, I'm really glad you're . . ."

He didn't finish the sentence, leaving it wide open for me to imagine what he was going to say. *In Los Angeles. Making music again. Still alive.*

What it came down to was that he didn't trust me.

His doubt left a bigger dent in my Teflon heart than I would have expected.

Eventually, Jeremy merely asked, "Can I come to the auditions anyway? To watch?"

"Only if you help me choose your successor."

"I'd like that."

Neither of us said anything about Victor. Maybe I was the only one thinking about how we weren't talking about him. Maybe it was easier when you hadn't been the one digging his grave. When you hadn't been the one to put him there.

— What about Victor, Cole?

Remember how we did everything together? I convinced him to become a werewolf with me. Now I'm in a loft in California and he's in an unmarked hole in Minnesota.

— He chose it, too. It wasn't all you.

Sometimes I pretend that's true.

"Cole, you still there?"

"I'm always here," I replied, though I hadn't been, really, for a moment. "Watching you sleep."

"I know you are. I feel it. What's the way? Today? What's your way?"

My reflection in the store window finally smiled. The way. The *way*. When we were on the road before, back before everything went to shit, every show was different. It wasn't just that we'd play a different set. It was that we'd come dressed as zombies, or we'd play a song backward, or we'd soak a pumpkin in gasoline and set it on fire. It was about the music, sure — that was always the most important thing — but it was about the game, too. The hook. Somewhere in there, we'd started calling it the "way." *What's the way, Jeremy? What's the way, Victor?*

Actually, it was always this:

What's the way, Cole?

"I was looking for props here, but it's useless," I said.

"Anything I can do?"

I was about to tell him no, I had to think more, but then, all of a sudden, my brain turned over and something caught.

I narrowed my eyes. "How are the speakers on your sound system?"

CHAPTER TWELVE

· ISABEL ·

Sometimes I took online quizzes to find out if I was a sociopath. Society thinks there are more male sociopaths than female, but that is a dirty, dirty lie perpetuated by the media. There are more unfeeling girls out there than they would like to admit.

Maybe I wasn't crazy. But if I wasn't, then everyone else was.

I didn't know why I kept being shitty to Cole. And by *Cole*, I really meant *everyone else in the world*.

He was only a few miles away from me. In California. In L.A.

At work, the minutes seemed fuzzy and timeless. I redesigned a sparse pile of mauve boat necks, and then I dusted the plants, and then I went into the back room. Sierra was not in, but she'd left evidence of herself in a pile of fabric scraps and "inspirations," which was what she called the weird things she collected to influence her clothing. Since I'd been in the store last, she'd added a glass milk bottle, a freeze-dried leaf of some kind, and, grotesquely, a seagull's foot.

I couldn't wait to hang up whatever bit of fashion was inspired by a dismembered gull part.

Pushing Sierra's stuff out of the way, I sat on the counter and pulled out my notes for my CNA class. The hardest part about the class, in my opinion, was trying to remember what CNA stood for. Certified. Nursing. Assistant. I'd been told that it was a good thing to have if you were trying to get into premed, but it was hard to imagine why. One of the browser windows on my phone was still open to a practice test question. It was this:

If you walk into a client's room and he is masturbating, what do you do?

a) laugh and close the door
b) ask him gently to stop
c) close the door and give him some privacy
d) explain the dangers of masturbation
e) report him to the head nurse

I was taking a class in this. I was taking a class in this.
I was going to college. I was going to college.
I was going to be a doctor. I was going to be a doctor.
If I repeated all of these things like a mantra, they would not only be true, they would start to make sense, or at least feel true, or feel like they made sense.

Hours thinned to minutes. The morning with Cole had been in color, and everything else was in black and white.

I sold a tank top.

My mother called. "Isabel? Are you wearing the white pants?"

The other day, someone had showed me a collection of portraits done by a photographer interested in familial similarities. Each face was actually two stitched together: a father on one side, for instance, a son on the other. If one had been done of me and my mother, nothing about the altered photograph would have struck viewers as unusual. We were the same height and weight, and we both had blond hair and blue eyes and one eyebrow that hated you. It was quite possible for us to share each other's clothing, size wise, although it rarely happened. I wasn't interested in smart skirts, and my mother wasn't interested in a bare midriff.

But the white pants we shared. They were high-waisted, pencil-legged, Hollywood-chic perfection. I wore them with cropped leopard-print tops that showed a tantalizing half-inch of skin. My mother wore them with a slinky black blouse that was, in my opinion, more suggestive than my version.

"Who are you trying to impress?" I asked.

"Don't be rude," my mother replied. "Is that a yes or a no?"

"I took them to the cleaners. There was something on them. It was disgusting. I don't want to think about it."

My mother clucked. "It was coffee. I'm going to the cleaners now. I was going to take them. When are you home tonight?"

"Eight, if there's no traffic. But I'm going right back out again with Sofia. When do you go to work?"

"Eight, if there's no traffic." My mother was on a series of night shifts at the moment. Part of it was because she was the new doctor in an old hospital and the night shift was given to the grunts, but part of it was because working the night shift meant she could sleep through the real world the next day. It saved on wine costs.

"Oh, well, see you tomorrow." I wasn't particularly crushed by this, nor was my mother. My graduation and initiation into the age of majority merely granted societal approval to our relationship. It wasn't that my mother was a hands-off parent. It was that she'd been so hands-on for so long that my psyche maintained the imprint of her palm even when she removed her hand from me.

The day dragged. Cole didn't call. I didn't call him. What did I want? I didn't know.

If you are considering getting serious with a rock star but he is filming a reality show that will probably result in death or hospitalization for one or both of you, what do you do?

a) laugh and close the door
b) ask him gently to stop
c) close the door and give him some privacy
d) explain the dangers of masturbation
e) report him to the head nurse

At the end of the day, Sierra's husband, Mark, came in. He didn't really serve a purpose, but he liked to come in and mess over the receipts like it was something. I wasn't exactly sure what he actually did for a living. Something male-modelish. He had the sort of face that sold sunglasses.

"Hey, gorgeous," he greeted me. It sounded funnier when he said *gorgeous* than when Sierra said it. Sierra used *lush* and *beautiful* and *dreamy* and *lovely* like other people used indefinite articles. I suspected Mark really did mean I was gorgeous, and I suspected he found all of Sierra's monsters gorgeous. But why shouldn't he? We were all hired to look a certain way, which was to say, we were all hired to look like Sierra, and he obviously found her attractive.

I didn't reply, but I raised an eyebrow, which was the same thing, for me.

"What are you doing?"

"Studying."

"What?"

I almost said *masturbation,* because it would be funny, but after Mark had just said *gorgeous,* it seemed like that would be flirting.

"How to save people from themselves."

Mark moved some papers around. He was doing absolutely nothing except messing up a system one of the monsters had devised. "They tell you about that on the Internet?"

Everyone in the world knew that everything in the world was on the Internet. I scraped listlessly at the bottom of my consciousness for any part of me that might care enough to think of an entertaining way to report this to Mark. I found nothing.

My phone buzzed. It was Sofia.

"Sofia, what?" I kept meaning to start answering the phone with *Culpeper,* because I liked the masculine idea of stripping my first name. And because it sounded less mean than *What?*

Sofia sounded abashed. "I'm sorry to interrupt you. It's just —"

Her apologizing for something that was clearly not even her fault irritated me even more. "Oh, God, Sofia. It's fine. I was just being a bitch. What?"

"I was just calling because I wanted to tell you that it's up. The first episode, I mean, of Cole's show."

Already?

"You probably already know. I'm sorry. I —"

"So*fia*. Stop saying sorry. What's the URL? Oh, right. With threes instead of *e*s. Don't forget about tonight. Wear something red."

After I hung up, I navigated to the website on my phone. The screen was tiny and the speaker shitty, but it would have to do. My stomach panged with a little nervous, wretched twist. Those crafty damns found ways to give themselves when I was least expecting them.

The episode had already begun; Cole was auditioning bass players on the beach. He had surrounded himself with dozens of speakers of all sizes. Every time a would-be player approached, Cole produced a communal bass guitar, shouted an announcement to the onlookers, and then made a little ta-da hand gesture. The gesture must've been some holdover from NARKOTIKA, because every time he did it, the gathered idiot fangirls made supersonic noises.

This annoyed me. It was like they had some intimate knowledge of him that I didn't. Didn't they know that had nothing to do with who he really was? They thought they knew him. Nobody knew him.

The sound of each audition spiraled out over the beach from the barracks of speakers. Leaning on the ancient, wood-sided speakers closest to Cole was a thin, rangy guy with shoulder-length blond hair and aviator sunglasses. He was so incredibly scruffy that he had to be either a hippie or famous.

Text appeared on the screen beneath his face: *Jeremy Shutt, former NARKOTIKA bassist.*

I wasn't sure how I felt about this bit of Cole's past appearing in his present. It felt like one step closer to that ragged rock star who'd collapsed onstage.

Mark pushed himself on the counter beside me to watch; I tilted my phone so he could see better.

A crowd had gathered around Cole. He was so electric, his body language so magnetic, that even on this tiny screen I could feel the tug of his spell. I envied the ease of it until I remembered that he'd had a lot of practice — he was meant to be exciting to watch from even the cheap seats in an auditorium.

Cords snaked like vines across the sand; Cole was encouraging people to plug in their own speakers. A variety of tiny iPod speakers studded the ground, as well as bigger, fancier speakers some people must have brought. It looked like an electric tree studded with weird fruit.

And the bass players kept coming.

I didn't know how they all knew to show up. Maybe Baby had used her contacts. Maybe Cole had. Maybe there was a core group of NARKOTIKA fans blogging his every move. Or maybe it was just because he had such a huge crowd and so many speakers and had somehow turned Venice Beach into his playground.

Onscreen, a little girl plugged in a small orange speaker and clapped delightedly. Cole St. Clair became just that little bit louder.

"I *heard* that while I was driving in," Mark said. "I wondered what it was. That's got to be so loud. That's got to be illegal."

None of the players satisfied Cole, though Jeremy shrugged approvingly at some. There was one guy, a crowd favorite, who kept playing and playing and playing. A winner?

But then Cole switched off the amp. He shook his head.

The crowd groaned, but Cole just twirled his hand. He turned away, and the guy didn't exist for him anymore. I'd always wondered how Cole got anything practical done, how he'd come so far, and now I saw. People were no longer people, they were just parts of the plan, in the goal. And parts could get moved around without thought or emotion.

It made me think about all the girls Cole said he'd slept with on tour. That had seemed like such an impossible feat to me, not because I disbelieved him, but because I couldn't imagine letting that many people have access to me. It sounded exhausting, frantic. Now I suddenly saw it, though. How he turned people into objects, and how easily he could be done with them.

Inside my heart was cool and dark.

"This guy is unbelievable," Mark said, but I couldn't tell if he was talking about Cole or the next player. A few dozen more speakers had been plugged in since the last time the cameras had focused on them. It was hard to tell where they were all getting their power from. Jeremy had to keep going away to tinker with something.

"I guess I remember some of their stuff. Are you a NARKOTIKA fan?" Mark asked.

"I know him. Cole, I mean."

"Is he really like that?"

Cole was like that. He was also not like that. It just depended on when you saw him. Wasn't that everybody, though? "Sure."

"Next Saturday, we're having a thing at the house," he said. "The others are coming. Are you?"

"Others?"

As Cole dismissed yet another bassist on the screen, Mark waved a hand around the shop. Oh. The other monsters.

"What sort of thing?"

Mark picked up the seagull foot. "Just a thing. No pressure. Think about it. Yeah?"

I kept all expression from my face, but inside I was a little flattered. I said, "I'll think about it." I tried to imagine going to a *thing* with Cole.

On the show, Cole turned away all comers as yet more speakers got plugged in. The cameraman walked along a string of speakers that trailed out for yards and yards: big black rectangles and palm-sized red ones and square gray ones.

The cops came, of course. They looked as if they expected trouble, but this Cole was not trouble.

"We're not hurting anyone," he said, gesturing broadly. "Look at all these happy faces."

The cameras swung over the crowd, who obligingly chirruped and cheered and leaped for attention. Cole was right: Most of them *were* happy. How easily he had surfed their individual thoughts and moods and replaced all of that with his noisy joy.

The cops informed Cole that he was violating noise code.

"I am glad to hear it," Cole replied, and he really did sound glad. "Do either of you play the bass?"

"I beg your pardon?"

"I need a bass player."

A cop laughed.

So did Cole. Then he stopped. "No, seriously. Give us a whirl and we'll shut this thing down."

The cops, captains of reason, eyed the cameras, the crowd, and each other. Cole smiled beatifically at them.

Reason died.

Of course the cops played. Did they have a choice?

One officer played. The other danced. The crowd was apoplectic. Officer Bass wasn't the greatest player, but it didn't matter. It was a cop playing a bass amplified by three hundred speakers and Cole St. Clair's smile.

The world belonged to Cole.

"Now you stop?" the cop asked. "That was the deal."

Cole said, "I still don't have a bassist."

Surely this wasn't how it ended. Not all of this fuss for nothing. The crowd was hushed.

In the quiet, Jeremy stepped forward. He shook his head, as if in disbelief. Tucked a bit of his blond hair behind his ear. "Fine, Cole. Fine. I'll do it."

For a second, a bare, bare second, I saw Cole's real smile, and then it dissolved into his show smile. He did a complicated man shake with Jeremy, and then grabbed his hand and held it over his.

"We have a winner!" he shouted.

He leaned close to Jeremy then, speaking quietly, as if it was just between them. But I knew Cole, and I knew he hadn't forgotten the cameras.

This was what he told us all: "Welcome back, man."

Credits rolled.

It was a brilliant little piece of TV.

I felt unexpectedly proud of Cole. He had been right, earlier, at least about one thing: He knew what people wanted. It didn't mean he was going to stay out of trouble, but he was very good at what he did. For one brief, crystal moment, I wished he was here, because in this moment, I could have told him that without any of my usual brittleness.

But he wasn't. So all I could think was: *Isabel, don't fall in love with him again.*

CHAPTER THIRTEEN

· COLE ·

"Dinner," I told the phone as I walked back to the apartment. I was holding a nine-dollar orange juice that Baby's budget had paid for. The sign outside the juice store had said CHANGE YOUR FUTURE WITH SUNSHINE IN A GLASS. My future was looking pretty great already, and I couldn't wait to see what would happen if I added orange juice to it. "That's the next meal."

"What?" said Isabel. There was something satisfying, really, about just calling her number and having her pick up.

"Dinner. Next meal. You. Me. What a delicious plan we have."

"I can't," Isabel replied. "I promised my cousin Sofia that I'd go out with her. She'll become a creepy old lady if I don't take her out."

"I like it when you're noble. You could come to my place," I said. It was hard to tell if the orange juice was changing my future, because I hadn't known where I was heading before I started drinking it. "There is room in the shower for three."

"I am not taking my cousin to your shower for a good time. What sort of lesson does that teach her? You could come out with us."

I didn't know what kind of a person this Sofia was, but I didn't feel up to small talk. Right now I was basking in the contentment of having done a job well and having earned a damn orange juice. "What sort of music is playing tonight?"

"I don't know."

"You live in L.A. and you *don't know*?" I actually didn't know who was playing, either, but it felt like something that I would know if I actually lived here.

"I don't like concerts. People jump around and smell, and the music sounds like crap."

"I don't know if I can talk to you if you're going to be spewing this blasphemy all the time." I paused to look at a sign that advertised a professional phrenologist. The sign also featured a line drawing of a bald man in profile with stars around his head. It was hard to understand what the product on offer was. "Have you never been to a concert that you liked?"

"Let me think about it; no, no, I haven't. Have *you* ever been to one you actually like? Or do you just think you ought to like them?"

"That's a ridiculous question," I replied, although possibly it wasn't. I hadn't been to a lot of shows until I *was* the show, and it turned out that the music industry disapproved of you missing your own concerts, even if you didn't think they were a good time. "Is Sofia real?"

"What? I don't even know why she is the way she is. Nothing in her childhood seems to support her level of neuroticism. Wait. You mean is she a real person? I didn't invent a cousin to get out of dinner, Cole. I'd just tell you."

I asked, "Are you going to pick up next time I call you?"

"I did this time, didn't I?"

"Say yes."

"Yes. Conditionally yes."

I finished the orange juice. I was trying to be magnanimous in light of the discovery that tonight wasn't going to involve Isabel Culpeper's lips. This juice had changed my future in unpleasant ways. "What conditions?"

"Sometimes you do things like call me forty times a day and leave obscene voicemails and that's why I don't pick up."

"Ridiculous. That doesn't sound like me. I would never call an even number of times."

"Also, sometimes you call only because you're bored and not because you have anything to say, and I don't want to be some sort of living Internet that you summon to entertain yourself."

That did sound like me.

"So go home and write your album and then call me in the morning and tell me where we're going this weekend."

"I'll be all alone."

"We're all alone, Cole."

"That's my little optimist," I said.

After I hung up, I walked back to the house.

I thought about kissing Isabel in the shower.

I thought about how I had the evening alone in this strange New Age paradise.

I thought about working on the songs for the album.

I thought about calling Sam.

I thought about getting high in the bathroom.

I crossed the yard to the stucco house where Leyla was staying. The sliding door to the yard stood open.

Inside, it was mostly just a white sofa and a lot of bamboo. The evening light through the front windows made it look like an elegant eco-car showroom, minus a car. Leyla sat in the middle of the floor performing yoga or meditation. I couldn't remember if they were actually different things. I thought meditation was the one that didn't require special pants.

I knocked on the doorjamb.

"Lily. Leyla. Can I talk to you a second about tomorrow? When we make the world a better place?"

Leyla blanketed me with a heavy-lidded, pacific gaze.

"Oh, you."

"Yes, me. Funny story: That is also the first thing my mother said to me."

Leyla didn't laugh.

"I just thought I ought to let you know," she said, "because I believe in honesty: I don't respect your work or anything about your personal sense of life."

"God. Well. That's out there now."

Leyla extended an arm and stretched. "It feels good, doesn't it?"

I wondered if it was some kind of milestone, to be dissed by a hippie. "I wasn't really reaching for the word *good*, but okay. Do you want to play any variations on that note, or was once enough for you?"

She switched arms. Her speed ranged between excruciating and sloth-like. "People are totally expendable to you. They're just, like, objects."

"Okay, and?"

"And you are in it for the celebrity, not the music."

"That is where you're wrong, my friend," I told her. "I am in it for the both of those things. Fifty-fifty, at least. Maybe even forty-sixty."

"Have you even written the album we're supposed to record in six weeks?"

"Now you're harshing my buzz."

It wasn't even fun to mock someone who couldn't tell that you were.

Leyla asked, "How do you know you're not going to hate my playing, too?"

I gave her the Cole St. Clair smile to buy some time.

The thing was, I could audition for new bass players because Jeremy, my old bass player, had been sitting beside me. I could get another bassist because I wasn't really replacing the old one. Jeremy hadn't gone, just moved. But the drummer from NARKOTIKA wasn't living in a house somewhere in the canyons. He was dead in a hole, dead in a wolf's body. And if I started thinking about drummers in an are-they-better-than-Victor way, I didn't think I could handle it. I had stuffed my guilt and my grief into that grave. I'd said sorry to a dead man, and it was over.

Tenuously over.

I said, "I have a plan. Everything's under control."

She closed her eyes again. "Control is an illusion. Animals have no delusions of control."

Suddenly, out of nowhere, I wanted to be with Isabel and only Isabel so badly that I couldn't believe I had to spend the evening alone here in this place with just Leyla to look at.

"You're a hippie freak," I said. I didn't care if the cameras heard me.

"There are no hippie animals," Leyla replied, "because every animal is, by its nature, at one with its surroundings."

I knocked on the threshold and I stepped back over it into the yard. Desire was still burning in me. "I might fire you tomorrow."

She didn't open her eyes. "I am fine with whatever tomorrow brings."

Which was a ridiculous sentiment. Tomorrow brought exactly what you told it to bring. If you told it nothing, nothing was what you got. I was done with nothing. I wanted something. No. I wanted *everything*.

CHAPTER FOURTEEN

· ISABEL ·

It only took about forty-five minutes before Cole called me again. I had just begun the final descent into the House of Ruin.

"I thought about your evening plans," Cole said, "and I thought, really, they weren't that great for Sylvia. Sofia? Sofia."

"I see you know her well. How is it they aren't great for her?" I backed the SUV into the driveway. I didn't look in the mirror. I had been straight when I started, and if I ran over old ladies, pets, and children, it was their fault. Fair warning.

"How is it — oh, look how you just played right into my reply here. Because they don't have me in them."

"And what, exactly, is your great plan that involves you?"

"All plans involving me are great. But this one is a surprise and you should bring Sylv — Sofia and a sweater and maybe some cheese cubes on sticks."

"I don't like ta-das." Already my heartbeat had sped up. Exactly what I was trying to avoid.

"This isn't a ta-da. It's a great plan. Oh, and there will be two other people there. But one of them is like Sofia because life is scary, and the other one is like you. Sort of. Except instead of sarcasm, he has religion."

"Cole —"

"Don't forget the cheese."

An hour later, I stood with Sofia and a bunch of dead people. Cole's great plan had involved meeting him at the Hollywood Forever Cemetery beside the memorial of Johnny Ramone. He — Cole, not Johnny — looked freshly washed and one-thousand-times-edible in a plain white T-shirt and very expensive jeans. He had brought two not-dead people: Jeremy and a man who seemed to be named Leon. The latter was old enough to be my father and was dressed in very nice slacks and a neat button-up with the sleeves rolled up. A manager, maybe? Jeremy, meanwhile, looked more hippie and less famous in person.

Sofia was not very happy to be in a cemetery. Neither was Leon. Both were obviously too polite to say it out loud.

I wasn't bothered because:

- The people here were long dead and beyond anyone's help
- I didn't know any of them, including Johnny Ramone
- It was taking a lot of my brainpower to not imagine when the next opportunity to make out with Cole would be

Also, the cemetery was not very creepy. The sun was blazing pink down behind the sky-high palm trees and white mausoleums. Vaguely mirthful tombstones grew up around pretty lakes. And there were peacocks. It was hard to be creeped out in the presence of peacocks.

Plus there were several hundred living people sitting on blankets between the graves.

"I'd like to send a card to the flamingo who died to make your coat," Cole told me, "because it is doing a great job being apparel. I would like to put everything not covered by it in my mouth."

That was a lot. It was not a very substantial pink jacket (and it was fur, not feathers). His eyes said everything he hadn't. I wasn't sure my face hadn't been saying the same thing back to him.

I was never going to make it out of this evening alive.

"Not in front of the children," Jeremy said.

Cole handed me his sunglasses. I put them on and looked at him through them. There was not a trace of his showman smile this evening, or possibly these sunglasses had been programmed to edit it out. He just looked . . . handsome, and cheerful, and like he would have sex with me right there.

Help.

But I was the only one around to help me.

He turned his attention to Sofia.

"Is there cheese in that thingy?" he asked her, waving a hand at the picnic basket she held. To this point, she hadn't said anything, her brain overloaded by the presence of so many other members of her species. Now this was too much, to be asked about the cheese. She stared back at him with round eyes.

"Just sandwiches," she managed. Then, a little louder, "Different kinds of sandwiches."

It was not just sandwiches. Because it was Sofia, it was an actual covered basket with a striped picnic blanket tastefully peeking from beneath the lid. It was ready for a magazine spread: *Plan your perfect picnic! Just add friends!*

"I want a keyboard on my headstone," Cole remarked, turning his attention to the statue of Johnny Ramone playing an electric guitar. He touched Johnny's face, which seemed sacrilegious. "Jeremy, what do you want on yours?"

Jeremy had been gazing at the Rob Zombie inscription on the side of the memorial: *A dedicated punk and a loyal friend.* "I'm going to be cremated. What good will this body do when I'll already be on my way to the next?"

"Of course," Cole said. "I'm going to have you stuffed, anyway. Isabel? How about you? A machine gun perhaps, or a tiara?"

I could not smile because the current game required me not to smile. But I liked his version of me. I replied, "Both."

"Leon?" Cole asked.

Leon was too kind for this, I could tell. He was the sort of earnest and pleasant man who would never let you know if you offended him, which only made me feel somehow pressured to not offend him. But he wanted to please Cole, because everyone wanted to either please Cole or kill him, so he answered, "I saw a grave once with an angel on it, and even though her head was like this" — he tucked his chin — "she was smiling. Just a little. It was nice. I'd like that."

"I could hook that up," Cole said.

Sofia realized a second before she was asked that she was the next in line for this question. Distress welled in her eyes.

"That's morbid," she interjected in a sweet voice only audible to attentive dogs. Luckily for her, Cole was an attentive dog.

"Death's not morbid," he said. "Everything else is."

"I don't think it's nice to talk about," Sofia said bravely. "There are so many beautiful things to talk about."

"Indeed," Cole agreed, to my relief. He grasped Leon's arm and pointed. "There. Leon. Yonder. That is the photo op of the day." Leon obediently plucked his phone from his slacks and framed the place Cole indicated: the palm trees, all slanted to the right, silhouetted on the glory-pink sky behind a white mausoleum.

"I took a photo with my mind," Jeremy said.

My mind's memory card was full. I had to delete an old mind-photo of a simpler San Diego sunset in order to take this one.

As a group of older women passed by us, laughing and gripping wine bottles, I asked, "What's your plan here, Cole?"

"Actually," Cole replied, "it's Leon's plan."

At this, Leon looked modest. "I read about it in the weekend insert."

Cole agreed, "The place where news happens. Apparently, they are going to project a motion picture on the side of that mausoleum over there" — he gestured to the photo op — "and we will sit like so" — he crossed his fingers on both hands — "and watch it."

The white mausoleum he indicated was massive and featureless, ideal for film projection. "Which film?"

Cole leaned forward, looking knowing. Desire stabbed me. *"Beauty and the Beast."*

He smirked. It was not actually *Beauty and the Beast.*

I narrowed my eyes. "I don't like it when you call me a beast."

Cole's grin was so wonderful that it hurt.

Leon broke in, "Folks, maybe we should find a seat?"

As Cole leaped ahead with Jeremy, Sofia hung at my elbow. She whispered, "Oh, Isabel, he's so *beautiful*."

Only she said it like she would say *terrible*.

Up ahead, the boys had found a place without too many tall people in front of it. Sofia spread the blanket and served everyone sandwiches, much to my annoyance — but the others didn't know to tell her not to. I watched her eat hers very quietly and precisely, tearing off small pieces so she wouldn't do it wrong with her mouth open. It just made me want to punch something. Couldn't she see that the others didn't care about how she chewed? How they were all prepared to like her before she handed them sandwiches?

I expected (feared?) there to be alcohol of some kind, but it turned out that Jeremy was some kind of straight-edge Buddhist, and Leon had given up drinking five years before, and Cole was also abstaining, and Sofia and I were us.

Cole, sitting beside me, put his hand on my back, under my jacket. His fingers wanted me and nothing else. I was absolutely dying.

"Would you like my jacket?" Leon asked Sofia.

"Oh, no, I'm fine," Sofia said, though she was clearly freezing and Leon had said it in a strictly fatherly way. Probably she didn't remember what fatherly looked like.

"Sofia," I said, lowering my sandwich from my mouth. The edge of the bread had a red mark on it from my lipstick. "If you don't take that man's jacket, I'm going to set something on fire."

Cole immediately came to life.

Jeremy shook his head slowly. "No, man. Not here."

He said it with such lazy, muted humor that it suddenly seemed obvious that they'd been in a band together. That he, anyway, knew Cole in a way that those fangirls did not.

I expected to feel jealous, but I felt more like I'd found another member of a survivors' club.

Sofia took the jacket.

The movie began. It turned out to be *Ferris Bueller's Day Off*, which we had all seen.

At one point I glanced over to Cole, and he was just — looking at me. His eyes were narrowed like he was trying to learn something from my face. He was silhouetted by the very last of the pink sky and the tall, leaning palms. It was impossible to think that California hadn't made him, because he looked like he had emerged from the ground here along with the palms and the peacocks and the memorial of Johnny Ramone playing his guitar.

He didn't look away.

God, I wanted to kiss him so badly.

I wished we were alone.

But there was Sofia, who needed me, and Leon, who seemed to be Cole's driver and date, and Jeremy, who — well, I didn't know what Jeremy was. He seemed like he could handle himself.

Partway into the movie, Sofia excused herself for the toilets. She was gone for too long, so I pushed myself to my feet with a sigh. I whispered, "I'm just going to go check on her."

I found her in one of the mausoleums. The wide aisle led me

under a high, domed glass ceiling. On either side of me, the skyscraping walls were divided into squares that looked like post office boxes. There were small urns attached to the front of them, because these were actually boxes of dead people.

Sofia was crying noiselessly next to an urn, Leon's jacket still over her shoulders. My heels clicked on the floor as I marched up to her.

"This is not what grown-ups do," I told her.

She turned her face and sniffled. "I'm not a grown-up."

"What is even the matter?"

"I don't know what to say to people."

"It's a movie. We're not saying *anything*."

"But if we *were* talking. I wouldn't know what to say."

I didn't know the first thing about how to cure a hypothetical problem that I would have barely understood even if it hadn't been hypothetical.

Which meant that a few moments passed, during which Sofia grew more upset and I grew more angry and thought more about dead people and how my brother was one of them, dead in a hole instead of in a clean white box in California.

"Hey," said a voice behind me. Against all reason, it was Jeremy. He was all unthreatening and hunched over, tucking one bit of hair behind his ear. "It's me. I came to see if everything was okay?"

"Oh, she's . . ." *upset with life.*

His presence pushed Sofia over the edge. She wailed, "Now I've really ruined things!"

I snapped, "You have *not*."

Jeremy said smoothly, "Oh, hey, no. Cole's just on his date with Leon; they're having a grand old time. So hey, hey, do you mind if I try something? It's this thing I learned in, like . . ."

He'd moved around me to face her. And something about his expression must have looked more comforting than mine, because Sofia gulped down the latest batch of tears and met his eyes.

"You just get overwhelmed, right?" Jeremy asked. He gestured while he said it. He had long, long fingers. Bassist fingers. He started to tap his breastbone with one hand, and with the other, he took her limp wrist and made her mimic the gesture on herself. "Tap here and just say something with me. Just say, like, 'We're all cool here. They like my smile.' "

What the hell.

Sofia offered him a shy smile.

What the hell times two.

"Now tap here," Jeremy said, and started tapping his chin. I expected Sofia to refuse — I would have — but she did as he did. "And say, 'We're all cool here. They think I'm nice.' "

Times three. What. The. Hell.

"Oh my God," I said. "Is this happening?"

"Isabel," Jeremy said mildly, "this is a positive space."

Sofia suppressed a startled and watery giggle. I rolled my eyes. "Will this be long?"

"Is eternity long?" asked Jeremy.

"Oh my —"

He grinned. "I'm totally kidding. It'll be five or ten minutes."

I pointed outside. "I'll be out there. Are you okay with that, Sofia?"

She was. Of course. Imaginary creatures are always happy with other imaginary creatures.

I had only made it a few yards out into the darkness when Cole appeared right in front of me. His eyes were hungry.

"Isabel —"

I just had enough time to feel his fingers seize my hand, pulling me aside, and then we were around the side of the mausoleum and kissing. It was such an instantaneous thing, something I'd wanted so much, that it was impossible for me to decide if he had begun it or if I had. Everything in my brain shut down except for his mouth, his body, his fingers banded tightly around my upper arm, the other hand hitching my skirt. His hand on my thigh was a question: My hands pulling him closer was the answer.

It wasn't really dark enough to hide us, Sofia could come out with Jeremy and see us, I was not supposed to be getting in too deep.

It didn't matter.

I wanted him.

A flashlight swept across our faces. A warning.

"Hey, kids," said a guy. Standard-issue security guard. "Get a room."

Cole stopped kissing me, but he didn't let go.

"Yeah," he said, flashing a tense smile at the guard, who moved on. Then he whispered in my ear, all tongue and teeth, "Come back with me."

My pulse crashed in my stomach and my thighs. I knew what he meant, but I said, "I was on my *way* back."

"Not that," Cole said. Then repeated, "Not that. After. Come back with me."

He wasn't talking about making out. He was talking about sex.

I said, "I have to take Sofia back home."

"I'll pick you up," Cole said.

My body hummed an answer for me. I tried to think clearly. "How would I get home?"

"Home?" Cole echoed, as if he had no idea what the word meant. "Stay. I'll take you back in the morning. Isabel —"

"*Stay!*" I whispered, suddenly hot. It wasn't staying that I was afraid of. It was that I might *like* staying, and then what happened when one of us got tired of the other? I'd seen those sorts of fights often enough at the House of Misery to know I didn't want it. Two days ago, he hadn't been here, and now he wanted me to spend the night with him. Maybe he was a cool-ass rock star who'd laid a ton of girls, but I was just a possibly ex-Catholic girl who had gotten to third base a few times. "What do you want from me?"

"I told you," he said. "Dinner. Dessert. Sex. Life."

Somehow hearing him say it sort of hurt, because of how much I *wanted* to believe it versus how much I really *did* believe it. I told him, "You're saying that because you think you look good saying it."

Cole made a dismissive sound. "I am, but I also mean it."

I removed his hand from my ass so I could think better. "Slower, Cole."

He sighed, noisy and melodramatic. Then he dropped his

head onto my shoulder, breathing into my collarbone. For once not moving, not needing, not asking, not doing. Just holding me, and letting me hold him up.

It was the most shocking thing.

It wasn't a question. It was a statement.

And here was what I was most afraid of: that Cole St. Clair would fall in love with me, and I'd fall in love with him, both of us human weapons, and we'd both end up with broken hearts.

CHAPTER FIFTEEN

· COLE ·

Isabel didn't come back with me, which meant I was still in the apartment alone, the giant moon observing me through the glass deck doors. I wanted her so badly that I couldn't think. There were an uncountable number of minutes between now and morning.

I looked at the keyboard, and it looked back. Neither of us was interested in the other.

In the kitchen, I investigated the cameras affixed to the edge of the counter, pointed at the floor. I crouched in front of one and said, "Hello. I'm Cole St. Clair. And this is my instrument." I straightened and gyrated my hips in front of it for a minute or two. The camera wasn't a satisfying audience.

I climbed onto the counter to see if I could reach the ceiling. I could. I kicked the toaster onto the floor to see what sort of sound it would make. Not much.

It wasn't morning yet.

I couldn't understand Isabel's resistance to my irresistibility. I could only stand being this furious with wanting her if I thought that she was somewhere wanting me, too. I longed to call her and ask her if this was the case, but even I could tell that such a phone call would violate every parameter she had set for me.

The bed was too much of a commitment, so I crouched on one of the chairs in the living room and picked at threads on the arm until I fell asleep. I dreamed of being awake in a chair that smelled like old ocean water, and I woke up alone with a crick in my neck and the moon still in my face. My heart and lungs were still eating me from the inside, so I got my things and went up to the roof deck.

This late-early night-morning Los Angeles was cool and violet. The moon was just past full, but it was still close enough to be a wide-open eye. I heard the sounds of people laughing from a bar several streets over.

I prowled the deck, running my fingers under the deck railing and the edges of the furniture and around the potted lemon trees. There were no cameras, and I was above most of Venice; all I could see were other roofs. The deck next door was vacant; I thought the entire house was, actually. A rental. And the deck on the other side of that, barely visible in the dark, was also empty.

It was safe. Probably. It was out in the open, so technically it was not bulletproof. But it was close enough. The margin of risk was not large enough for me to even pretend I cared about it. I would get away with it for five to seven to twelve minutes.

I injected and I swallowed and I waited.

When I was a wolf, the space felt smaller. My senses felt fragmented. I kept remembering a young man with a jittering pulse and I saw the world out of his eyes, higher, and then I forgot him. I paced the edge of this space, trapped high above the hissing ground below. The leaves of the lemon trees murmured to me. The smell of nearby food was hot and sweaty. Overhead, a star smeared noisily from one side of the sky to the other.

I put my paws on the edge — sand gritted under the pads of them — and looked down below. Too far to jump. But the world stretched out invitingly nonetheless. I whistled in soft frustration.

Everything in this place called to me, but I was trapped up above.

I fell back into my human body beside the lemon tree's decorative pot. Lying on my back, I looked up through the leaves of the captive fruit tree. My thoughts and memories slowly reassembled themselves.

Even as a wolf, I wanted more.

Chapter Sixteen

· COLE ·

Here are things that never get old: the first word said into a recording studio mic, the rough cut of a song, the first play on the radio.

Here are things that do get old: me.

Whatever part of me that had been able to pull off all-nighters or something close before had evidently been left behind in my ill-spent youth, or maybe just in Minnesota. I slept until the sun was high and then discovered I had nothing but an empty donut bag of bored ants for breakfast. I clearly couldn't work under those conditions, so I went out on foot to hunt/ gather (lyric possibility? Jot in notebook) (*gather/hunt* more interesting as it is unexpected).

(*I gather/you hunt/we both miss the trap*)

By the time I got back to the apartment, the sun was even higher and Baby was waiting for me.

She sat in one of the two white vinyl chairs in the vestigial sitting area, working away on her iPad. When I slid open my door, she looked up.

"You're supposed to be working."

I slid the door shut behind me with my elbow. "I was working."

"What do you have there?"

I looked at my hands. I couldn't remember everything I'd gotten. "Stuff. For things. For. Work."

She watched me unload my arms onto the table in front of her chair: a small wicker basket that crackled very intriguingly and would probably crackle even better into a microphone, a fake ivory candelabra, a not-gently-used Hawaiian shirt in extra large, and a small purple Buddha statue as a welcome-back present for Jeremy.

"This isn't *The Bachelor*," she told me. "I don't have the budget to stalk you. So you're going to have to do interesting things when my cameras are there. Or call me when you're about to do something. Meanwhile, my feelings are hurt that you fired the musicians I picked out just for you."

I headed to the keyboard. It was a Dave Smith. Maybe my Dave Smith. I didn't know if it had been liquidated or something when I was reported dead/missing/werewolf (lyric possibility?) (too on the nose) (another word for *werewolf*?) *(beast) (unicorn) (suicide)* (jot in notebook?) (nothing to see here).

I pulled out my notebook and wrote *nothing to see here* in it. "Cole."

"What? Oh. I didn't want a guitarist, and the bass player was totally wrong."

Baby tapped at something on her iPad. "For the record, he was chosen by users on the show's forum before you even got here. They knew him by name. It was their way of being involved."

This was the way I preferred my listeners to be involved: buy the album, come to my shows, know all the words.

I turned on the keyboard. Lights flared across the board. For a moment, I rested my finger on one of the knobs. Just to feel what it was like again. It had been so long. Even though, chronologically, I had spent much more time playing my keyboard on tour than I had playing it at home, it was those early days I remembered now. My first keyboard, my bedroom, morning sun across keys, cell phone photos snapped of the settings, songs hummed with my eyes closed. It was like NARKOTIKA had never happened.

"Get out your phone," Baby said, "and call him back. Tell him you've made a mistake."

I didn't even bother to turn around. "No."

"This is not optional."

I bristled inside, but I kept my face blank and my voice careless. "Is making a good album optional?"

No answer.

"They didn't like the first episode?" I knew they had. "They didn't like Jeremy?"

"I didn't mean for this to be a NARKOTIKA reunion show. Is Victor going to appear out of the woodwork?"

I could feel the song drain out of me. "I can pretty much guarantee that is not going to happen."

There was a very long pause from behind me. I heard Baby tapping away at her electronic life while I flicked on the speaker and concentrated on making the biggest, fattest, meanest synth-swell this apartment had ever heard.

The chord grew and grew until I was imagining the album

cover and the number of tracks on the back and the feeling of releasing it out into the world to sink or swim — only they always swam; it was only ever me that sank — and wondering what in the world I would call myself if I wasn't called NARKOTIKA.

Finally, Baby said (loudly, to be heard over the biggest, fattest, meanest synth-swell this apartment had ever heard), "Here is the deal. You aren't going to take Chip back?"

I released the chord I'd been hitting. The sound slowly trailed off. "Who the hell is Chip? Oh. No. I'm sticking with Jeremy."

"Then here's the deal," she said again. "This is yours now."

I turned. In her outstretched hand was a phone. "What's this?"

She didn't answer until I'd taken it, reluctantly. "Your new work phone. I just signed you up for every social media avenue on the Internet. And I told the world you're going to be handling all those personally. You want to be able to call the shots on the band? You're going to have to work twice as hard for it."

I stared at the phone in my hand. "You have murdered me."

"You would know if I'd murdered you."

I groaned.

"Don't even," Baby said, standing. "Don't act like I'm your jailer. Because we both want the same thing. This show does well, I get to do another one. This show does well, you don't have to tour for the rest of your life. So get to work and don't forget you have studio time booked for this afternoon."

I got to work.

Because she was right.

CHAPTER SEVENTEEN

· ISABEL ·

"What's the next meal?" Cole asked me.

"Lunch," I replied. I glanced at the classroom door to make sure it stayed closed as I walked in the direction of the girls' restroom. Bathroom breaks were the only allowed excuse to escape my CNA class, a fact that seemed to trouble only me. The other students in the class seemed genuinely engaged, a concept I could only understand if I told myself they hadn't read the textbook closely enough to note the redundancies in their learning experiences.

In any case, Cole's number on my vibrating phone screen was more than enough to make me play the bathroom card. In the hallway, I tried to breathe through my mouth. It takes a certain sort of intestinal fortitude to willingly enter another high school after you'd graduated from your own. The sheer smell of the hall triggered a variety of feelings, any one of which would have been a good topic for a therapy session.

Cole said, "Tell me you want me."

I pushed into the bathroom. "I have a very short lunch break."

"I forgot that you were being educated. Teach me something you've just been taught."

"We're working on professional courtesy. It turns out that no matter how friendly you are with the clients, you're not supposed to call them *sweetie*."

"You are going to make a great C-A-N. C-N-A. Right? Although you do have a great C-A-N."

In the mirror, my mouth smiled. It looked mean and happy.

"Doctor," I replied. "I am going to med school. This is just a necessary evil." Although that wasn't strictly true. I could probably get into a fine premed program without it. But I didn't want fine. There was very little point to fine.

"Come get me," Cole said piteously. "In your car. My car makes me look like a loser."

"That's not your car," I said, and Cole snickered at himself. "I'll come get you. But I'm picking the place this time."

I hung up. I didn't want to go back into class. I didn't want to do my clinicals this week, either. I didn't want to roll old people over and clean whatever was left beneath them. I didn't want to be told by my instructor that I needed to smile when I introduced myself to clients. I didn't want to have to put the gloves on and have that gross hand-glove feeling that happened after I pulled them off. I didn't want to feel like I was the only person in the world who hated people.

You're taking a class in this.

You're going to be a doctor.

This is life.

In the mirror, I looked stark and out of place in front of the worn stall doors. I wasn't sure if that was actually how I looked or just how I stood, with my elbows tucked so that nothing in the room would accidentally touch me. That was the rule: Nothing was to touch me.

I didn't know why I kept letting Cole break it.

An hour later, Cole and I were headed to lunch at an obscure L.A. food establishment.

I wasn't sure why people still got credit for "finding" obscure places to eat. Friends of your parents took you and your mother to some tiny place that made great omelets or something, and the friends preened as if they'd invented omelets, and your mother's all, "How did you *ever* find this place?!" I could tell you the answer: the Internet. Five minutes, a zip code, and cursory access to the Internet would grant anyone the secrets to culinary obscurity.

It pissed me off when people called common sense a magical power. Because if it counted, I was the most magical creature I knew.

I took Cole to a place that I'd discovered with my magical powers, a hole-in-the-wall pie shop that was easy to drive by if you didn't know where you were going. Outside, the front was painted a deep purple. Inside was L.A. at its most visually appealing. The skinny eat-in area was concrete floors, sparse white walls, and reclaimed wood benches. The air was coffee and butter. The ordering area was tiny and quaint: a cooler with interesting drinks, chalkboard menu, a pie case full of delights. I had tried them all, from the velvety citrus tarts to the salty caramel drizzle chocolate pies.

It was so far from the gross high school classroom that I'd

started the day in that it felt as if one or the other must not be real.

We stood in line. I kept finding myself standing too close to Cole, close enough that my shoulder blade pressed into his chest, and then I would realize we were both inhaling and exhaling at the same time.

I didn't want to go back. I wanted to stay here with him. Or I wanted to take him with me. I was sometimes so damn tired of being alone —

I suddenly felt strangely and unpleasantly tearful.

I took a deliberate step to one side. Without my body to anchor him, Cole restlessly turned to the drink cooler and then to the shelves of merchandise and then back to the drink cooler and then back to the shelves of merchandise.

"I'm not really a sweets person." He fingered a T-shirt that I could already tell he wanted to buy purely because it said THE PIE HOLE on it.

I said, "Don't be a bastard."

"Then tell me what to get. Apple? That's a pie."

"Shut up. I will order for you. In fact, you're making me crazy pacing. Go get a table out front."

"Da," replied Cole, and vanished.

When I came outside, I found him at a tiny metal table in dappled shade, staring at two phones he'd set on the tabletop. There were two other tables, one of which was occupied by a cheerful but very ugly woman and her beautiful but very pissy-looking little dog. The third table was occupied by a camera guy, who I gave the finger. He waved back at me with a guile-less smile.

I put Cole's coffee in front of him and sat down with my back to the camera.

"What did you order for me?" he asked, not lifting his eyes from the devices.

"I'm not going to tell you. It'll just have to surprise you when it comes out. It's not apple. What's that other phone?"

Cole glumly explained Baby's mandate.

"That's not that bad," I said. "So she wants you to talk to your fans?"

"I don't want to talk to them," he said. "All they want to talk about is whether I'll take their virginity or write another song like 'Villain' or come play a show in whatever impossibly small place they live in. Did you put sugar in this?"

"No. It's a grown-up coffee. I made it for you the grown-up way. Also, you don't have to be one-on-one. You could just update them in general."

"Update them! *I'm being brilliant. Now I'm being amazing.* How tedious that would be for them."

"Oh, it's tedious already. Baby knows I'm not on the show, right?"

Cole glanced up at the camera. "Legally, she can use the back of your head but not your face. All that" — he gestured to the street — "is too loud for him to pick up any audio, but — do you want to go inside?"

I thought about how there was a certain dark pleasure to anonymously marking my territory, letting the fangirls know that he already had someone. And my hair looked great from the back.

"No," I replied. "Drink your coffee."

Cole took another sip. He looked pained. I slid a sugar packet I had been hiding from behind my mug and he leaped upon it. As he sprinkled its contents into his absolutely already-perfect latte, I picked up the Baby phone. It was a rather nice one.

"Look at the way it sits in your hand." Cole squinted critically at the phone in my palm. "It respects you. You could be Cole St. Clair, you know."

I laughed, a little crueler than was strictly necessary. "Oh, I don't think so. That position is already filled by someone incredibly overqualified."

"I mean, you could be my voice. Try it. Say something."

I gave him a scathing look. But the truth was, although Cole was a complicated creature, his projected self was quite simple. I opened Twitter and typed: *hi hi hi world.*

I hit POST.

I had to admit, it was vaguely thrilling.

"What did I say?" Cole asked.

I showed him.

"I don't use punctuation," he said. "I also use a lot of these things." He cupped his hands on either side of his face to demonstrate. "Parentheses."

"Did you even read it?"

"I did. I know. I was admiring it. Let me see it again. Yes. This is a great idea. It will free me up for all kinds of things."

"Like lying around on your floor and firing nice people?"

"Hey, I don't talk smack about *your* work. For the record, I'm going into the studio this afternoon."

I studied his expression to see how he felt about this, but he was facing the camera, so his features were handsome and regulated and fixed into a studied, arrogant relaxation.

"You could come," Cole said. "And be my — what is it called? Naked person. No. Muse. You could be my muse."

I raised an eyebrow. "I have class. Maybe if you do all your homework, I'll come by and give you a gold star."

"Oh," he said. "I could give you one, too. I'm all about sharing."

"That's big of you."

Cole held his fingers eight inches apart, then reconsidered and made it ten.

The girl from behind the counter appeared with a tray. "Here's your st —"

"*Shh,*" I said. "It's a surprise. For him, I mean. Close your eyes, Cole."

Cole closed his eyes. Smiling at both of us, the waitress set the plates down. She left us there, but I noticed that she waited by the other side of the door, still with the same pleased, anticipatory smile on her face. It felt strange to be the genesis of such a pleasant expression.

"Open your mouth," I ordered Cole. I worked to create what I thought was a bite-sized forkful of strawberry graham tart. It took longer than I expected.

"It is open," Cole said. "In case you didn't notice."

"Keep it that way. I didn't tell you to close it."

I sat there for a long minute, watching Cole fidget, waiting to see if he would lose patience, while I smirked at his closed eyes and looked at the way his neck disappeared into the collar of his T-shirt. He shifted. His eyeballs looked back and forth beneath his eyelids. Anyone wanting to torture Cole would only have to tie him to a chair and do absolutely nothing. He'd beg to have his toenails removed just for something to entertain himself.

"Culpeper," Cole said finally, and I felt a rush of blood in my cheeks at the way he said it. "I'm going to open my eyes."

"No, you aren't." I put the bite in his mouth.

He rolled the pie around for quite a while before he swallowed. He sighed deeply.

"Don't open yet, there's more," I said. "Verdict?"

"Mmmm."

"Ready for the next?"

"Is it chocolate?"

It was the chocolate-caramel crostata, crusted with sea salt. It was the best food ever, if you were in a food-eating mood. "Mostly."

"Just a small bite, then," he warned.

"Good. I barely want to share this much with you anyway."

He opened his mouth obediently, and I placed a small forkful of the caramel-drizzled-chocolate in it. I reminded him, "Eyes still closed."

Savoring the chocolate, he sighed even more deeply.

"That one," he said, "would be the one I would happily let kill me. Eyes still closed?"

"Yes," I said. "Open your mouth."

I kept him waiting again, while I looked at the lines of his cheeks and his jaw and his eyebrows, all of them so purposeful and dazzling and at home here in this place of purposeful and dazzling things. Then I leaned across the table and kissed his open mouth. It still tasted of caramel. I felt him say *Mmmm,* the sound vibrating against my lips, and then he pressed his hand against my neck and kissed me back, earnest and certain.

My heart felt so full I thought it would explode. It was unfamiliar with pumping blood instead of ice.

I sat back. Cole wiped lipstick onto a napkin. I waited for my pulse to return to normal.

I said, "Also, here's this."

I pushed a Pie Hole T-shirt over to him.

Cole sighed a third time, as if this was his favorite flavor of all. He rubbed the shirt against his cheek. Then he picked up his fork and ate his pie in two bites.

I took longer to eat mine, first, because I chewed, and second, because I explored his new phone while I ate. I thumbed through various apps, all of them with Cole's name over them. "Do you really want me to be you online?"

Cole smiled. His real smile. "I trust you."

CHAPTER EIGHTEEN

· COLE ·

By the time I got to the studio with my retinue of cameramen, I had already e-mailed music concepts to both Jeremy and Leyla, and formed an idea of what the episode would look like. I figured as long as I kept them interesting, Baby wouldn't try to make things unpleasant.

The way www.sharpt33th.com worked was this: Each "season" was six weeks long, and most of them had six to nine episodes that could appear at any time. It didn't seem like the most logical way to run a show, but it had been running that way before I arrived and I guessed it would keep running that way after I was gone. Baby had developed a core viewing audience with the SharpT33th app installed on various devices, and those core watchers were rewarded for their dedication by being the first to see the irregularly timed episodes. The idea was that when Baby's disastrous subject did something heinous, it could be posted immediately to the Internet, and if you were sitting by your phone, you could be the first to know. After that first blast out onto the web, the shows got archived and could be watched at any time by anybody. The ideal was once a week, but my contract specified that I could be asked to do up to two a week "if material and demand warranted."

Those extra episodes were always when her subject melted down.

I wasn't going to do those.

The recording studio, close and gray and soulless, was unfamiliar to me, but known to Leyla, who gripped hands with the sound engineer when we arrived, and then immediately sourced kombucha from a fridge. Joan and T lurked with their cameras.

"Hello, man," said the sound engineer. "I'm Dante. How's it hanging?"

Jeremy and I exchanged a look.

"A little to the left," I replied. "How much time do we have?"

Both Leyla and Dante looked insulted at the immediate introduction of business talk, but here was the truth: Studios made me anxious. It wasn't that I didn't like being in one; it was just that for as long as I'd been in music, I'd always been on deadline in one. It didn't matter how big NARKOTIKA got; in the end it was always a new album squeezed into a set number of studio hours before I was scheduled to go back on tour again. There was never enough time to get the songs like I wanted them. Nothing had ever gone out as a disaster, but it had come close. Close enough that I never forgot what the stakes were.

Also, it was freezing cold in the studio. Like a systems test on my wolf-strained nerves.

"Do you want to, like, get to know the equipment?" Dante asked. "I mean —"

"What I'd like," I said, "is to put down my gear and have

those two people over there start hooking in to your equipment while you pull up your Wikipedia page so I can tell who else you've recorded and I can see if we're going to be best friends or mortal enemies by the end of this session."

Dante looked at me. Leyla looked at me. The cameras looked at me. Jeremy set down his case and flipped open the snaps to get his bass out.

No one was moving.

Jeremy looked up. He said, very pleasant and surprised, "Oh. Didn't you know? Cole doesn't do small talk."

Sometimes I can be an asshole. Sometimes I don't care.

Everyone went to do what I said.

"Also," I added, "can we have it warmer in here? I can't feel my goddamn fingers."

Jeremy stood up and adjusted the strap of his bass. He played a soporific bass riff and paused to tune. "Just like old days."

"Almost," I said. I didn't say *Victor*, but I was thinking it. My eyes were on Leyla as she messed around with the drum kit.

"Which of those things are we doing?" Jeremy asked. He meant the files I'd sent. "I fooled around with a few of them."

"Which are you feeling?"

Jeremy glanced at the cameras. He glanced back at me. In a low, casual voice, he asked, "Depends. What's the way?"

God, I loved smart people.

"Special guests," I said, turning my phone so he could see.

"So, noisy," Jeremy confirmed. "That third one, then. It does this?"

He played a little snatch of tune until I could tell which one he meant.

"Do you hear that?" I said to Leyla, who looked up with dislike on her face. "That's the one we're doing. Put your thinking cap on."

I didn't know if a thinking cap would fit over her dreads.

"Cole?" David — Derek — Damon — Dante? asked from overhead, his voice coming from everywhere. Behind a glass panel, I saw him moving behind an array of boards and computer screens. "Can you guys hear me in there?"

"Da."

"My guys are bringing out your headphones. Let me know about the levels in your ears, and then we'll do some levels in here. We're all hooked up. What's the working title for this track?"

" 'Gasoline Love,' " I replied.

Dante typed it in. "Nice."

"Predictable," replied Leyla from behind the kit.

I bristled. "There is nothing predictable about either gasoline or love, comrade. Why don't you go back to not caring what tomorrow brings?"

Leyla shrugged and played a bit of drums.

It wasn't bad. But —

I want Victor

I want Victor

I want Victor

I let myself think it for just a second, and then I shivered and turned to my keyboard. Misgiving still hung inside me. I thought about Isabel's open mouth on mine, back at the pie shop.

Then we got to work.

Recording in a studio is nothing like playing live. Live is everything all at once. There's no redos, no problem solving, just powering through. In a studio, though, everything becomes a puzzle. It's easier if you do the edges first, but sometimes you can't even tell what the edges are. Sometimes the hardest part is telling which track to lay down first — which track is going to be the skeleton to pack flesh onto. The vocals? But what if they're not on the beat or if they drop out for measures and measures? The drums, then. But that left you with a track so spare that you might as well start with nothing, or just a click track. The keyboard, then, establishing the chords and the tone. It would have to be rerecorded, but at least it was something.

Mostly I liked it to start and end with me, anyway.

We worked for an hour, during which I hated Leyla more and more. There was nothing wrong with her drumming. It was fine. But Victor had been the best instrumentalist of us all. Other bands had always tried to poach him from us. *Magic hands.* Leyla was just a person with a drum set.

How stupid I'd been to think I could just go into a studio with any other musicians and come out with something that sounded even vaguely like NARKOTIKA. Not stupid. Cocky. NARKOTIKA was me, but it had also been Jeremy and Victor.

After an hour, "Gasoline Love" was sounding more like "Turpentine Disinterest."

I was in a pretty bad mood by the time my guest stars arrived.

"I thought about bringing coffee," Leon said as he stepped in. The shocked cameras swung to him — impotently, because

Leon hadn't signed a release, and wouldn't. "But I thought that kids these days probably drank these newfangled things instead."

He offered me an energy drink. I was unreasonably glad to see him.

"Leon, I love you," I said, accepting the can. "Marry me and make an honest man of me."

"Oh, well," Leon said. He offered another one to Jeremy, who shook his head but said, "Thanks anyway, man." He'd brought a mason jar of green tea.

Leyla sniffed and took a drag of her kombucha. "Who's this?"

"Special guests," I replied.

She said, "Every guest is special," but halfheartedly.

Then Leon's passengers stepped in: the two cops from the first episode. In uniform. One of them, I knew, had actually ended her shift a half hour before arriving here, but had agreed to come in uniform to improve the general appearance of the shot. I wasn't an idiot. I knew no one would recognize them without the uniforms.

I hoped Baby was impressed by my sheer cunning. Surely she had to realize just how no-holds-barred brilliant it was to bring the cops back. I had really wanted to ask Leon to be in it as well, but I knew he would say yes to make me happy and then would hate it when he was recognized in the grocery store. So I hadn't asked him, even though, in my head, Leon would make a great recurring character on the show. Everybody's dad/brother/uncle/guy.

But I wanted Leon to be happy. That was the mission. Well, one of them.

I exchanged pleasantries with the cops, just polite introductory things like asking them if they had ever gone skydiving or petted a hairless dog. Then we got down to business.

The trick was that I had to find parts for the cops that they could perform in the studio without any particular skill. Sure, the one cop could play the bass badly, but that wasn't going to cut it for a studio track. They could do percussion, though. It would get in the way of the drums, but really, anything that irritated Leyla was a bonus.

I got the cops all set up on the stomp-clap routine, and it turned out the girl-cop (Darla? Diana?) had opera training, so we went a bit wild with that. Dante had no concept of how to use a mixing board, or maybe he just had no idea of how to mix us, but that was all right, because someone whose name sounded like mine was a wizard with a synth and could run a voice through there like no one's business.

It was turning into something quite good. It wasn't a single, but it was beginning to sound like one of those off-the-wall tracks some fans got religious over, the cult classics that somehow managed to get played long after the big ones had burned everyone else's speakers out. A few hours in and I was feeling pretty good about life. This was not quite the point — Isabel was the point — but it was a subpoint, and it was working well.

Then the power went out.

In the false darkness, Jeremy and I looked at each other. Girl opera cop swore, just one short, filthy word, sort of like a scream. Someone sighed. I thought it was Leon.

To the darkness, I said, "Tell me you had this on autosave, Dante."

Dante did not reply, because he couldn't hear me. Without any power, he was just a guy behind a glass wall.

Leyla took a drink of her kombucha — I heard her do it, and it infuriated me. Jeremy tucked a piece of hair behind his ear.

Then the power came back on.

The headphones still weren't working, so I ripped them off and charged into the engineering room. Every computer was beeping and whirring as it came back to life.

"Give me good news," I said.

Dante looked at me. There was a thin rim of white all the way around his pupils. He shook his head.

"Any of it?"

He said, "The drum track?"

It took a long moment for the truth to sink in: Everything weird and one-of-a-kind we had just done was gone. We could redo it, but it would sound like we had redone it. It was like today had never happened. Like someone had just taken my time and thrown it away. Like the pressing deadline that was always there had been shoved closer.

"And it didn't occur to you to save along the way," I said. "You're working with a six-figure project, and you didn't think at some point after the drum track, *I will hit these buttons here on this fancy machine and save it?*"

"I *did* save," Dante insisted. "The power cutting off has messed things up. Like, it's corrupted stuff. That machine won't even start back up again."

I wasn't even certain which machine he was pointing at. I *was* certain that Baby had done this. I was also certain that she had done it to get me to implode on camera. I was even more certain that she was going to get what she wanted.

"Show me," I said. "Show me the corrupted files."

Dante scrolled through a bunch of empty screens. "It's gone, man. I don't know. . . ."

"That is the most obvious thing you have said all day. Is this your *job*? Have you seen one of these things before? Tell me how it is that we still have a drum track."

If he had been in on the plan, he was doing a good job of looking shell-shocked now. He fumbled through some more screens and muttered, "That's, like, the last save that it paid attention to; I don't know, I don't know. . . ."

I gestured toward T, who stood at my shoulder. "I hope you're happy that your total incompetence is being broadcasted to the planet."

I stormed out. In the recording room, Jeremy was packing away his bass because he knew me, and Leyla was still sitting behind her drums because she didn't.

"We could redo it," the bass cop suggested.

Girl opera cop shook her head. She knew.

Leon clapped his hand on my shoulder and then got his car keys.

"It was meant to be," Leyla said. She didn't look surprised, but it was hard to tell if that was because she was in on Baby's plan, or because she was baked, or because she really did believe that it was meant to be.

"I know that you're trying to get me to kick your drum set in," I warned her, "but I'm onto you."

Jeremy told the cops how glad he was that they had come and that at least the cameras had caught their contributions. He made sure that he had their telephone numbers. He shook Leon's hand. He closed the door behind them all. He was good at this.

I called Baby. "This is not the way to get me on your good side."

Baby said, "What?"

"Oh, come on."

"I'm not a mind reader."

"I know you want drama. But you mess with the album again," I said, "and —" I stopped because I couldn't think of what to end the sentence with. I didn't have half an ounce of leverage. I was right back where I'd started. I'd thought I'd been so clever to circumvent the system, to make an album without a label as overlord, and here I was again, just merchandise.

I thought about how she'd been so concerned at the beginning.

I kicked over one of the microphone stands. It barely made a sound in this pointless, generic studio. This wasn't a place to make music. It was a place to record commercials for music.

I didn't even know what the hell I'd been thinking.

"And what, Cole? I don't really like being threatened, and for no reason. I'm working. I have a call on the other line. I don't know what has happened, but I'm happy to help."

I wanted to snarl *This is war!* but the fight was going out of me. I couldn't believe the track was gone. I just couldn't believe it. What a damn waste of everything.

"I want my Mustang," I told her. "That's how you can help. Get me my Mustang."

I hung up. I felt like a toothless dog.

If Victor had been here, I would've turned to him and said, "Let's go get high."

But he wasn't. And I was on camera. And that wasn't me anymore. That wasn't me anymore. That wasn't me anymore.

I looked at Jeremy.

He said, "What are you thinking?"

I said, "I wish Victor would come through that door."

The camera was right on me. Baby was winning this game uncontested. My brain whirred, looking for some kind of traction, some way to turn this to my advantage, but nothing caught.

Jeremy said, "That's not gonna happen. We have to work with what we have." He paused. "What's the way, Cole?"

It was a ridiculous question, because that ship had sailed so miserably away.

A text vibrated through on my phone. It was from Isabel. It just said, **you'd better be recording something I can dance to**.

I *had* been, but it was gone. I pictured it, the way that track would have sounded as she danced to it. Because it was both a fantasy and a memory, I knew precisely what it would feel like to have her hips pressed up against mine. Isabel Culpeper, perfect ten.

I wanted that gold star.

And then it was like a bank of mist cleared from my brain. I turned to T's camera. "You've been filming this whole time, right?"

"Oh, hey," T said, looking alarmed. "You know, it's my job, I —"

I waved my hand to cut him off. "I just wanted to make sure you had what I needed. Let's do this thing."

Jeremy grinned.

CHAPTER NINETEEN

· ISABEL ·

That first day that I was Virtual Cole St. Clair, I spent a lot of time on the Internet. Not because I was posting updates, but because I was researching the way Cole looked on the outside. I realized I'd only heard a few of his songs, so I listened to some with one earbud while my CNA instructor showed movies in a darkened room. I listened to the rest on my drive over to .blush. I had never read an interview with him, so I queued up web pages and scrolled through them on my phone while Sierra pinned various bits of clothing on me in the back room. I listened to NARKOTIKA *Behind the Band* segments as she pulled them off. After she had left me to close down the shop, I watched videos of the bands Cole thanked in his liner notes or mused on as influences in interviews.

I learned that the little hand gesture I'd noticed in the first episode meant that Cole was about to reveal something new or pull off some virtuoso bit of playing or dancing. I made a note of it. Or rather, I made a mental note that he never accidentally did the hand gesture when he was with me. It wasn't a real-Cole gesture he had co-opted for his shows. It had to have been a gesture that he invented for them.

I learned that he had a long-running inside joke with interviewers where they often asked him what he was afraid of and he always replied "nothing."

I learned from a two-year-old interview that he wrote most of his songs in the car or in the shower or while in movie theaters or making out with soon-to-be-ex-girlfriends.

I wasn't interested in learning much after that. So I looked up Baby North instead.

Near the end of my shift, I called Cole. When he picked up, I heard tinny music in the background, including Cole's recorded singing voice. The sound of it gave me a strange little crawl up my skin. "Did you finish your homework?"

"Nearly. It got complicated. I really want my gold star, though."

"There's no partial credit," I replied. I clicked on a hyperlink for an article on Baby. Her face smiled out at me, open and honest, beside a headline that said DEATH BY BABY. "I'm practicing being you. What's one thing you know you would never say in an interview?"

Immediately, he replied, " 'I'm sorry.' "

I didn't have to see his face to know he was pleased with his answer. "God, you are unbelievable. Like, do these lines just come to you, or do you actually see *in your head* how your words look printed before you say them?"

"What a superpower that would be. Like a thought bubble?"

I demanded, "Do you say *anything* without thinking whether or not it sounds good?"

"I don't even know why I'd bother opening my mouth otherwise."

"Yeah. You know, this whole thing where interviewers ask you what you're afraid of and you always answer 'nothing,'" I said. "That's such a lie."

Cole was quiet. It was impossible to tell if it was because he was picturing a clever answer in the thought bubble above his head, or because he was doing something while he was talking to me, or because he had no answer.

Finally, he replied, his voice very different from before. "It's not a lie. It's super clever. It's why I'm still here on this planet. I'm surprised you haven't figured it out with your giant brain. It's a riddle. Like how to get my Mustang out here from Phoenix without having to ever speak to my parents. These are puzzles, Isabel, and I think you should solve them all for me." His voice had returned to normal. Over-normal.

"I don't like puzzles," I told him.

"That's because you are a puzzle," Cole replied, "and you don't like your own kind. It's okay. I don't like other me's, either."

I didn't believe him. Cole got along great with a mirror. "Don't you have homework?"

"Hey, you called *me*."

"Tell me what to tell the world."

"Tell them," Cole started, then paused. "Tell them I am making them a present. And tell *me* that you'll dance to it."

Chapter Twenty

· COLE ·

That night, I returned to the apartment, too tired to be restless. I was the sort of tired that came from finishing something, from emptying myself. I'd chased this feeling before, too, with fancy drinks and cheap drinks and pills that made you slow. But just like how the drug highs could never quite match the highs of creating music, the induced lows could never match this real peace that came from *having* created.

If I were always making an album, I would never be unhappy.

I lay on my bed and put my headphones on and listened to the track on repeat. It was impossible to get tired of listening to a new song the first day I breathed it into life. I texted Isabel. **I did my homework.**

She texted back: **I'm checking your work.**

In the end, I'd pulled the imperfect, lo-fi audio from T's video footage and used it as a scratchy intro. Then I'd had us rip into a harder version with the tinny operatic singing pieced through. It sounded like we'd meant for it to turn out this way all along.

I was glad Isabel was checking my work. But I didn't need anyone else to tell me I'd gotten a passing grade.

I drifted off with the song still playing in my ears. I dreamed about drifting off with the song still playing in my ears.

I woke to the sound of my door opening.

Isabel —

I heard a breathy giggle.

Not Isabel.

I had locked the door, I thought. I had been tired, but I remembered the action of turning the bolt.

My headphones hissed; my music player battery had died. I pulled them off an ear and heard another little snort. The giggles were traveling in packs. I felt like I was living a memory.

My wolf ears heard hands scrubbing over walls. Smelled perfume and sweat. The light came on.

Three topless girls stood in my living room area, peering at me through the see-through IKEA bookshelf into my bedroom. One of them had artfully written my name across her breasts. *COLE* on one. *CLAIR* on the other. *ST.* in small letters on her breastbone.

"I think you have the wrong place," I told them pleasantly, not sitting up. This inspired another round of giggles. They remained in my apartment. They remained topless. I remained in bed.

In the old days, this wouldn't have been a problem. Bored and horny and high, I would have entertained them all if not myself, and then passed out on the deck.

But now I was not only on camera, but I very much wanted Isabel Culpeper to keep taking my calls. I was working arduously and single-mindedly toward my gold star, and there was nothing about this situation that was going to get me that.

"I'm sure I locked that door," I said, sitting up.

One of the girls held up a key. She flashed a million-dollar smile at me.

Oh, Baby.

The girl with my name written large informed me that she was a virgin.

"I'm proud of you," I said. I held up a finger and called Isabel, keeping one eye on my half-naked visitors. "Pumpkin, do you have Virtual Cole with you?"

"Pumpkin," repeated Isabel.

"Da. Yes. Pumpkin." I got up, glad that I had fallen asleep fully clothed.

"I do, but I'm driving. I'm pretty sure there's a cameraman following me. Isn't that funny?"

The girls drifted closer. They were astonishingly drunk. Every camera in the apartment had a shot of boob. I was so untempted that I felt positively saintly. I wasn't sure how I could be so slain by Isabel clothed and so disinterested in these girls.

"Everything about today is funny," I replied. "Could you please broadcast to the world that there are better ways to show your support of my album-making efforts than showing up on my doorstep? Also, why are you driving? Surely there is nowhere in the world you long to drive to at this hour besides me."

I heard a petulant honk from outside the window. The three girls and I all looked out the window. Isabel's SUV was pulling up in the alley behind the apartment. A van pulled up behind with Joan inside.

The timing was tediously coincidental.

"I think you ought to go," I told the girls, who were all invading my personal space in very unself-conscious ways. I began to herd them back the way they came. I paused to pry one from my arm. "It's about to get unpleasant."

As if on cue, the door burst open, the sound in perfect timing with the explosion of my heartbeat.

Isabel Culpeper clicked in, sporting a cropped leopard-print top, black leather pants, and a pair of boots with heels to stab usurpers. She also wore crocheted gloves that went up to her elbows. Nothing about her was out of place. There was not an integer in this world to represent how many times sexier she was than the half-naked girls.

I could not believe that Baby had had the gall to ruin the moment with three topless fans. I felt rather old and weary just then. How many lives had I lived in order to get to a place where these gigglers were merely an inconvenience?

Isabel pursed her red lips. The girls looked at her with the fearlessness of the drunk. Joan and her camera peeked in the doorway.

"Did you broadcast my special request?" I asked Isabel.

I felt strangely nervous that Isabel wouldn't believe my innocence.

"I did," she said. "Pumpkin." Her eyes had found my name jiggling on the intruders. I was no prude, and history will support this claim, but at the moment I was very uncomfortable with the number of bare breasts in the room. It was as if all of my hard-won cynicism had been murdered, orphaning a far more naive sixteen-year-old Cole, nervous that his crush wouldn't agree to go out with him.

This seemed like a very dangerous place for that Cole to reemerge.

Please don't be angry. You have to know this isn't real. Please, Isabel —

I wasn't sure what I could say, not with Joan's camera watching us carefully from just outside the apartment. The cameras inside the apartment watched carefully from everywhere else.

"I think you should give me that key," I told the girls. "And you shouldn't accept keys from strangers. You never know what you'll find on the other side of the door."

"Chop-chop," Isabel suggested, her voice so cool that a nearby semitropical plant dropped dead.

"Are you his *girlfriend*?" the girl with the key asked, her voice ugly. "Because really —"

Isabel interrupted, "Don't say anything we'll both regret later. You can give the key to me, actually."

She held out an imperious gloved hand. The girl relinquished the key with a sort of hiss. The virginal one crept by Isabel. The third spit at Isabel's boots on her way out.

There was a pause. The spitter stopped just beyond Joan, a challenge in her face.

Isabel laughed, nasty and dismissive. I suddenly had a very clear idea of what she must have been like in high school.

"Oh, please," she said.

She slammed the door shut, right in Joan's face.

Silence.

My heart was thudding in my chest. I almost couldn't believe how nervous I was, when I'd done nothing wrong, when I didn't care what anybody thought, when I had spent so long being numb.

"Let's have a little discussion in your office," she said, throwing a hand toward the bathroom. I couldn't tell what she was thinking.

I closed the door behind us and, as she opened her mouth, held a finger to my lips. Joan and her camera had come into the apartment. My wolf hearing could pick up her breathing on the other side of the door and then the shuffling as she worked to get the boom microphone as close to our voices as possible.

Isabel went to the sink and turned the tap on full blast, the movement of her wrist crisp and vicious. I leaned into the shower and spun the knobs.

Then, with the hissing white noise of wasted water behind us, we gathered by the toilet, heads close.

"God, you smell nice," I said, low and hushed, because someone had to say it, and to let some of my anxiety escape.

"You smell like —" Isabel stopped herself. She said, "What's going on here, exactly?"

It was not at all the reaction I'd expected. Not much stopped Isabel in her tracks. I lifted my palm to my hand and inhaled.

Wolf.

Earth and musk, night and instinct.

I didn't know why it was there, only that it was. It was as if the wolf in me seeped through my pores, released by my anxiety. Part of me wistfully thought of that wolf body and how just a minute in it would instantly ease all of my jostled feelings.

"Isabel —"

"This is not okay," she interrupted. "I'm not okay with any of this."

"It wasn't *me*. Baby —"

"I know it was Baby!"

"Then I don't get it."

We looked at each other. My fingers had that feeling like my arms had been asleep but now they were waking up. Somehow I was both obviously innocent and obviously in trouble. I still couldn't tell from her face what she was thinking. She was wearing enough eyeliner to black out the finer points of most emotions.

"I will never feel good about walking into a room with you and three half-naked girls, Cole. I don't want to see that *ever* again."

The problem was that this was part of being *me*, part of being Cole St. Clair, part of having a band, signing up to be on a voyeuristic TV show. "I can only control myself."

"Can you?"

"I just said it."

"Can you control *yourself*?"

Hadn't I *just*? "Do you not trust me — is that what this is?"

Isabel opened her mouth and then shut it. She turned away, crossed her arms, scowled into the shower. "I haven't been with one hundred other people, Cole. I haven't seen a hundred other people naked. I don't know what —"

She shook her head like she was mad. But I knew Isabel, and I knew that every one of her emotions looked like anger from the outside. It didn't make this any fairer, because I hadn't invited the girls over, nor had I known Isabel when I'd slept with all the others. But I'd known when I started this whole thing that we were different in this important way: Isabel had spent her teen years caring who touched her, and I hadn't.

"I'm not here for anybody else," I said. This seemed too earnest for her to handle, so I added, "Culpeper. I came here for you."

She still didn't look at me. The light came through her ice-blond hair, lighting her cheek and chin and neck. I still wanted my gold star, even though I knew there was no way I was getting it tonight. She answered, "Me and that little show you're doing."

"That's my job."

"Hiding in bathrooms?"

"Making music."

"I could handle dating someone whose job was making music," Isabel said. "But I don't think that's what your job is."

I thought I could remember having this conversation with Leyla, and I hadn't liked it much better then.

"Nobody *just* makes music. You can't make a living *just* making music. I thought this would be better than a label. I thought I'd have more control. You know what? I've said all these things. I can remember my face saying them."

Isabel laughed, as mean and thin as she had when the girl spit, but I was relieved, because it seemed to somehow soften her. She pulled out Virtual Cole and began thumbing through screens. "You thought signing up with *Baby North* would be better than a label? Even though all of her people end up twitching and drooling on the floor. Nobody makes it out."

"I'm not like anyone else."

Isabel stopped scrolling. Her voice was wry and sexy as she said, "Thank God."

We looked at each other. Her kohl-rimmed eyes were sky blue and unblinking. I hated that I could still feel the remnants of the anxiety batting around inside me. I didn't want her to go, though I could tell by the way everything had happened and the way she was standing and the way Joan was outside trying to eavesdrop that she had to.

I didn't want to be alone anymore.

I wanted to tell her *Isabel, stay.* And I wanted to tell her, *Isabel, I love you.*

I hadn't said anything out loud, but Isabel shook her head a little, like *don't.*

So I just said, "What about my gold star?"

"Ha!" Her laugh was bitter and annoyed. "Baby has taken your gold star. Breasts have taken your gold star."

"Do you want, at least, to hear my brilliance? Like, as it is meant to be heard?"

She didn't say *yes,* but she didn't move. So I turned off the shower, wiped down the tiled seat inside with a towel, and folded another towel to act as a cushion. I tossed my useless battery-dead headphones into the sink. Then I sat on the shower seat, pulled my MP3 player from my back pocket, and patted the spot beside me.

"This has to stop," she told me, but she joined me, crossing her epically long legs as she sat. God, she was so beautiful I couldn't take it.

"Sure," I agreed. "Earbuds?" She handed me her purse, and I rummaged for them (they were leopard print). Plugging them into my player, I put one bud in my right ear and one bud in her left ear. I scooted closer so that our shoulders were crushed together. As she readjusted the earbud, I checked the screen and then hit PLAY.

For the first minute, she listened. Then her head moved, just a little, the memory of dancing. She could make even that look sexy. I watched her — her eyes were closed, she was just listening, her lips parted a little. I couldn't get it. I felt like I could only pull off sexy when I thought about it, but I was just as attracted to her when she was *trying* to attract me as when she wasn't.

The song looped around; I had forgotten I had it set to repeat.

Isabel's eyes opened.

"Well?" I asked.

She kissed me.

There was no build to this kiss. No gradual confession of desire conveyed through body language. It was nothing, and then everything. Her hand was on my hand, dragging it over her bare stomach and pressing my palm into her ribs and making it feel the ridge of her hipbone at her belt. Her fingers asked mine to unwrap her. I barely had any breath at all, and her mouth was taking the rest of it.

I stood up, lifting her so that she was never any farther than the earbud cord. I didn't want her body to stop touching mine, anyway. As the song clanked and stomped jaggedly in my right ear and in her left, we kissed and kissed, her tongue warm on my tongue, her skin smooth under my fingers, her legs curved around mine.

Isabel dragged me toward the door. "Bed."

I didn't argue. The song looped again. I fumbled for the doorknob.

On the other side, Joan's camera looked at us.

I had forgotten. Isabel didn't flinch, but her eyes fluttered closed for just a moment, lashes dark on her cheek, and then when she opened them again, she was ready for the camera, all truths erased from her expression.

"Hi, Joan," I said. "Are you staying long? Can I get you a coffee?"

Isabel removed herself from me. Joan, who, for the record, was a humorless trundle elf, merely took a few steps back to allow us to exit the bathroom.

"I'm going to go," Isabel said.

"Oh," I protested, "that's crazy talk."

But it was true that the forgotten surprise of Joan had had a somewhat deleterious effect on my favorite instrument.

Isabel removed the earbud from my ear and pulled the cord free from the MP3 player. She went to get her purse while I glowered at Joan.

"Thanks for nothing," I said.

Joan switched off her camera. "Ditto."

Isabel reappeared. She had reapplied lipstick. I snatched for her on her way by and missed. She stopped at the door, though, and a smile sort of lurked around her mouth. "I think you should get a new job."

"Doing what?"

"Making music."

CHAPTER TWENTY-ONE

· ISABEL ·

On the way home, after the buzz of Cole had worn off, I kept finding my thoughts returning to breasts. I'd looked at mine in the mirror before. They didn't look anything like the three sets that I'd just seen in Cole's apartment, and not just because they had never had Cole's name written on them. It wasn't the size, really. It was the shape and the placement and the level of hang and sway versus perk and vengeance. It was the size and the shape and the color of nipples.

Different. But better? Worse? It was hard to attach a value judgment.

Ultimately, it just made me angry. What did anyone care *anyway*? Cole stood around shirtless all the time. It wasn't even really a thing for those girls to arrive without a top. It was an arbitrary decision culture had made to make our nipples salacious.

But it was a thing. And it did matter. And I couldn't stop seeing them. That made me angrier than anything, that I couldn't talk myself out of reliving the moment.

"Isabel, don't you think you should tell people when you're going to be out late?"

My mother's voice carried from the living room as I stepped into the foyer of the House of Dismay and Ruin. I knew what I'd see before I'd even gotten to the end of the hall and rounded the doorway: my mother reclined elegantly on the sofa, hair cascading over her shoulders, wine glass in hand.

I was not wrong, though I hadn't guessed that my aunt Lauren would be there as well, matching wine glass in her hand. She waved at me a little, turning her head very slowly, looking weary behind the bandage taped between her eyes. She'd just gotten a nose job, and she was always saying that sudden movements gave her a headache.

"No," I said, standing at the end of the sofa. On the television, a bitter soldier in a helmet peered into the distance. My mother watched war movies when she was feeling low. Probably because the excessive bloodshed and bitter victories reminded her of my father. "Because I'm over eighteen."

My mother sighed. It was not particularly disappointed. She already knew this was an argument I was good at. I knew the rest of it, actually.

MOM: *But you live under my roof.*
ME: *I'm happy to move out.*
MOM: *You'd have to get a job for —*
ME: *Yahtzee! Also, you told me I should find some friends.*
MOM:

My mother also knew the rest of it. So she just tipped the wine glass at me. "Want to try?"

"Is it any good?"

"No."

I shook my head. "What's that smell?"

My mother looked at Lauren. Lauren answered, "Sofia's making cinnamon rolls."

It was ten o'clock at night. I guessed there was nothing really wrong with baking at ten o'clock, but there was nothing really right about it, either.

"Is he cute?" Lauren asked me. "You were out with a boy, weren't you?"

I blinked at her. I'd thought about what would happen when my mom and Lauren found out that I was dating Cole, but I hadn't really expected how unpleasant it would feel to hear Lauren talk about him. Somehow it felt like it sullied him in a way he hadn't been before. Dusted him with the sterile House of Ruin relationship powder, the grown-up version of love.

"Yeah," I said. "He's like a damn panda."

On the television, a tank shuddered as a round erupted from its gun. The camera shifted quickly to its target, a small bunker that exploded in a shower of cinder block and shattered dreams. My mother began to cry softly. I went into the kitchen.

"Sofia, why are you making cinnamon rolls at ten o'clock at night?" I demanded.

My cousin turned from the counter. She was wearing duck-printed flannel pajama bottoms and her hair was down. She looked approximately twelve years old. Her T-shirt was covered with flour. I tried not to think about breasts.

"I was making them for you. So you could take one to class with you in the morning."

I opened my mouth to snap something about carbohydrates, realized I was about to be a bitch, and shut it again. Maybe Cole was a good influence on me.

"Right," I said. It was not *thanks*, but it was a lot closer than I usually got. "At the end of the week we should go buy you some shoes. I'll take you to Erik's."

Sofia blinked at me. Her eyes luminesced.

"Shoes are the things you put on your feet."

"Just us? Or Cole, too?" Right after she said it, she added, "Because I don't mind. I mean, if he comes. It's okay. It doesn't have to be just us. I appreciate you asking either way. Because —"

"Sofia," I snapped. "Stop."

"Are you going to marry him?" Sofia asked.

"*Sofia*," I snapped, with slightly more teeth. "Way to escalate. What the hell. This is not a Disney movie. Have you learned nothing from the example of our elders?"

She turned back to the counter and began to operate the standing mixer, her shoulders slumped. Powdered sugar surrounded her in a cloud. Without looking at me, she said, "Dad called."

Ah. This explained some of the wet-towel atmosphere in the House of Ruin. I tried to think of what an actual human would say in this situation. I asked, "Are you okay?"

Sofia began to cry, which was exactly why I generally tried to avoid being a human. I wished I had stayed with Cole.

"Yes," said Sofia as tears dropped off her nose. "Thank you for asking." She glopped a huge spoon of frosting from the mixing bowl onto a cinnamon roll and handed the plate to me.

"For the love of God," I said, taking it. "Get one of those things and come on."

"Come on where?"

"My room. Let's go call Cole."

We did. Up in my room, I put him on speaker and made him sing his latest song to us. When he found out Sofia was listening, he started swapping out his real lyrics for funny ones, and soon she was laughing and crying at the same time. Finally, I got up to plug my phone in because the battery was dying from all the singing, and Sofia went off to bed, happy and sad, which was at least better than just sad.

I took the phone off speaker and climbed onto my bed. I put my head on the pillow and laid the phone on my ear. "We're alone. You can swear again."

"I wish you were here," Cole said.

I didn't answer right away. Then, because it was a phone, and he couldn't see my face, so I could be as honest as I liked, I admitted, "Me, too."

"Isabel —" Cole said. He stopped. Then he said, "Don't hang up."

"I haven't hung up."

"Keep not hanging up."

"I still haven't hung up." I heard a bird shrill on his end of the phone. "Are you outside?"

"I'm in the alley. Waiting for Leon. He's done at midnight and we're going to go get food on a stick and I'm going to win him a stuffed monkey on the Pier. These are the things I do when you leave me alone, Isabel."

I said, "Don't break Leon's heart."

Cole laughed. His real laugh was a funny sound — not funny like ha-ha, but funny strange. It was percussive rather than tonal. He said, "Tell me you'll see me tomorrow."

"I'll see you tomorrow."

"Tell me you'll see me the next day. And the day after that. And the day after that."

My heart thumped convulsively. It had happened. Against my will, despite the naked girls and the smell of wolf and all of the things that hinted at future misery, I had fallen back in love with Cole.

I said, "Good night, Cole."

"Good night, Culpeper."

I hung up and closed my eyes. Later, later, I knew that I'd probably regret all of this. But right now I couldn't feel afraid. I just kept hearing his silly lyrics and his real laugh. I kept remembering the feel of his hands on me. I tried to tell myself that everybody in the House of Ruin and Misery eventually cried themselves to sleep, but right then, in that moment, I let myself imagine I wasn't like anyone else.

Chapter Twenty-Two

· COLE ·

In the morning I woke up and discovered there was really nothing wrong with the world at all, apart from waking up with barbecue breath. I boiled eggs and drank a carton of milk, and then stood on the roof deck for an hour trying to piece together a lyric that would say exactly all that while not saying *exactly* all that. Baby called me and said, "Why aren't you picking up your work phone?"

It took me a moment to realize that she was talking about Virtual Me, which of course was not in my possession. I stretched and closed my eyes. The sun was straight overhead and pointed only at me. I replied, "Because I only use it for, like, connecting with the Internet. Don't cross the streams, Baby. Why haven't you got me my Mustang?"

"Ha-ha, this is me laughing, Cole. I want that girl on the show."

It felt slightly less sunny out here. "I hope by *that girl* you are referring to my car."

"The Internet loves the idea that you're dating someone. They want to know if she's the one, Cole. She's a very pretty girl. Think about what it would do for viewership."

I didn't have to think. I knew exactly what the world would do with it, because they'd done it with every other girl they'd ever spotted me with. The idea of trying to date in public tweaked exactly the same part of my brain as the idea of speaking to my parents or old friends from home. Which was to say the same part of my brain that was always contemplating blowing myself away or jumping off a bridge or eating some pills.

It wasn't a part of my brain I liked to engage. Until very recently, I thought I'd lobotomized it from my skull, but apparently it was still in there.

Baby said, "Convince her to be on the show and I'll get you a Mustang."

I laughed before I'd even though about it, because it was such an obvious devil's bargain that there was no danger I'd fall into it.

"We need to have dinner, Cole," Baby said. "I think that is the thing. Bring her. Tonight. Clear your schedule."

"I'm not feeling very dinner-y," I replied. "Seeing as my track nearly got screwed over yesterday and I had a bunch of topless girls in my apartment last night."

"That sounds exciting. I like exciting."

"I was being plenty exciting without that."

"Were you?" Baby asked curiously. "Are you being exciting now?"

"Yes," I lied.

"Great. I look forward to seeing it. Dinner tonight, don't forget. Also, pick up your other phone when I call it."

She hung up. I called Isabel.

"Culpeper," she answered.

It never got old, her taking my calls.

"It thrills me when you answer the phone like that," I told her. I walked to the edge of the roof deck. I could see palm trees and more roof decks. The rest of them were empty, so it was just me and the sun. "Please tell me you are naked."

"I'm at work, Cole."

"Naked? Well, it is Santa Monica. Do you have Virtual Me?"

"Of course I do. You just tweeted."

"Was I funny? Did the Colebots like it?" I watched a little boy appear on one of the roof decks one house away, on the other side of the empty rental. He had a little plane in his hand, and he was flying it up, up, up as high as he could get.

"Oh, please," Isabel replied. "Also, I think Baby tried to call Virtual Cole."

"I know. I know everything. Could you possibly use your skills to find me a Colebot who's having a party in the L.A. area today? Or getting married? Or divorced? Some sort of festive occasion that might involve music?"

I watched the little boy on the deck sail his plane around the table. He was deeply content in a way that I couldn't ever remember being. If it had been me, I would've flown that plane to the edge of the roof deck and jumped.

"I thought you knew everything." Isabel sighed noisily. "What's in it for me?"

"My eternal admiration of your superior intellect."

"I'll see what I can do."

"Also, Baby wants to have dinner with us."

She made a noise that I couldn't interpret. Then she said again, "I'll see what I can do."

After she hung up, I noticed the boy had come to the edge of the roof deck and was staring at me.

"Hey," I told him. "We're twins."

It wasn't as creepy as it sounded. We were both wearing khaki shorts and no shirts and were tan with sun-kissed brown hair. I couldn't decide if he was four or nine or twelve. I had no idea of the specifics of children. He was too young to drive, but old enough to be able to turn doorknobs.

"Are you a time traveler?" he called warily.

"Yes," I replied. I was pleased that he had also noticed the similarity. Already I was shaping this into a song. "But only forward."

"Are you me?"

"Sure," I said.

He scratched his stomach with the plane. "What is my future?"

I said, "You're famous, and you have a Mustang."

We both looked at the Saturn parked behind the building. With a frown, the boy hurled the plane at me. It careened through the shimmering air before disappearing somewhere into the roof crevices of the rental house, palms hiding it.

"Well, now you've done it," I said. "You've probably broken it."

The boy looked dismissive. "It's not about the landing. It's about the flying."

I narrowed my eyes at him. I felt agreeably goose-bumpy, like I was creeping myself out on purpose. "Maybe you *are* me. Are you real?"

On the chair behind me, my phone rang. It was Isabel, calling me back. I pointed at the boy and turned to answer it.

"I found you a wedding," she said.

"I think I just talked to younger me from the past," I replied. I turned back around, but the roof deck opposite was now empty. "He was flying a plane."

"Great. I hope you told him to not do drugs. Do you want the address or the name or what?"

I tried to see where the little plane had landed. I sort of wanted it. I made a note to break into the rental house if at all possible. "Give me the everything. Oh, tweet that. That's something I would say."

"I'm hanging up now." She did.

I called T.

"Cole!" he said gladly.

"Life is about to happen," I said, with a last glance toward where I had seen younger me. "I'm just putting on a shirt."

He and Joan arrived so quickly that I suspected he had been lying around waiting for me to call. Together, we made the odious journey across the courtyard to Leyla's part of the compound. Joan and T trailed me, cameras on shoulders.

"Hey," I said to Leyla.

She was sitting at the island in the kitchen, eating a plate of chopped-up raw vegetables, her dreads hanging around her long face. She blinked at me and then at the cameras. I had not knocked, but she didn't say anything about it. I tried not to hate her, because it felt like a victory for Baby.

"Today is the day we make magic happen," I said.

Leyla ate a piece of something green. She chewed. We all got older while she swallowed. "What did you have in mind?"

"Grand things. Where's your kit?"

She just looked at me. I couldn't tell if she was high or stupid or simply hating me back. None of those things were mutually exclusive.

"Your drums? These things?" I air-drummed. "Get them. Put them in the Saturn. Come with me into the future."

She put another vegetable in her mouth. She chewed.

"Since we started this conversation," I said, "two hundred babies have been born on this planet. And what have we accomplished? You have eaten that thing."

Leyla swallowed. "You didn't hurry to get over here until now. Time is continuous, Cole. It doesn't speed up and slow down. Do not let yourself be fooled by whims. Contentment is constancy." She drew a slow, even line in the air with something I thought was a zucchini.

I said, "Sure. Okay. But we're on a schedule now. Drums. Saturn. You and me, baby. Bring your garden there. You can eat it on the way. Do you have a wheelbarrow or something? I'll chuck it in there for you while you get your kit together."

She didn't move. "What am I playing?"

"Music."

"What kind of music?"

"Mine."

"Do I know it?"

"There is this thing called *jamming* and it means you play a piece of music with other people even if you have never heard it before, and if you tell me you have no idea how that's done, put down that carrot because I'm firing you."

Leyla ate the carrot. "Music is inherent, man," she said. "And you don't have to be such a hole all the time. I'll get the drums."

Jeremy was at band practice with people who were not me when I arrived to fetch him.

It wasn't that I didn't understand Jeremy getting a new band while I was missing/dead/etc. I was sure I would have done the same thing in his position. Well, I would have *started* one, not *joined* one, because I don't really like team sports unless I've invented both the team and the sport. But I didn't begrudge him for finding some new people to play music with. It's what we do, after all. We can't get this out of our blood. The music.

But it didn't make me feel any better about having to share him. Especially since I wanted better for him than this: a fairly boring band playing inside a fairly boring garage attached to a fairly boring house in a fairly boring part of L.A. I could hear their efforts as I pulled the Saturn up to the worn curb. They were clearly just a high-class cover band with an unimaginative guitarist, a drummer who had learned everything he knew from pool halls, and a singer named Chase or Chad.

That bass player was top-notch, though.

I got out and stepped over a hose snaked across the concrete drive. It was attached to a listless sprinkler that showered the small, brown yard.

That sprinkler, I thought, was a lot like Jeremy. That water wasn't going to improve that yard any more than Jeremy was going to improve this band. What a waste.

The music died as I approached. The only sound was the *cha-cha-cha* of the sprinkler. The dim interior of the garage reminded me how much I wanted the Mustang. The smell of it reminded me how much I missed Victor. Our garage practices had been works of art.

"I'm here for Jeremy," I announced. "Jeremy Shutt. In the case that there are two Jeremys here."

The humans in the garage simply stared at me, so I explained a few self-evident facts. (1) A band practice is moveable, while a wedding is not, and (2) no amount of practice was going to make this band interesting enough to get a label on board, so (3) really I was just saving them all a lot of time.

The singer, who looked even more like a Chad or a Chase up close, didn't seem to appreciate my insight. The drummer and guitarist just sort of waved. It turned out I knew both of them, even though I couldn't remember either of their names. The drummer used to play for a band called ChristCheese, which had been more successful than you might imagine, and the guitarist had been with Pursuit Ten until their percussion guy had OD'd in a bathtub in Oklahoma, which is a sad story no matter how you look at it.

To the singer, I said, "In conclusion, it will make no difference in the relative scheme of things if Jeremy comes with me now."

The singer was clearly trying to behave himself in front of my cameras, but his voice was a little strained. "You can't just disappear and then expect to come back and find all your toys where you left them."

I said, "Don't be like that. I will not break Jeremy. He's clearly too valuable for that. You'll have him back, and you can continue on this grand old path to playing high school proms. We all have to share."

"Don't play all, whatever, high and mighty now," the singer said. "You can't act as if you're being gracious while you diss my music."

"Diss!" I replied. "If you want to hear a proper diss, I can prepare some words for you. But no, my friend. I was merely placing things in perspective for you. You are doing *that*, in *there*. And I am doing *this*, with *them*." I gestured to T and Joan. Even with the dimming presence of the Saturn, it seemed quite obvious to me that Cole > Chase.

The ChristCheese drummer and Pursuit Ten's ex-guitarist both looked at singer Chad/Chase to see what his next move would be.

"Yeah, I know what you're doing. I know about the *show*," he told me. "You think you're all that because of who you were. But no one cares if you were big once, dude. Your singles are so old that grandmas are humming them. You're only famous now because you're a total loser."

Very evenly, I said, "Also because of those three multi-platinum albums. Let's be comprehensive."

"Oh, come on! Don't pretend you don't know why people are watching the show. You know I'm right," the singer scoffed. "Or you would be with a label instead of Baby North. Come *on*, man. Don't even pretend it's about the music."

His words wedged their way into my heart. Once upon a time, I had written the soundtrack for everyone's summer. Once upon a time, my face had been on the cover of magazines. Once upon a time, all of these guys in this garage would be shitting themselves to hear my voice in person. What was I doing now?

Just get the show over with. Make the album. Disappear into the Los Angeles sunset with Isabel. But that didn't feel quite right, or true. I asked, "Don't you have an Eagles cover to be practicing, or something?"

ChristCheese drummer rattled a cymbal. Pursuit Ten guitarist looked at him sharply, as if warning him not to get ugly. I kind of hoped it got ugly. I wanted to hit something, or to get hit.

The singer said, "I'm not going to take that kind of shit from you."

"You just did. Now, if you don't mind, I have to go do a real job now. Jeremy, what's the verdict?"

I turned to him. It wasn't a challenge. It was just a question. There was no point gaming Jeremy. Did you game Gandhi? No.

"Jeremy, if you go with this joker," the singer said, "don't bother coming back."

"Chad," Jeremy said gently.

I knew it.

"I'm serious," said the guy. The Chad. I *knew* it.

I said, "Don't make Lassie choose, Chad."

"You, shut up. Pick, Jeremy."

Years ago, I'd dated Victor's sister, Angie. Pretty seriously. Our breakup after my first tour had been ugly and nasty and entirely because I had slept with anything that took its shirt off in my presence. It was the first time I'd really realized I'd lost my soul and that the beauty of not having a soul was that you couldn't seem to care that you no longer had one. Even though the band had just gotten back, we already had studio time booked for the next album. Angie had wanted Victor to quit. I had wanted Victor and his magic hands to come with me and never return to Phoenix, New York.

I made him choose between us.

I didn't think it would kill him.

I didn't think at all.

Dirt kept falling over the wolf's muzzle. Somewhere, Victor's grave was always being filled in.

My day was approaching ruination.

"Jeremy," repeated Chad. "What's it going to be?"

Jeremy tucked a bit of hair behind his ear. He sighed. His eyes were on his bass and on my car.

I interrupted. "Stay here." I hadn't even realized I was going to say it until I said it. And then even after I said it, I couldn't believe that I had. It didn't sound like something I would say.

Every face in the garage turned to me.

I plunged on. "I'm not going to screw you over, Jeremy. If this toolbag won't take you back just because I need you now, I'll figure something out today without you. I'll catch you on the next one. No big deal."

I felt so virtuous and so awful. If this was the right way, I didn't like it. I needed to make a note to never do it again.

Jeremy nodded. He didn't say anything for a moment. Neither did Chad. He didn't seem to understand what had just happened.

Cole St. Clair had failed to be an asshole — that was what had just happened.

It continued to feel terrible. It felt exactly like that first night, when Isabel had told me to drop dead, and when I had realized that I wanted desperately to become a wolf and could not anymore. No, *would* not anymore.

I told myself now that I'd feel great later. Noble.

Then Jeremy said, slow and serene and Southern, "Sorry, Chad, but I think I'm going to go with Cole. I might come back, if you ask me, but I would have to give a lot of thought to the emotional manipulation you brought into the conversation today. You know that's not how I like to work. Give me a moment, Cole. I need to get my sandals."

He had picked me. I hadn't asked, and he'd still picked me.

This feeling was almost worse than feeling shitty. Really, it was the difference between the two emotions that was hard to navigate. The sudden lift from crap to joy.

"You bastard," Chad said. It was unclear if he meant me or Jeremy. He clarified, "You no-talent boy-band wannabe."

I saluted at him with two fingers.

Jeremy joined me with his bass case. We performed a lengthy handshake, which helped ease my tremendous, painful joy. In a rather perfunctory way, I hooked my foot into the garden hose and twisted the sprinkler round. Artificial rain blasted into the garage's interior. *Now* the guitarist and drummer made some noises.

Chad knew a lot of swearwords.

I turned with Jeremy and headed back to the Saturn to where Leyla waited. T was filming everything. I imagined the shot framed gloriously, soaking wet musicians in the background like a car explosion in an action movie.

"That was nearly reasonable of you," Jeremy said. He added confidently, "They'll call me."

A drumstick hurtled by my head. It rattled on the concrete as it landed.

Jeremy leaned to pick it up. "But probably not you."

CHAPTER TWENTY-THREE

· COLE ·

After we'd done the episode but before Isabel was off work, I hung out with Jeremy in his old beat-up pickup truck, parked in the middle of a beach lot. It was just the two of us. I'd sent Leyla back with the Saturn because I didn't want to see either of them ever again.

The sounds were traffic and someone else's boom box and the surf and the slap of arms on a volleyball. I lay in the truck bed on a dry, crinkly tarp, and Jeremy sat on a tire, looking at me and the ocean. Overhead, the sun pierced the jet trails, baking cracks into the asphalt down below. I was still wound up from performing and now would've been a good time for a beer. Jeremy offered me some unsweetened iced tea.

"I don't want your witches' brew," I told him, but I took it anyway and set the jar down by my head. For several long companionable minutes we did nothing together. Jeremy leaned his head back and watched the sky, looking like a wizened Australian guy in the full sun. I closed my eyes and let the heat bake my eyelids. Here with Jeremy, it would be easy to pretend the last three years of my life hadn't happened, and I could restart without any of my sins. Only then I wouldn't have met Isabel, and I wouldn't be here in California. I wondered if there had ever been a more direct route to this place. Maybe I'd been on it and ruined it. Maybe if I'd just stayed on the straight and narrow all along, I would've met Isabel at a show.

No, because she didn't like concerts, and neither did I.

I thought of those three topless girls in my apartment and how they would never be Isabel and Isabel would have never been them.

I couldn't keep my eyes closed because my brain was moving faster and faster instead of slower and slower. I opened them and said, "All of the girls look old now. When did that start? All I can see when I look at them is what they're going to look like when they're forty. It's like the worst superpower ever."

Thoughtfully, Jeremy replied, "Really? I always see people as kids. Since I was in, like, middle school. It doesn't matter how they're acting or how old they are, I can't not imagine them as kids."

"How awful. How can you possibly flip someone off if you're imagining them as a toddler?"

"Exactly," Jeremy said.

"Tell me. Why is Leyla so unacceptable?"

"You know I don't like to judge people."

"We all do things we don't like."

He picked a nub of rubber off the tire and flicked it onto my chest. "She's not really our thing. Style-wise."

"Musically or ethically?"

Jeremy said, "I'd rather not perjure myself."

"Do you even know what *perjure* means?" I wasn't 100

percent on it myself. I had a very specialized knowledge base. "I want to fire her. I really do. But what's the alternative?"

I regretted saying it as soon as it was out of my mouth. Because the alternative was dead, and I didn't want to talk about it. *Don't say anything, Jeremy. Don't say his name.*

So you ready to do this thing?

— *What?*

NARKOTIKA.

I didn't give Jeremy time to answer. "You wouldn't be with me if it wasn't about the music, right? I mean, you wouldn't be doing this with me if it was just about me jerking off on camera as a loser, right?"

"Is this about what Chad said?"

"Who's Chad?" I asked, as if I couldn't remember. "Oh, him. No. I was just thinking because of . . . maybe. Possibly. I'm on a road of self-evaluation. This is one of the side streets."

Jeremy thought about it. He thought about it for so long that the sun moved a little overhead. A family went by us on their way to the beach. One dad was in a wet suit with a surfboard under his arm. The other dad was in the world's geekiest swim trunks. The children trotted behind them making gleeful supersonic noises and punching each other.

"Jeremy," I prompted, because I couldn't take it anymore.

He said, "What we just did wasn't about the music. The way's never been about the music. The *way* is about the show. The gig. This is just another gig. The studio was about the music."

"Can I do the music without the way? Like, and still sell anything?"

"I think you like the way too well for that."

"Hey."

Jeremy said, "I'm not saying it's bad. You're good at it. But sometimes I think you've forgotten how to stop doing it. Do you think maybe you should get out of the city for a little bit?"

"Is that a suggestion or a question?"

"Just to get your head back together."

I rocked my head to look at him. I could feel the knob at the back of my skull grinding and crackling against the tarp and the ridges of the pickup bed. It was sort of satisfying. I shook my head back and forth. Not disagreeing with Jeremy, just feeling the crunching on my head. "What makes you think my head is not entire already? What a glorious time I'm having in this state."

Jeremy took a drink of unsweetened iced tea. He said, "Chip died."

"Who the hell is Chip?"

"Chip Mac."

"Are you even using words, man? Or are you just communicating with a series of clicks and whistles?"

Jeremy repeated slowly, "Chip. Mac. The guitarist Baby hired for you."

"I didn't know his name. How'd he die?"

"OD'd."

It didn't mean anything at first. Then I made the connection, but the wrong one. "That was totally not my fault."

"No," Jeremy agreed. "It wasn't. He'd just gotten out of rehab, and he'd been in the hospital, too. Did you know the bass player?"

"He was just some kid."

"Picked up for dealing last year," he said. "I asked around."

It was rather heartwarming to imagine Jeremy asking around on my behalf. "So, what? You think Baby was trying to get me wingmen."

He made a noise of affirmation. It wasn't really surprising. It did make me feel a little strange, thinking how the guitarist was now dead and he'd just been alive and angry at me. And also thinking about how things might have been different if I hadn't fired them that night. No wonder Baby had been so aggravated that I'd fired Chip, perfectly poised for a disaster on television. "What if I hadn't fired them? Lucky."

"Luck," Jeremy scoffed softly. "There's no luck."

"Then what?"

"Your feet take you where you need to be."

I thought about this. "My feet have taken me to some pretty rough places."

"That was your dick, dragging your feet along with."

I laughed. A flock of pelicans flew by, ungainly but beautiful, reminding me I needed to call Leon and make him ride a Ferris wheel. A word appeared in my head, unbidden: *home*. Was that what this could be? Was that what I wanted?

"I don't want to give you back to Chad," I said.

There was a very long pause. Even by Jeremy standards. Then he said, "I can't tour with you, Cole."

Just as before, when he hadn't trusted me, it wounded. I didn't care if the rest of the world didn't trust me, Baby and America and all that. But Jeremy — Isabel —

"I've changed."

"I know," he said, and he got out the truck keys. "But some things you can't change."

CHAPTER TWENTY-FOUR

· ISABEL ·

In our clinicals today, we'd been going over codes. Codes are basically shorthand for terrible things that happen in hospitals. They're mostly standardized in California.

Code Red: Fire

Code Orange: Hazardous Material Spill/Release

Code Yellow: Bomb Threat

Code Blue: Someone's Heart Has Stopped

A few of the more twittering idiots in my class had been transported by fear at the idea of a code possibly going down during our clinicals. Part of me was sort of hoping for one, though. I was going out of my mind with boredom. A hazardous material spill seemed like a good time. The big thing about the codes was to not panic, anyway, and I was excellent at not feeling emotions. The point was to gather all of the information you could, and then act on it.

Baby was basically a code. I couldn't decide if she was a Code Gray: Combative Person or Code Silver: Person With Weapon/Hostage Situation. In either case, there was no harm at all in finding out more about her. Which was why I agreed to go out to dinner with her, as long as I chose the place. I wanted it to be on my territory, not hers.

I picked Cole up and we headed to Koreatown, a place that many of Sierra's monsters were afraid of because they were silly little weaklings who believed what their mothers told them. My mother had also told me to not go to Koreatown on my own, but she'd never been, so how would she know? The news was full of lies and, anyway, the food was great.

Everybody wanted something in Koreatown, and nobody was pretending they didn't. It wasn't really attractive, but it felt satisfyingly urban to me. The streets were wide and treeless; everything that wasn't an apartment building was a strip mall, and everything that wasn't a strip mall was made out of concrete. There were more walls tagged with graffiti than not. Not the feel-good graffiti of Venice, either. It was all gang tags and well-done murals about ugly things. One of my favorites was a mural of wolves at a kill. There was no blood, though — just butterflies. That felt like Koreatown to me. It came at L.A.'s prettiness all real and brutal, but in attacking Los Angeles, it just became part of the prettiness. That was the hungry magic of Los Angeles. It defied all comers and turned them all into yet more Los Angeles.

I parked the SUV, swiped a credit card at the meter, and in we went on foot. On our way to the restaurant, a bunch of cute Latino guys on the opposite street corner hooted. I thought it was directed at me until one of them flipped Cole the bird and shouted "NARKOTIKA!" to make sure Cole knew it was personal.

Cole, wired and hectic from whatever had happened during his shoot today, looked over his shoulder at them. For a moment

I was afraid he was going to do something that got him stabbed, but he just flashed a peace sign at them. Then he turned away, despite their shouted replies. Done with them. Just, done.

The restaurant, Yuzu, was a Japanese place located in an apocalyptic shopping mall on the edge of Koreatown. It was four half-abandoned, dimly lit levels connected by ancient escalators. Every store that *was* still open had signs in Korean out front.

I liked coming here because the food was good, but also because it felt like a place that you couldn't just use the Internet to find. You had to use something real. And you had to actually and truly not give a damn about what other people told you.

We rode an escalator up. I was wearing a lace top, and Cole's hand had snuck under the edge of it to rest on my bare lower back. I returned the favor. His back felt smooth and cool beneath his PROUD TO BE CANADIAN T-shirt. He was distracted, though. His eyes were narrowed as his gaze flicked from the stores to me. A little muscle moved in his jaw.

"What?" I asked. "Just say it."

He said, "I think I've been here before."

"Think? Seems pretty memorable to me."

"I might not have been in a remembering mood."

I didn't like to think about Cole coming here to score while on tour, so I didn't say anything else. We rode up the escalator in silence, then took two steps to the next escalator, and rode that one up in silence. I walked him to the front of Yuzu. Cole pointed to the sign out front, which read: WE RESERVE THE RIGHT TO REFUSE SERVICE OR ADMITTANCE TO ANYONE.

Inside, we were led past a translucent screen into a surprisingly intimate seating area. We were early, because I was always punctual or better. Baby wasn't there yet. I slid into one side of a dim booth, and Cole threw himself into the other. He leaned across the table on his elbows, invading my personal space, knocking the paper lantern askew and sending the menus sprawling.

"Just say it," he said. I lifted my hand. *Say what?*

At the head of the table, the host cleared his throat. He looked very unamused by Cole. "Something to drink?"

"Water," Cole said. "And Coke. And more water."

I cut my eyes to the host's. "Water for me, please. Don't bring him a Coke."

Cole protested, "Hey," but the host seemed to agree with me that Cole didn't need any more sugar or caffeine in him, because he nodded at me curtly and swept away.

"Oh, hey," Cole hissed to me, leaning forward, hitting his head on the light. "Go time. Is that a phrase still? Because it is. Go. Time."

"Hi, kids," Baby said. She had manifested at the head of our table, her smile wide and dimpled as always. I kept imagining that she should loom and look like an evil genius, and she kept . . . not. "Where do you want me?"

Cole leaped up and slid into the booth beside me, crashing our shoulders together. He gestured to where he had just been. "There. Take everything that was mine."

She sat down. She still wore the private, amused smile, like life entertained her. "I haven't been here before."

"We'll get you a menu. A guide to the food in this place. A description of all the . . ." Cole lost interest in his own sentence. He drummed his fingers across the table; I put my hand over his hand, pressing it still.

Baby didn't have Cole's manic energy, but somehow her gaze kept subtly shifting so that I got the idea that she was taking in the entire restaurant. Mostly the people. Her eyes stuck on little interactions: one of the sushi chefs lifting his hand to gesture at another chef. The delivery boy at the door raising his eyebrows at the hostess. My hand on Cole's hand.

I wondered if she saw us all as players.

Cole's leg was jiggling beneath the table. I pressed my thigh up against his and it stilled.

A neatly dressed young woman with a red streak dyed in the front of her black hair came to the end of our table. She peered closely at us.

"Oh, we're not ready," I told her.

Her nostrils flared. "I am not coming for order. Masaki asked me to check on you."

Something about her tone was enough that if it had not been my favorite sushi restaurant and if I had not been in front of Baby, I would have offered to give her something better to check on. But instead, I just said, "We're okay. Thanks." I couldn't keep all of the chill out of the *thanks*, but I defrosted most of it.

The girl's lips tightened, and then she left us alone.

"Weird," Cole said.

"Interesting," clarified Baby. "What's good here?"

I flipped over the menu. There was an unsaturated and unappealing-looking photo of a California roll on the front. "All of the sashimi," I said.

Cole ran a finger down the menu like a kid learning how to read.

"Have you ever had sushi before?" Baby asked him.

He shook his head. To me, he said, "You'll have to show me how to use these. The pencils." He'd removed the chopsticks from the paper sleeve and now he walked them toward me. I resisted the temptation to snatch them from him.

"Nice job on the filming today," Baby said. "Mostly."

Cole's fingers stilled completely. "The Saturn ran out of gas on the way to the gig."

"How inconvenient," Baby said.

"I know it had three-quarters of a tank," Cole said. It was strange to see him when he stripped away the performer and the humor.

Baby didn't look sorry, though. She tapped a line on the menu and then she said, "It made excellent TV."

"So did our wedding gig," Cole said.

"No," Baby replied. "That made fine TV. Everything has to be turned up really loud to make good TV."

Icily, I said, "Like hiring some topless girls to bust into his apartment?"

Baby looked genuinely shocked. "I didn't hire them!"

"Oh, come on," Cole said. "Enough with the playing pretend."

"Why do you think I wanted you, Cole?" Baby asked.

He regarded her, chin tilted arrogantly. I felt his leg still quivering beside mine, a bare fraction of the jiggling he wanted to do with it.

I answered for him, "Because you think you can destroy him on TV. For good TV."

Her eyes widened. "You don't believe that, do you, Cole?"

He just kept looking at her.

"You ruined the rest of them," I said. I knew it would hurt Cole's feelings, but I went on, "You want Cole because you think he's an easy mark."

Baby's expression never stopped being shocked. "I wanted Cole because he was a performer. Because he knows how to work a crowd. Look, do you get it? He *was* a mess. But look at him now. He's pretty again. Pretty makes good TV."

I remembered what Cole had said when I'd first seen the list that Baby had made for him. *She wants me to look like a disaster.*

"Did you really think all those people on my shows collapsed and went crazy?" Baby asked. "That *I* did that? Nobody's that good. No, they all knew what the world wanted."

"They were fake?" I said, and hated the look Baby gave me, like she couldn't believe how innocent I was. Of course I knew that reality television wasn't real.

"They were *curated*," corrected Baby. "They gave the viewers what the viewers wanted."

Cole said, voice empty, "And the world likes us better falling down."

Baby shrugged one shoulder as if this were an unchangeable fact. "Not real destruction, though. Do you know what's bad

TV? Someone passed out on a floor, drooling. Rock stars vomiting. Being too drunk to go to the studio. If I got a real disaster, I'd have no show. You ever seen an addict? Shitty work ethic."

It was so the opposite of how I'd expected this dinner to go that I couldn't quite comprehend it. On the one hand, what she said made complete sense. But on the other hand, I'd seen three topless girls in Cole's apartment the night before.

"I don't believe it," I said. "Then why the half-naked girls, if not to tempt him?"

Baby said, "Tempt? Look at this —" She pointed to the two of us. I wasn't sure what she was trying to indicate. Proximity, maybe. "Tempt? I saw those fangirls wandering around and simply pointed them in the right direction. I figured Cole had enough of a brain on him to make it into a good scene. I don't cut and paste my shows to make drama. I just . . . line up the edges. Put people in situations and film what happens."

Cole said, "But I've been making situations."

"Not big enough," Baby countered. "So I just throw in some variables when it occurs to me. Have I tried to trick you? Did you find drugs in the bathroom to tempt you? Beers in the fridge? Have I done anything to pull you off the wagon?"

Cole frowned. "The musicians. The ones I fired. That one is dead. Chuck."

A ghost of something fluttered over Baby's face. "Chip."

"Yeah, well, Jeremy told me he was dead. And the other kid was into shit. That seems pretty — engineered."

He hadn't told me this. I wondered if that was because he hadn't known what to do with the information yet or if it was because he hadn't wanted me to know.

"They were disasters," Baby admitted. "You can't really predict someone's crisis point, but you can guess. I figured Chip would work his way into the hospital during some gig. And that you'd have a giant shouting match with Dennis over you being clean now, and maybe someone would get hit. I don't mind hiring real disasters for scenery pieces."

"Does that mean Leyla has skeletons?" Cole demanded.

Baby laughed. "No. You're just supposed to hate her."

"Well done."

"I did my research. Isabel, you're still looking unhappy."

I wasn't unhappy, but I was suspicious. The other meltdowns had been so complete. So convincing. Was it just because I was like the rest of the American public, so ready to believe that a disaster was never truly cured? Or was it because I was just so ready to believe that Cole in particular wasn't cured? "So, you're not the enemy."

"Isabel," Baby said, "I'm not in this to get sued. If there's something that ruins my heroes, it's something they've done to themselves. I told you. I just put my people in situations. What they do with that situation is up to them. If there's an enemy, it's inside them."

I shouldn't have been surprised. Everything about Los Angeles was a cover for something else. The ugly masqueraded as pretty, and it turned out that now the pretty pretended to be ugly. I wondered if there was anything in this entire world that was real.

"So, you want me to try harder," Cole said finally. "You want the show. The Cole St. Clair show."

"I know you know how to do it," Baby said. "I did my research, like I said."

"Does it have to be down?" he asked. A little wistfully, if you knew him.

"Make it good. That's all I care about. Ah —"

A different young woman stood at the table. She looked, if possible, slightly less welcoming than the last girl. She demanded, in a very unwaitress-y way, "What do you want?"

I dragged the menu toward me. "I —"

She shook her head. She was looking at Cole. "What do *you* want here?"

His expression was still puzzled. "She can order for me."

Her gaze shot to me. Then back to him. "You're here for food?"

Now his face cleared. "Oh. Oh, now I see. Yes. *Food*. This is her favorite restaurant. I like the look of those round ones in the photo." With his index finger, he made little circles around the bloodless photo of the California roll on the front. Baby watched everything attentively.

The girl looked eight degrees more unfriendly, and then she vanished.

I turned to Cole. "You've been here before?"

Cole sounded a little bewildered. "When I said I thought I'd been here before, I didn't mean *here*. Like, this place. I guess it could have been. They must have recognized me. Maybe they think it was . . . like before."

Like before. Meaning that before, he would walk into a place and they would remember that he was a guy who wanted some cocaine with his entrée? I felt sick. I couldn't even blame anyone but myself. I knew exactly who Cole had been before I met him.

Baby, however, just kept wearing that same private smile. And why shouldn't she — Cole was only demonstrating his pedigree.

The host was back. Hovering behind him was the girl with the dyed hair.

"You are Cole St. Clair?" asked the host.

Cole nodded his head. Just one little jerk. He was all certainty and arrogance now, completely back in his public persona. He had become too large for his side of the booth; he'd turned this restaurant into a backdrop for his personality. This was what the rest of the world got from him.

"We told you before to never come back."

Cole cocked his head. "Back?"

"We tell you that you were not welcome here anymore. Not you or your other friend, either. You ruined everything. I don't forget your face after that."

Sudden recognition, and something more pained and empty, flickered across Cole's face. The latter so fast that only I saw it. "Oh. That. Look, that was a time long time ago. That's not going to happen this time. I'm clean. I just want to have a nice dinner here with my girlfriend."

I could have killed him for the casual way he threw the word out there, in the middle of all of this. *Girlfriend.*

The host was unsmiling. "Clean is not rumor."

Now Cole was losing his good humor. "And what is the rumor, my friend?"

The girl with the dyed hair said, "You have moved on from China White to something better."

Baby kept smiling. The world loved a loser.

"I am here," Cole said levelly, "for some goddamn sushi."

"Get out," the host replied. He stepped back to allow us room out of the booth. "You are not welcome."

"Well, my friend," Cole said, gruesomely expansive, "that seems like rather shitty business sense. Do you normally do background checks on your patrons before they sit down? Is this a saintly restaurant? Only for nuns? Buddha? Any lesser angels who wander into Koreatown? However do you stay open turning away all the sinners?"

He had acquired the full attention of the sushi chefs and the waitress. They stared at both of us. I knew forever on after this, no matter what happened, I was going to be *Cole St. Clair's girlfriend* to them. There was absolutely no good ending to this.

I could never get sashimi here again.

"Most sinners do not linger in our memory like you," the host said coolly. "Out."

I snapped, "What did you *do*, Cole?"

Baby watched each of us, back and forth, like a tennis match.

"It was *a long time ago*," he repeated.

The host said, "Not long enough."

I was as humiliated as I would have been if *I* had done something. "This is perfect. Let's just go."

Something burned furiously in Cole's eyes, but he shoved out of the booth and tossed his napkin contemptuously on the table. "Rumor works both ways," he told the host.

One of the guys behind the counter twisted his knife in the air slowly, just so the light caught it.

"Oh, I see you. I am *terrified*," Cole said. "Keep your shorts on. We're going."

I couldn't remember the last time I had been so embarrassed. One of the perks about not giving a damn. I couldn't even put words together.

I had spent so many afternoons doing homework at Yuzu, just being alone there where nobody knew me or what my facial expression normally looked like, and now my time there had gone from *present* to *past* in just a few minutes.

Out in the deathly fluorescent end-of-the-world mall, Cole told Baby, his voice cool and remote, "Rematch. I've lost my appetite."

"Are you sure?" Baby asked as we headed back down the escalator. "Now would be a good time to shoot some good TV."

"Yeah," Cole said. "Yeah, I'm sure. I can think of something better."

Baby said, "Do it, then. I've got the greatest surprise for your birthday, but you have to earn it."

We parted ways with her on the sidewalk. It was shockingly concrete white after the dim, timeless mall. We didn't speak until we were back to the SUV.

"What was that?" I spat. "What did you do to those people?"

In the passenger seat, Cole shook his head. "I don't know."

"How can you not know? I saw your face. You know."

"Isabel, I don't *remember*."

"Don't *lie* to me!" I snapped. "I saw it! What did you do?"

"Victor and I —" In the passenger seat, Cole pinched his nose and, a second after, threw his fingers outward like he was chucking an idea away from himself. He had been restless before. Now he was rattling around inside his own body.

I guided the SUV through a traffic light, past an apartment building with a pagoda roofline. "I hope that means you're trying to figure out how to tell me why I can't ever go back to my favorite restaurant."

Cole said, "Isabel, Jesus, give me a second."

"Also," I snarled. Now the rage was developing properly. *"Girlfriend?"*

"What, you want an apology for that, too? There's probably an application I should've filled out before I was supposed to say it, right? Jesus. Of all the things —"

Of all the things. Maybe he'd had girlfriends before, but I'd spent a lot of time intentionally being no one's. And now I didn't even know if he'd been saying it just to put a suspicious waitress at ease or because he thought I was really his girlfriend. And I didn't even know, after that, if I even wanted to be. I didn't know if it mattered if your boyfriend wasn't a mess if everyone else in the world thought he was.

Cole rested his temple on the window, his eyes cast toward the cloudless sky. "I'm trying," he said finally. "I'm trying and it doesn't matter to anyone. I'm always going to be him."

"Who?"

"Cole St. Clair."

It seemed on the surface like a stupid thing to say, but I knew exactly what he meant. I knew just how it felt when your worst fear was that you would be yourself.

Chapter Twenty-Five

· COLE ·

Here's what I knew: If I went back to the apartment by myself now, I'd go into the bathroom and slide a needle under my skin, and even though it was not drugs, even though it was so much *cleaner* than drugs, it would remind me of that person I had been not so long ago. The person who had gone to Koreatown to score and trashed a sushi restaurant when things went sour. I couldn't take hating myself like I'd hated myself then.

So I begged Isabel to take me back with her, at least for a little while.

And she must have known me, because she did, even though she was angry.

Isabel's mother lived in one of those houses that would be a lot nicer if the houses that flanked it weren't nice in exactly the same way. It didn't look like California to me — it looked like Upper Middle Class, USA. Isabel backed her huge SUV into the driveway; she did it so neatly and proficiently that I was sure she must have intended to crush the flower bed on the right. When she climbed out into the evening yard, her lips parted dismissively, and I knew I was right. This was guerrilla warfare:

Isabel versus the suburbs. She hadn't figured out yet that the only way to succeed was retreat. Or maybe she *had*, only her retreat was blocked. So she had decided to go down fighting.

It made me feel tired just looking at this neighborhood. It reminded me of my parents and Phoenix, New York.

We stepped into the center hallway, which smelled like air freshener. The decor was endlessly nice, and I forgot what it looked like the moment I moved my eyes. Isabel was out of place here: an exotic. She pursed her bubble-gum paradise lips and then we heard her mother call, "Isabel?"

Isabel had warned me that her mother would be home and that she would take care of it.

But then there was a lower rumble: a male voice.

Isabel's eyes narrowed at exactly the same moment that Sofia appeared on the carpeted landing above us, looking equally out of place here — a drowsy-eyed transport from a silent black-and-white movie, complete with one of those side-curl hairdos and words printed in fancy font on the bottom of the screen. Her white hand gripped the stair rail.

She mouthed words. They would have been printed on the bottom of the screen like so: *Your dad!*

Tom Culpeper.

I'd last seen him over Victor's dead body, two thousand miles away and a million years ago. Culpeper hadn't known it was a guy in wolf's clothing, though. He had just been trying to kill things with sharp teeth. So Victor's death wasn't really his fault. It was mine. Always mine.

I should have gone back to the apartment.

"Isabel? That was you, right? Sofia, is that Isabel?"

Both girls looked at me. Sofia silently scooted down the final stairs and started to touch my arm. Then she thought better of it and made a little hand-wheeling gesture. Words on the screen: *Follow me!* Isabel put a finger to her lips — *Shhh (air kisses, baby/air kisses/follow my breath)* — and stepped into another room.

As Sofia whisked me down the hall and straight through a fine, nice, forgettable kitchen toward an open patio door, I heard Isabel say coldly, "Oh, how wonderful. All of my DNA is here together again."

Sofia didn't stop until she'd led me two steps across a small deck and directly into a tiny wooden playhouse that butted up against it. It was the sort of playhouse with a green plastic slide and a climbing wall, and usually a wasp's nest inside. The interior was about four feet square, and was dimly lit by the porch light. Sofia crawled into the far corner and curled her arms around her knees, and I sat in the other corner. I realized that we could still hear the Culpepers, especially when they came into the open-windowed kitchen a moment later. The small, green-shuttered window even gave us a view of the festivities — Sofia and I weren't visible to them, but they were lit like a television screen.

"I see you picked up the dry cleaning," Isabel said, voice still cool. She got herself a glass of water. She didn't say anything to her father.

Isabel's mother smoothed a hand over her hips. She wore a pair of meticulous white pants and a low-cut black blouse. She was one of those glorious women who was *put together* but not *constructed*. Usually mother-daughter pairings felt like before/

after shots, but in this case, the two of them together just left the room in collective awe over the excellence of the genetics involved.

"Your father would like to know if we'd like to spend the weekend with him," Isabel's mother said.

Beside me, Sofia made herself into a smaller ball. All I could see over her knees were her enormous eyes as they gazed at the kitchen. They had a sheen as if she was crying, but she was not crying. I wondered how old Sofia was. Fifteen? Sixteen? She seemed younger. She still had that mysterious thing young kids had that made people want to take care of her instead of date her.

"Here?" Isabel said in the kitchen. "Or in San Diego?"

"Home," Tom Culpeper said. He leaned in the doorway with his arms crossed, looking lawyerly. "Of course."

Isabel smiled nastily at her glass. "Of course."

Sofia whispered, "I wish I were like Isabel."

I brought my focus back into the playhouse. "How do you figure?"

"She always knows what to say," Sofia said earnestly. "When my parents fought, I just blubbered and looked stupid. Isabel never gets upset."

I didn't know about that. I thought Isabel was always upset.

"There's nothing wrong with blubbering," I said, and added untruthfully, "I blubber all the time."

Sofia raised an eyebrow and smiled at me behind her knees. I saw just the corner of it, shy and disbelieving. She liked that I'd said it anyway. I pulled out my tiny notepad and wrote down the air kisses lyric before I forgot about it.

"Are your parents divorced?" I asked.

She nodded.

"Was your dad a dick lawyer, too?"

She shook her head. Her sheen-y eyes were a little sheenier. "Not a lawyer, and not a dick." She couldn't even say *dick* in a hateful way. She said it very carefully, like she was talking about anatomy, and she didn't want anyone to hear her.

In the kitchen, I heard Isabel say, still very chilly, "Driving two hours doesn't give you a particular claim on my time. I have plans. If you and my mother would like to enjoy a weekend of adult activities and flotation devices, however, I'm fine with that. You're big people."

"Being eighteen doesn't give you a free pass to be rude, Isabel," Tom said. I closed my eyes and thought about the different ways I would like to hurt him, starting with the easiest and working toward the cruelest: with my fist, with my words, with my smile. "Do you speak to your mother like this?"

"Yes," said Isabel.

I opened my eyes and asked Sofia, "How long have your parents been divorced?"

Sofia shrugged and rubbed her finger on the interior of the playhouse. In the dim light, I saw that she was touching the words *Sofia was here*, written with a spidery font. She was sad in a way that didn't ask me to do anything about it, which made me *want* to do something about it. I felt in the pocket of my cargo pants until I found a marker, and then I leaned past her and wrote *Cole was here*. I signed it. I'm good at my own signature.

Her teeth made a tiny crescent in the darkness.

I heard Teresa's voice rise, and both Sofia and I leaned to listen again. I missed the end of her sentence, but Tom's reply was unmistakable through the open windows and door.

"You and I both know that love is for children," he said. "We're adults. Compatibility is for adults."

"Compatibility is for my Bluetooth and my car," Teresa replied. "Only they get along just fine, and my car never makes my Bluetooth feel like shit."

"Well," Isabel said, thin and mean and condemning, "I'm going to leave you two here. I have things to be doing, like drilling a hole through my own temple. So long."

Tom broke off his death stare toward his wife to look at his daughter. "I drove two hours to see you."

Isabel's back was to us, so I saw her arms crossed behind her back instead of her face, and I could see how she so savagely pinched the skin of her right arm with her left hand that the skin flushed red. But her voice was still glacial. "And now you've seen me."

She clicked out of the room.

Tom licked his teeth. Then he said, "I see your parenting has done wonders, Teresa."

There was no universe in which Tom Culpeper and I would be friends. Sofia ducked over her phone, texting rapidly. I saw nothing but Isabel's name at the top of her screen.

A moment later, Isabel appeared around the side of the deck and squeezed into the playhouse — I had to crush right against Sofia to make room. Isabel looked carved from ice. Her eyes were pointed at the place where I'd signed the playhouse, but she wasn't really looking at anything at all.

"Here," I said.

I offered her the marker, but she didn't take it. She said, "I want to forget I was ever here."

Sofia volunteered, "I can go in and get some cookies if you want them."

Isabel snapped, "I don't want you to go get me any god-damn food, Sofia!"

Her cousin somehow managed to shrink without actually occupying any less space. Isabel closed her eyes, her mouth thinning.

I was sandwiched between two miserable girls and I had no car of my own to go anywhere else, and even if I did, it was a Saturn. And once Sofia had said *cookie*, I really did want one, because our dinner had been reneged by suspicious sushi chefs. But now Teresa and Tom Culpeper were having a proper scream fest in the kitchen and really, nobody could go inside without risking civilian casualties.

"I would take a cookie," I said to Sofia, "but I'm watching my weight. Camera adds twenty pounds, you know, and there's really no point to life if I can't be handsome on camera."

Isabel snorted. Sofia snuffled and murmured something.

"What?" I asked.

"Lens distortion," Sofia sniffed. "That's why it adds twenty pounds. Every — *sniff* — lens is technically a fish-eye so it makes the middle of everything bigger, like your nose and stomach and stuff. And all of the lighting and flash and slave flash and — *sniff* — whatnot gets rid of shadows and edges, so you look even fatter."

"Well," I said. "The more you know."

The fight in the kitchen escalated. (Teresa had just shouted gloriously: *Isn't* lawyer *just another term for* whore? And Tom had replied, *If we're talking about women who work all night long, I think the term is* doctor.)

I retrieved my phone. "Want to see the episode we did today?"

Sofia said, "What's it about?"

"That's a surprise. I could tell you, but then I'd have to edit you out of the world's fabric."

Isabel opened her eyes. I thumbed through screens on my phone and navigated to the website. Both girls leaned a little closer to the illuminated screen in the darkness.

The episode began with my fight with Leyla and proceeded apace to the fight with Chad over Jeremy.

"What a jerk," Sofia said.

"Doesn't he know Jeremy was married to you first?" Isabel added hollowly. I knew she was saying it for Sofia, to sound like she was into the video-watching and to be forgiven for being mean earlier. It worked, too, because Sofia badly wanted to forgive her.

After I secured Jeremy, the three of us headed to the address Isabel had given me. It was the wedding of a super-fan in Echo Park. Well, according to Isabel it was a super-fan. A lot was resting on Isabel's ability to both play me on the Internet and also know how to do her research. Because if this turned out to be just a normal person's wedding or a casual fan's wedding, we were heading to disaster. Timing was tight, and the Saturn mysteriously ran out of gas on the way. We were forced to walk for gas to a station where the attendant just happened to recognize me.

I paused the video. "So this is the part where I got to find out if Isabel really did know everything."

Sofia said, "Why?"

"She's the one who found the wedding."

Sofia's giant eyes turned to Isabel.

Isabel said, "Good thing for me I know everything."

And she did. We eventually made it to Echo Park, where both the bride and the groom turned out to be super-fans, and the bride fainted wonderfully and mostly on camera when she saw me and Jeremy climb out of the car. Much to the horror of all of the parents involved, we jammed and played the couple down the aisle. Leyla wasn't even terrible on the drums. It really was a fine bit of television.

Sofia sighed happily. "It's so romantic. Was it that romantic in real life?"

"Sure," I said.

Isabel was scrolling through the video comments on my Virtual Me phone. There were a lot. Too many to read all of them, even if you wanted to. Isabel squinted at the most recent one. It was a paragraph long, full of love for NARKOTIKA and weddings and asking if I would ever write another song like "Villain."

As we were both looking, another comment came in. Comment number 1,362, and just one line:

cole st clair facedown is how I remember him

Isabel pursed her lips. She didn't look at me. I felt trapped between that comment and the confrontations in the sushi restaurant and with Chad. It felt like my past was getting closer and closer instead of the other way around.

Sofia was still in rapture from the glib ending of our episode. "Do you think you'd have a rock band at your wedding, Isabel?"

"I'm not getting married," Isabel said, clicking off the work phone and putting it away. She still wasn't looking at me or at the house or at anything. "I don't believe in happy endings."

Later, in the empty apartment, that was all I could remember clearly. The aborted dinner with Baby was a blur of humiliation and anger. The conversation with Chad a smear of doubt. The smiles of the wedding guests: forgotten.

I just remembered the one person I wanted to be with saying she didn't believe in happy endings.

When I got into the Saturn late that night or early that morning, the radio was playing "Villain." My voice snarled at me as I backed it out into the alley:

> *Didn't you always want me this way?*
> *On-sale late-night going-out-of-business*
> *I'm so much cheaper.*

The roads were eerie and deserted. Even the bars were closed. The lack of people and sun somehow emphasized the lack of grass and foliage beside the sidewalk. This place was carved from concrete. On the radio, my voice was still bitter. I didn't turn it off.

Don't pretend you like me

The beach parking lot was empty, and when I opened the car door, the air was frigid.

That this is about me

Frigid was good. It would make this last longer.

I'll be just a story in your wild youth

I took my things and padded barefoot across the sand toward the ocean. I stripped down. There was no one to see me except for the black, starless sky, and the blacker silhouettes of the palms at the edge of the parking lot. I put the needle into my skin.

God you're a villain a villain

I could be caught, of course. Someone might see me as I ran through the surf as a wolf. Or someone might see me in nine or fifteen or twenty-two minutes when I had turned back into a naked human. Or possibly, very possibly, someone could see the very moment of transformation.

But they wouldn't. Statistically, they wouldn't.

And the threat wasn't enough to stop me. I waited as my veins began to howl and my nerves started to shudder. If there was a way to make my thoughts go before the pain, the screaming pain of the shift, this would be the perfect escape. The cleanest drug, the sanest mental vacation.

Sometimes I forgot how filthy the drugs had made me. But it was like Baby said. I was pretty now.

Villain villain villain

And then, finally, I was a wolf. The sand on my paws, cool and damp and endless. No colors to miss on the night beach. Just sound and smell and wind hissing past my ears as I ran. Every thought was an image.

I came to crouching in the freezing surf. There was no one around. The beach was still empty. I had gotten away with it, which somehow made me feel worse. It was only me who knew the truth about me, but that was enough. Everyone else had already guessed.

I was always him, always Cole St. Clair.

And I could still hear Isabel's voice as she said, *I don't believe in happy endings.*

CHAPTER TWENTY-SIX

· ISABEL ·

INTERNET: *Hey, Cole St. Clair, is it true you got kicked out of Yuzu?*

VIRTUAL COLE: *for being awesome*

INTERNET: *My buddy said it was because you were shooting up in their bathroom.*

VIRTUAL COLE: *you need new buddies*

INTERNET: *LOLOL love you man*

VIRTUAL COLE: *really who doesn't*

INTERNET: *Will you ever do another song like "Villain"?*

INTERNET: *Who is that girl we saw on the last episode?*

VIRTUAL COLE: *superhot alien*

INTERNET: *dump her! I luv u cole!*

VIRTUAL COLE: *superhot alien would destroy planet*

VIRTUAL COLE: *really im saving the world (no really)*

VIRTUAL COLE: *thank me now*

INTERNET: *she wouldnt have 2 know haha lol*

INTERNET: *Are we ever going to see Victor again? NARKOTIKA rocked!*

VIRTUAL COLE:

INTERNET: *Great to see you and Jeremy playing together!*
How about Victor?

VIRTUAL COLE:

INTERNET: *OK let's have Victor now!!!!!!*

VIRTUAL COLE: *you guys are going to give leyla a vegan breakdown*

INTERNET: *hahaha no but really NARKOTIKA 4EVER*

INTERNET: *What do you want for your birthday?*

VIRTUAL COLE: *to stay young forever*

Cole texted me:

Actually I want you

CHAPTER TWENTY-SEVEN

· COLE ·

Baby called me and said, "Happy birthday. Are you ready for your surprise?"

I was standing in the rental house next door to my apartment; I'd broken in right after I'd had breakfast. And by breakfast, I mean a banana lying in a hot dog bun, and by breaking in, I mean I found out that one of the rear sliding doors was unlocked. I wasn't thrilled with the idea that it was my birthday, even though I couldn't say exactly why. I said, "Am I going to like it?"

"I worked very hard on it."

"Can I get a hint?"

"Just enjoy the ride," Baby said. "You might want to put on pants for this. I hope you've been writing some music."

The first surprise arrived on my doorstep at ten A.M. Actually, it didn't quite arrive on my doorstep. It arrived in the alley behind the house and made really loud noises until I climbed up onto the roof deck to see what was happening.

Down below was a brilliant cerulean Lamborghini revving its engine repeatedly. For a brief moment, I thought, *That's quite a present*, and then I realized that the present was actually sitting behind the driver's wheel in the form of a small, gorgeous Latina with white aviator sunglasses on. She looked both richer and more famous than me, because she was. My heart gave an involuntary lurch.

Oh, Baby, you clever bastard, I thought.

"Magdalene," I called down. "How nice of you to stop by."

When I had first met Magdalene, she had just been discovered in some small town in Arkansas or Georgia or South Carolina, the daughter of a sometime mechanic who entertained herself joyriding and singing in shopping malls. She'd just graduated from high school and released her first EP and was looking for some exposure.

She recorded "Spacebar" with us and then we went our separate ways. By which I mean, I went on to make NARKOTIKA famous in a few different countries and then pass out in my own drool. And she went on to record one of the top five selling dance albums of the decade, marry and divorce two actors and one actress in two years, lose and regain her driving license for running a street-racing ring, and star in one of the movies in the Clutch franchise — the only one that made any money. I still had a poster she sent me. With a metallic blue marker, she'd written on it:

Shut up (and Drive), Cole

I understood that she had the largest collection of sky blue supercars in North America.

She was also the nicest drunk I'd ever known. Once upon a dangerous time, I'd had the biggest crush on her. I was quite certain Baby knew both of these things. I wondered what she was hoping I'd do with this episode.

"Happy birthday, Cole St. Clair!" Magdalene gave the Lambo another rev. Wind came from somewhere and lifted her black hair. The ripple of the strands suggested that they had been constructed by a team of specialists. "Get in this car before I run out of gas!"

I leaned over the railing, taking in the blueness of the car. I noticed that T was parked behind her in a van, recording every second. Also, Magdalene had a tactful little mic clipped on her glittery tank top.

"Where are we going?" I asked loudly.

"Baby told me we were recording a song?"

"Oh, did she."

"I only record in my place. I hope you've got something that's gonna make me sound good."

"My drummer's not going to fit in that car."

"She can take that," Magdalene said. Contempt oozed off her voice and pooled around the tires of the Saturn.

The image of Leyla being forced to drive the Saturn again was a powerful motivator. I pushed off the railing. As I headed for the stairs, I texted Isabel. **Virtual Me might heat up. Episode is happening.**

Isabel texted back. **The internet never sleeps**

I shot back: **you could come**

Isabel: **damn class til late**

I texted: **tell them it's my birthday**

She didn't reply, but I didn't expect her to. I called Jeremy. "I'm sending a car for you. An episode's happening."

Jeremy asked, "What's the way?"

I said, "I have no idea."

. . .

Magdalene took me down to her studio space in Long Beach. I couldn't even call it studio space. I didn't know what to call it. It was a warehouse near the Long Beach Airport, all concrete floors and giant doors meant for driving semitrucks through. It was big enough to fit an entire Venice block. Half of it was lined with sky blue supercars. I didn't know what most of them were. Flat cars with big engines and spoilers that looked like torture devices. The concrete floor between them was marked with big loops of tire marks, some smeared sideways.

The other half was a studio. It was the biggest, fanciest studio I'd ever seen, and I'd seen some pretty big and fancy studios. There were isolation booths for singers and isolation booths for drum kits and a piano and an upright hipster piano and a rack of synthesizers and an array of guitars and bass guitars and cellos all propped up in stands, waiting to be used. The walls were covered with acoustic padding and the ceilings were hung with microphones on tracks. For a second, I thought I smelled a hint of wolf among the mixing consoles, but then it was gone and maybe it had just been me. Above me, a huge pair of shiny 3-D lips, complete with lip ring, hung on the wall. They were larger than any of the cars and red as the blood in my beating heart.

It was excessive even for excess. I turned to Magdalene. She was already drinking something out of a tiny little glass.

Quick tip: Things in tiny little glasses punch harder than things in big ones.

She smiled at me. It was a smile that had seen ten thousand cameras. Two of the ten thousand were already trained on her.

"You want something? I probably have something that will interest you."

"I'm clean," I told Magdalene.

"Good for you." Magdalene laughed, and her laugh was a little hoarse, like mine was when I'd been touring a lot. "The world needs more priests."

I wondered if Baby was hoping we'd fight. I let it pass. "Look at all these toys you have here."

The most insane part was that this place was clearly a concrete manifestation of her imagination. She was so over the top — huge hair, huge eyes, tight sparkly tank top, elaborate belly-button piercing, belt wider than my hand, bell bottoms, and combat boots — that she fit right in.

"Wait till the boys get here," she said. "Play me something."

She gestured to the piano. It was a nine-foot Steinway. Because seven-foot Steinways are for posers.

There is only one option if you are presented with a nine-foot concert grand Steinway, especially if it is sky blue, as this one was.

I sat at it.

I wasn't always a rock star. It wasn't synthesizer lessons I'd asked my parents for.

I played a little fragment of Bach. Intentionally slow and stilted and soft, like a creepy clown or a joke involving Bach. The piano was incredibly tuned. It practically played itself.

"Come now, Cole," Magdalene purred, leaning on the piano. She rolled her eyes toward the cameras. "We're all alone here. Surely you don't have nerves."

I smiled at her — the Cole St. Clair smile — and trilled out another snatch of messy Bach, fast but proficient, and then I crashed into the chords of "Spacebar."

Magdalene grinned wildly, recognizing them at once. She pulled the glass from her lips and sang the chorus as I got to it: "Hit it, hit it, hit it!"

Each time she repeated "hit it," she ratcheted up the scale. Man, she had a set of pipes. And she'd gotten better since we'd first recorded that track, too. She tapped out a beat on the edge of the piano as I tripped and plummeted through the refrain of "Spacebar," trying to translate the synth chords into a piano bit on the fly. It had been a million years since I'd played it.

But it was still catchy.

Whoever had written this song had known what they were doing.

My reflection smiled cunningly at me from the sheen of the open piano lid.

Magdalene kept singing.

And oh — oh, it was good to be playing again. To hear someone else riffing off your tune, to throw a bit of an improvisation back at them, to come back again and again to those same crashing four chords that, for two glorious weeks, America had sung over and over until they were dreaming them.

Then we'd sold the rights to a car commercial and moved on to something else.

Magdalene screamed up the last bit of the scale at the same time that I crashed down to the very bass range of the Steinway, and when the last ringing note died, she got herself another drink.

I wondered if she was supposed to be the disaster at the sidelines.

I heard slow clapping. Jeremy and Leyla had arrived, as had "the boys" — the sound techs. The oldest of the techs was the one clapping. An assistant had been filming us with his phone.

He asked, "Can I put that on the Internet?"

Magdalene said callously, "Why not? He's written something better for later, anyway." Then she turned to me. I was still a bit destroyed by hurling myself onto the shores of the tune. She put a small hand on my cheek. "Ah, Cole. I forgot what talent sounded like."

Chapter Twenty-Eight

· ISABEL ·

I could say that I had never missed a CNA class before and that I was making an exception for Cole, but I'd be lying. I had always considered class to be a negotiable concept. The only thing that mattered was the grade. Ever since I hit high school, I constantly skated that fine, dangerous line between knowing all of the material and getting in trouble for failing to participate.

Still, so far the only time I'd cut CNA class had been on my dead brother, Jack's, birthday, but I hadn't really been thinking about that when I cut. I was just thinking that sitting in someone else's high school for another six hours was going to make me violently and physically ill.

I cut this time for another birthday: Cole's. I didn't want to surprise him until he'd actually had time to get some work done, though, so I found myself with a beautiful stretch of day with nothing to fill it. Ordinarily, these huge swaths of time would invest me with anxiety and hatred of the planet, but today, the hours seemed benevolent. I decided to pick up Sofia from her erhu lesson and make her buy some sexy boots before I drove myself to Long Beach and Cole.

I couldn't tell what this thing was inside me. Was it a good mood? It seemed like it could be.

But when I headed down the stairs of the House of Ruin, prison keys jingling merrily with the melody of escape, I saw my father standing in the foyer. He looked tidy and powerful, a barely sheathed knife in a gray suit.

I hesitated. That was my mistake. My father had been bred and trained to sense weakness. His eyes were on me in a second.

FATHER: *Isabel.*
ISABEL: *Father.*
FATHER: *Don't use that tone with me.*
ISABEL: *This is my voice.*
FATHER: *You know exactly what I'm talking about.*

I contemplated if I could go back to my room and rappel out the window. Physically, I could. Practically, it would stain my skirt. The point was to look excellent for Cole later. Hopefully, this wouldn't last long.

Down below, my father gazed up at me. His eyes looked hectic, like they did when he was working on big cases.

FATHER: *We need to talk to you.*
ISABEL: *I'm on my way out.*
FATHER: *This isn't optional.*
ISABEL: *I encourage you to plunder the definition of the word* optional *as I leave.*
FATHER: *Isabel — please just — please just come down. This is important.*

His voice had gone strange. I came down.

I felt an unpleasant jitter inside me, like when I'd heard the news about Jack.

I followed him into the kitchen. Because it was day, all the lights were turned off, but the sun was high enough overhead that it didn't make it in the windows. It made the room seem cool and hostile. My mother was already arranged inside, leaning against the counter with her arms crossed. She had dressed herself in contempt. Not her best look, but better than tears.

My good mood felt like an endangered species.

I tried to imagine what could possibly put those expressions on my parents' faces.

I thought I knew. I just didn't want to —

"We've decided to get a divorce," my mother said.

There it was.

All of the suggestion and postulation and threatening and, finally, there it was.

"Of course you are," I said.

"Isabel," my mother chastised.

My father looked up sharply. He hadn't heard what I'd said because he had been busy cutting the throat of my good mood on the center island. Luckily, the granite had been chosen to provide a wipe-clean surface for blood, orange juice, and disappointment.

I tried to think of how it would change things. I didn't know if it would really make things worse. Or better. Or different. Mostly I thought of how it meant now when I went away to college, I'd have to visit two separate houses if I wanted to see both parents. And I thought of how if Jack somehow magically returned, he wouldn't recognize his family, because it had disintegrated. And I thought of how statistically pointless love was and how unsurprising this all was in the relative scheme of things.

"Are you crying?" my mother asked.

"No," I replied. "Why would I be crying?"

"Lauren said that Sofia cried a lot when she found out about her and Paolo."

Both my father and I looked at my mother.

"When?" I asked, but I knew it was a pointless question as soon as I asked it. A divorce wasn't like a wedding or a birthday party. You didn't set a date and buy flowers. I thought about the photographs that used to adorn the entire entry wall back in our home in Minnesota. An assortment of wedding and honeymoon photos. My genetic material was quite attractive, and they were a striking couple in every photo. I'd like to say that even in those early images you could see the seeds of discord, but I'd be lying. They were beautiful, unposed photos of two beautiful young people in love with each other. They were in love before they got married and in love at the wedding and in love when they had baby Jack and baby Isabel.

But not anymore.

My father said, "Do you want to talk about it?"

"We *are* talking about it."

My mother shot my father a look as if this must be obvious.

"What about Christmas?" I asked. It was a stupid question. A child's question. I was immediately angry at myself for asking it. "Never mind. I answered my own question."

My mother said, "Oh, honey, I don't know. That's months from now," which made me wonder if I'd even said the *never mind* part out loud. I thought about it and I was pretty sure I remembered the action of forming the words.

I wondered if I should retrieve the body of my good mood for a proper burial, or if I should just leave it here in the House of Ruin.

My mother wasn't wearing her wedding ring. I noticed it just then. My father wasn't, either. I felt like laughing. A really hideous, cold laugh. Instead, I sneered a little. My face had to do *something*.

"What do you need from us?" my mother asked. She asked it with the exact cadence in her voice that meant she had been told by her therapist, Dr. Carrotnose, to ask me that. Divorce-by-numbers.

"Your genetic matter," I replied. My skin felt sort of hummy. "And I already got that. So thanks. Congrats on your impending breakup. Well, making it official. I'm out."

"This is unacceptable," my father announced. He was right, but there was nothing really left to do but accept it.

"Isabel —" my mother said, but I was already gone.

Chapter Twenty-Nine

· COLE ·

That day, the acoustic version of "Spacebar" wound its way through the Internet as we wound our way through "Air Kisses," the track I'd decided to attempt to record that day. I had to redo the lyrics on the spot — they were better with a female vocalist, anyway, but some of it was meant for me when I wrote it, and I didn't want to hear Magdalene singing about Isabel, even if only I knew that's what it was. While the others broke for lunch, I sat with headphones on, ducked over the Korg, writing a brand-new bridge. I recorded and rerecorded my pulsing synth heartbeat. I made Leyla record and rerecord and rerecord her drum part, which she did without complaint or brilliance. Jeremy observed silently through the first few hours and then, in hour four, wrote a bass riff that made us all quiet. After that, Magdalene strutted into the booth and caressed the microphone and belted a vocal track that made us all loud.

She was very drunk.

Two years ago, I would've been, too.

What's the way, Baby?

Then, while two of Magdalene's boys worked on mixing the refrain, she opened up one of the massive doors so that we wouldn't all die from carbon monoxide poisoning, and we drove her beautiful cars around in circles in the warehouse and then in the chain-link fenced parking lot.

The sun had gotten high and then gotten low somehow as we worked. A whole day vanished into a microphone. Dust buffed up into the air in big, choking clouds, all of it orange and violet in the sunset, everything beautiful and industrial and apocalyptic with the warehouses and the sky blue cars.

Maybe this was the only point of the episode. Enviable and beautiful excess, good music and pretty people.

As I got into car number four or five — a Nissan GT-R, or something flat and mouth-shaped like that — Magdalene climbed into the passenger seat beside me.

"Take it down the road and back. See what it can do!" she shouted, pointing down the perfectly straight road that ran in front of her warehouse. "We'll be back in two minutes, boys!"

Then she turned to me and said, "Punch it, kid."

I didn't know what it was, but it wasn't the Saturn, and that was great.

I let it charge to the edge of the lot. Just before we squealed out onto the long, straight road to the airport, Magdalene ripped off her mic and threw it out the window. In the rearview mirror, I watched it roll into the gravel and become invisible.

"Vandalism," I remarked uneasily. "Baby won't be pleased."

As the speedometer climbed and the warehouse disappeared in a fresh cloud of dust, she said, all messy and sexy, "Are you enjoying your cage?"

The engine howled. In the rearview mirror, I saw that the cameramen had stepped out into the road to film our short escape. "What cage?"

"The one they watch you prowl around in. I have something for you," she said. "Once we get out of view."

I screwed a gear shift. What the hell did I know about driving? And what the hell was this car anyway? We were already going eight thousand miles an hour, and I was pretty sure we were only in third gear and had very little marked road left. "If you're talking about substances, my dear, I am clean."

The road dead-ended in a massive parking lot. Before I could hit the brake, Magdalene leaned over and snatched up the parking brake. The car immediately spun. For a single moment, we were weightless. It was life and death and stopping and going at the same time. The car sailed sideways, the steering wheel meaningless, but there was nothing for it to run into.

Chaos without consequence.

Magdalene released the brake. With a jerk, the car finished its spin. We faced back the way we came. Dust rolled by us in herds.

"I am the greatest," Magdalene observed. "Cole, you have never been clean."

"I'm not using," I said as the windshield cleared. "Give me some credit."

"You're an addict," she said. "You'd be an addict if no one ever invented a drug. *I* saw you before you started using. You aren't any different now."

The car was so loud, even idling. "I'm sober now."

"You were sober back then, too. Maybe the world thinks you loved heroin, but I know what your real addiction is."

I looked at her. She looked at me. I wanted her to say *music*, but she wasn't going to. We'd started this as the same thing: ambitious teens with no idea of what to do once the ceiling was removed from the world.

She asked, "Have you seen those big black-and-white monkeys at the zoo? They sit around all day picking their butts *hoo hoo hoo*, until a crowd comes along. And then they pick up all the toys in their cage and start throwing them and clowning around. They do it for the laughs. They do it because there are people watching. It's not even about the toys. It's only about the crowd."

She meant the *way*. She smiled then, sharp and beautiful, just the girl I remembered appearing in the studio on day one, back before it all went to shit.

Magdalene opened up her hand, and in it was some ecstasy. "Who's your friend? I am."

I hated how much I wanted to take it. My heart was crashing as if I already had.

But even more than that, I hated how Magdalene believed in that old version of me. She was so certain I'd already toppled. The world didn't want me to reinvent myself. Not a single person in it.

"Did Baby give that to you?" I asked.

She made a dismissive sound. It was accompanied by a very alcohol-scented breath. She was such a lovely and friendly drunk.

"Oh, Magdalene, Magdalene. What did she say when she asked you to be on the show?"

Magdalene smiled at me, her other hand on my face again. This smile was a real one, not her camera-ready number from before. Her obscenely beautiful lips parted to reveal that she was slightly gap-toothed. I suddenly remembered Jeremy saying that everyone looked like kids to him, and just like that, I could see her as the little girl she must have been before she ever got discovered. It was the saddest thing I'd ever imagined. I couldn't comprehend how Jeremy could stand it.

"She told me to be myself," Magdalene said.

I closed her hand back over the ecstasy. Her eyes widened in surprise.

Cole, what's the way? Nobody but me was going to tell me how to be Cole St. Clair.

"Yeah," I said. "Yeah, me, too."

As the camera van approached us, I put the car back in gear and screamed back the way I'd come.

CHAPTER THIRTY

· ISABEL ·

I was not in the mood to pick out sexy boots. I was not even in the mood to stare at famous people and dissect what made them look famous. I was in the mood for lab work. Back when I'd been taking AP Biology, I'd discovered there was nothing like plucking and dicing and observing to occupy the more active parts of my brain. If nothing else, biology was relentlessly logical. You could not change the rules. You could only work within them.

But this was not biology. This was Sunset Plaza, which was sort of the opposite of biology. It defied logic. It was famous for being filled with famous people, but apart from that, it really wasn't that exceptional. In fact, the inside of Erik's didn't look like much of anything. The narrow store boasted thin, high-traffic carpet, clear plastic, and dull lights that did nothing to replace the sun blocked by the yellow awning out front. .blush. was way nicer, in my opinion.

But the shabby was how you knew Erik's was an institution. If you survived in this city without being drop-dead gorgeous, it meant you were really something. While this ordinary shop continued on with age and cunning, the brand-new, beautifully stark storefronts next door kept coming up for lease as their pretty new tenants got eaten by Los Angeles.

"Sofia," I snapped, pulling her out of the way of a rogue Escalade. "Watch where you're going."

Sofia's gaze fluttered to me, but she was still mostly watching the rest of the people on the Strip. "Did you see that woman over there? I think it was Christina —"

"Probably," I interrupted. "Movie stars. That's the view here. Unless you're one of them, I wouldn't recommend walking out in front of traffic. It won't stop."

Sofia kept goggling, so I kept her arm and walked her, seeing-eye-dog-style, from our parking spot across the road to Erik's. Once inside the dim store, I released her into the wild. As she walked slowly past the racks, I pulled out Virtual Cole and looked to see how the world was reacting to the acoustic "Spacebar."

Well. They were reacting well.

In fact, they thrashed and squealed and hated and shouted and clapped delightedly. The music blogs disseminated it. Sound bites of the song provided soundtracks for animated GIFs of long-ago Cole throwing stuff out of a hotel room window. Words flashed at the bottom: *COLE ST. CLAIR IS BACK*.

The four chambers of my heart were all vacant.

I updated Virtual Cole, replying and re-disseminating where necessary, but my mind was wandering back to Minnesota. Cole dragged himself down the hallway of a house I couldn't forget. He was a boy and a wolf and then a boy again. He begged me to help him to die. To die or to stay a wolf.

My mind moved down the hall, past Cole, into another memory in that house. My brother Jack, dying in the bedroom at the end of the hall. Crumpled on the bed, burning up, determined to stay human, or to die trying. Everything smelled like wolf and death. Maybe there wasn't a difference between the two.

COLE ST. CLAIR IS BACK. Was the wolf back, too?

I realized I'd been trailing around after Sofia, eyes on my phone, for quite a while. I looked up to see that she was staring at a pair of strappy sandals that she would never wear. She stared at them for so long that I realized that she wasn't actually looking at them.

"Sofia," I said. "Are you waiting for them to speak?"

She rubbed her own cheek and blinked her dark lashes at me with an apologetic smile. "I'm just distracted. Dad's coming for a visit!"

Immediately, I thought about the conversation in the kitchen with my parents. I couldn't remember any of it as well as I remembered my father's voice going strange when he told me we needed to talk. I felt like smashing some shoes off the shelves. People who say throwing shit when you're angry doesn't help have never thrown shit while they were angry.

"What a bucket of kittens that will be," I said.

Sofia began to nod before she realized I was being sarcastic. Then, all earnest, she said, "Mom said she might go out with us."

Her face shone.

I couldn't take the hope in her expression. "Oh, please! They aren't getting back together, Sofia!"

My cousin looked like I'd smacked her. Her cheeks turned as flushed as if I had. "I didn't say they were!"

"But your face said it. That's not how the real world works."

Predictably, her eyes shone with the threat of tears. "It's not *about* that. We're just going to spend the day together."

"Really? Not even a little tiny bit of you thinks they will get back together?"

Sofia shook her head fiercely. She swiped the back of her hand across her eyes. They still looked fine, but she had a line of black mascara on her hand. She insisted, "I just want to spend time with him again. That's all I care about."

"Well, great," I said. "I'm sure it won't be awkward at all."

She looked at her feet. I hated that she never fought back. I wouldn't feel like such a jerk if she bothered to hit back. But she just smeared a hand over her skirt, smoothing it, and then over her hair, and then placed one hand in the other, like she was comforting it and sending it to sleep.

"I'm not in a good mood," I told her.

"That's okay." She said it to her shoes.

"It's not okay," I said. "Tell me to shut up."

A tear dripped onto Sofia's shoe. "I don't want to. You always say the truth, anyway."

She didn't mention the other half of the coin, though: that sometimes the truth wasn't the most useful thing to add to a conversation. I knew *now*, minutes after I'd started the conversation, that the proper way to reply to "Dad's coming for a visit!" would have been, "Cool! Where are you going?"

"Right," I said, "Yeah. Are you going to buy shoes?"

"I don't need shoes."

I bit my tongue before I asked her why she'd even come. She'd come because I'd asked her. "Let's just go before traffic gets bad. I have to get to Long Beach."

It was hard to remember my mood of this morning. It was harder still to imagine any sort of birthday surprise going well enough to make up for the dismal expression on Sofia's face. The one I'd put there.

As I pushed out of the door, I almost ran into Christina. After she swore at me and said, "Excuse *you*," I realized it wasn't actually Christina, just one of the dozens of interchangeable famous young women who frequented this place, women who looked gorgeous and slender on screen and were all knobbed elbows and big feet and huge sunglasses in person.

"Oh, please," I told her, and clicked out onto the relentlessly sunny sidewalk.

Sofia, behind me, couldn't look the fake Christina in the eye. Sofia's hand was on her waist. I could tell she felt lumpy, because fake Christina was skim and Sofia was 2%. I could tell she felt sad, because her cousin was a bitch. I could tell that, despite it all, she was still a little excited about her father coming to visit.

I hated this place.

CHAPTER THIRTY-ONE

· COLE ·

I sat in the recording booth with the headphones, my legs resting on the music stand in front of the swivel chair, and listened to the track. I'd added my vocals to the chorus at the last moment.

I sounded good. The whole thing sounded good. Not just good, but *good*.

Though it had been hours and hours and I should have been exhausted, I felt like I'd just woken up. My heart had burst into frenzied life. Or my brain. Or my body.

Sometimes when I was done with a track, I had this moment where I knew it was going to take over the world. Was it about subjectivity? Knowing you'd just done something that would sound good played overhead at a roller-skating rink? Or was it a kind of telescoping sixth sense that only traveled through speaker cables?

I took out my phone. I called Sam, who didn't pick up, and left a voicemail that was only the song. I called Grace and did the same.

I didn't feel any more complete than I had before. I called Isabel, even though I knew she was in class. I didn't expect her to pick up, but she did.

"I have just done something magnificent," I told her. I wanted her there with me, in a raw, sudden, endless way that was like the song in my head. "Come bask in my glory."

"I'm in class," she said in a low voice. "Paraphrase it."

I'd taken off my headphones, but the music kept playing through them. I could feel the bass pulsing a beat against my thigh. It felt like the end of the world. Or like the creation. Something was exploding. I needed angels to attend me. It was not good for man to be alone in this state. "I just did."

"Use your words."

My words were *I need you right now I need to kiss you I want to have you here I want to just have you* but I struggled to translate. "I've just recorded my first real track since I died and it is going to eat every dance floor in the country and it's not even the best one I've written so far and someone is paying me to go into the studio and record the others and I can't wait, I just can't wait, I want to do it tonight, and I want you here because it is stupid to do it by myself."

I didn't know how many of those words I said out loud, or if those were even the ones I used. My brain was tripping over itself, all sudden adrenaline and feeling and music music music, and my mouth couldn't keep up.

"Are you high?" Isabel asked suspiciously.

I laughed. I was high, but not the way she thought. "I did it. I made a thing, Isabel!"

"Well done. I alr — dammit. I have to get off the phone. Just remember" — she paused, and I thought I heard honking, but probably it was just voices at her class. I tried to tell myself that I was lucky that she had even picked up at all — "when a client is a different faith than you, it's not an opportunity for you to evangelize, even if he's on his deathbed."

"Am I a CNA now?" I asked.

"Yes," Isabel said. She hung up.

In the headphones on my lap, I heard the track loop back around to the beginning. I felt like I had put my foot on a gas pedal and had nowhere to go. Up up up.

Magdalene threw open the door. She grinned wildly. "Now," she said, "we celebrate."

Chapter Thirty-Two

· ISABEL ·

It was taking forever to get to Cole. First it was an accident, and then a huge event of some kind in the city, and then rush hour, and then another accident. The cars inched and stuttered along the freeway. My forty-five-minute drive turned into an hour and a half turned into two hours. The sky pinked and then blazed and then blackened.

My mood went from bad to worse to the worst.

I told myself it would be worth it for the look on his face when I appeared in the studio, assuming he was even still *at* the studio when I got there.

I turned up my radio as loud as I could stand, trying to drown out the continuous loop of the scene with my parents in the kitchen. All the words were gone, leaving just their gestures behind. Like a television show with the sound turned down. The name of the episode: "The Culpepers Get a Divorce."

I didn't know why I cared. My father hadn't even been living with us. I was about to go off to college. They hated each other, and this is what grown-ups who hated each other did. It changed nothing, except for making it all official.

I couldn't convince myself not to give a damn, though.

I focused on navigating to Magdalene's studio instead. It hadn't been a hard thing to find the address on the Internet, but I wasn't sure what to expect. It looked like an old warehouse in the photos. An old warehouse in the middle of nowhere.

When I got there, it looked like a dance club.

The parking lot was full of cars. Dozens upon dozens of them, packed in, parked sideways, parking one another in. People had spilled into the parking lot, laughing and drinking.

A party.

I shouldn't have been surprised, but I was.

I wasn't really in the headspace for a party.

For a brief, selfish second, I thought about turning around and going home. Cole couldn't be disappointed, because he hadn't known I was coming.

But then I thought about what was waiting for me at home.

I should've just gone to class.

I closed my eyes, then opened them and checked my makeup in the rearview mirror. I tried to imagine what I'd find on the other side of those doors. A big party full of people having a great time, and then Cole feeling sorry for himself in a recording booth, sad and alone in a crowd. Cole always liked to see himself as alone, no matter how much the circumstances disputed it.

The only thing that made me move at all was the idea of how happy he'd be to see me. I got out of the car.

Inside, the massive warehouse seethed. Music pounded overhead. The floor was alcohol-slicked sticky. There were a million people dancing. A lot of girls. Everything smelled like beer. Over everything was a pair of giant red lips.

Then I found him.

Cole St. Clair was sitting on a sofa being carried by four other guys, and a girl was sitting on the other side of the couch, and she was famous and she was beautiful and she had her lusciously golden arm around his neck. The cameras gazed adoringly.

My stomach felt it first. I couldn't move.

I tried to be fair. I told myself it wasn't like he was making out with someone else. I told myself he had only sounded high on the phone, that I didn't know for sure. I told myself that I had only thought I'd smelled wolf on him before; I hadn't actually seen him shift since he'd come here.

I told myself it was possible he was clean and he was not a cheater and that he wasn't NARKOTIKA's Cole St. Clair.

But I couldn't take my eyes off him sitting on that couch with that impossibly beautiful girl. Because he sure as hell looked like NARKOTIKA's Cole St. Clair to me.

Humiliation and anger clawed inside me.

He didn't know I was here.

I was going to go.

I was going to go.

I was going to go. As soon as I could look away.

Cole saw me just as I managed to rip my feet from the floor and turn, my hand fumbling in my purse for my car keys. I saw his eyes find me, just for a second, and then I knew I'd stayed too long. Because now it was going to get —

"Isabel! Hey! *Hey.*"

I kept walking. The door to the warehouse felt miles away. I could see it, but it never got any closer. I didn't turn around. I kept going. People moved out of my way.

"Isabel!"

Outside, in the black night, I sucked in breaths of empty air, trying to fill this hollowed-out cavity.

"Hey." Cole grabbed my arm, stopping me. This close, I could smell the alcohol and weed. And wolf. Wolf wolf *wolf.* It was all over him.

I'd never left that house in Minnesota.

I spun. "Let. Go. Of. Me."

In the dark of the lot, his eyes were bright and glittery, but there were bags beneath them. He was tired and awake. High and low. Going up and burning down. Turning people into objects and throwing them away.

"What is your problem?" he asked.

"That question is not even remotely appropriate for this situation," I replied. I felt like I needed to shout to be heard over the music, but really it was just that I could feel it in my feet from inside the building.

"What situation is that? Are you going to clue me in?"

I flicked a finger at him. "You! You are the situation!"

Cole narrowed his eyes. "So the situation is *awesome?*"

The wire-framed industrial light on the outside of the warehouse was twitching and trembling to the beat inside. Every time I thought of him with that girl on the couch, every time I inhaled and smelled the beer, something inside me did the same thing. I didn't know why I thought I could do this. "You know what? Just — I'm not even."

I jerked my arm out of his hand and started back toward my car. It was parked near the edge of the lot. It hadn't seemed so far away when I'd gotten here.

"So now it's a crime to exist," Cole said. "That explains a lot."

The indignation was too much. I snapped, "Call me when you're sober. Or actually, don't."

There was a long pause, long enough that I unlocked my car and opened the door.

Then he said, "Sober? I *am* sober."

This was so ludicrous that I turned to face him. "Come on, Cole. Don't insult me. I'm not an idiot."

His face was a broad expression of absolute persecution. He spread his arms out. "I haven't been drinking."

"I can *smell* it on you!" You didn't grow up in my house without knowing the smell of hard liquor and beer and wine. Without knowing how exaggerated it made the drunk. How they became a caricature of themselves: silent if they were quiet, a hurricane if they were irritable.

"There is beer in the building," Cole said. "There was beer on the couch. There is not beer inside me."

"Right. And that girl?"

"*What girl?*"

"You were wearing her? That one?"

Dismissively, he said, "Magdalene. She's a sloppy drunk. That was nothing."

Nothing. Maybe to him. Maybe to him it didn't count unless you were naked. But to me, who had never been someone's *girlfriend* — I was so done. I had driven out here for this stupid surprise, this birthday surprise, and I was tired, and I wished I'd never come and seen it and I wished he hadn't ever come into .blush. in the first place and I just couldn't do it anymore. I wanted to go back to not giving any damns. I missed that Isabel. Everything hurt. "And the *wolf*?"

He didn't answer right away. His eyes flickered an answer, swift and guilty. God, I couldn't take it. I'd known it all along, and I'd just been playing pretend.

"So you're just Cole again, is it?" I demanded. "Cole St. Clair is back!"

"What? Oh. It's not like that."

I fired back, "Sure looks like that."

"*Looks* and *is* aren't the same. Otherwise they'd be the same word. Precision, Culpeper. I thought that was your thing. If you'd been here instead of always saying you weren't going to be part of the Cole St. Clair show, you'd have seen what really happened here today. Not just been part of the audience, believing the hype."

"Don't try to make me feel guilty about not being a player in your life."

"If you feel guilty, it's because you put it there, not me. I never asked you to be on the show."

"Asked! You didn't have to. It's like a giant cloud that follows me around!"

"What, so now I'm in trouble for things I didn't even say? For *thinking* I want more time with you?"

My eyes seared, like they were close to tears, even though I couldn't feel any accompanying emotion. "Yes! You always want more from me. Be okay with naked girls in your apartment. Be you on the Internet. Be happy with you smelling like a goddamn wolf. More, Isabel, more! Well, I don't have any more! I'm giving you what I can give you without completely . . . And this is what you do?"

Cole laughed in a very unfunny way. "This? *This?* I don't even know what *this* is. Breathing! Living! Being me! What a grand day this has become!" He did the little NARKOTIKA hand gesture that said he was revealing something new. "Happy birthday, Cole! Happy, happy birthday."

"I'm *here*, aren't I?"

"Telling me I screwed up!"

This was too much. "Because you *did*."

He stepped right up next to me. I could tell he was angry, but I didn't care. Wolf wolf wolf. "I. Am. Sober."

Did he think I couldn't smell him? "Whatever."

"Whatever?" he echoed. "How about you take my word for it?"

"And why should I do that?"

"How about because you trust me?"

"*Trust you?* Does anyone do that? Of all the things I would do that are crazy, Cole, you can be sure that will never be one of them."

Just like that, he was gone. His body was still there, but his eyes were empty. Cole St. Clair had left the building. A very tidy party trick, and the most cunning objectification of all: when he took the person that was him and threw him away. I would have felt guilty, but I had seen what I'd seen. I wasn't making any of it up. I could smell the wolf, smell the beer, remember the girl's arm draped possessively around his neck.

I would not feel bad.

I did not feel bad.

"Don't call me," I said. "Stop doing this to me. I'm not your — stop doing this to me."

I got into my car.

I didn't look back to see if he was still standing in the lot.

CHAPTER THIRTY-THREE

· COLE ·

I was sober.

I had told the truth, and it hadn't mattered. In the end, she'd bought into the same story everyone else had.

Did it matter if you'd changed if no one believed it?

After Isabel left, I walked through the party in a haze. I knew I said something to Jeremy. I knew I smiled at a joke some guy told me. I knew I signed someone's hat. I didn't remember the fine details of anything. They were all lost in the hiss in my ears.

I moved through the people until I found Magdalene on the couch beneath the giant lips, making out with one of her boys.

"Farewell, pet," I told her. My smile was a corpse that I resurrected briefly for her. "I'm out."

Magdalene slapped the boy away. "It's early! I think it's early? Don't go."

"I must," I said. "Come, give me a sisterly embrace."

She staggered to her feet. "How boring that you're sober! Stay."

She threw her arms around me in a way I wouldn't have put up with from my sister, if I'd had one. I removed her fingers from my mouth. I needed to go before I felt-did-was something stupid. I needed to get out of here and I needed to call Isabel and I needed to not be angry and I needed to not think about the many ways I knew how to distract myself from this feeling —

"But wait, wait," Magdalene said. "It's your birthday."

"I remember."

"You have to stay for your present."

I looked past her. T was there with his camera, unable to hide his pleased smile. Joan had hers, too. I realized the music had been turned down for this moment. The partygoers, chattering in low anticipation, had parted in an uneven line toward one of the warehouse doors. It was rolled all the way up, and I saw the night sky and a thousand bitter stars.

Jeremy stood by the door, the only one not grinning. His face was watchful.

I asked, "Will I like it?"

Magdalene led me down the aisle of people to the door. T backed down ahead of us to get my facial expression; Joan followed up behind.

I got there and faced the nighttime parking lot. Three floodlights lit my present.

It was my Mustang. Black and shiny and tricked-out and new — well, not new anymore. It had been new when I'd gotten it, back when I'd rewarded myself for my first album going platinum, back before I realized you couldn't bring a Mustang or your soul on tour. It was not new, but it was still pristine. I could tell it was my Mustang from Phoenix, not just a rental, because there was still a St. Christopher medal dangling from the rearview mirror, just like when I'd left it.

It looked molten in these lights. The black of the paint reflected the black of the sky until it was just a void sitting there.

The doors opened.

My mother got out of the passenger's side.

My father got out of the driver's side.

T trotted around to keep getting my face.

It reflected the car that reflected the night sky that was a slice of the universe that contained infinite nothing.

There was nothing wrong with my father except his face looked a little like mine, and nothing wrong with my mother except she wore matched separates, and there was nothing wrong with the two of them together looking at me except it felt like the suburbs had moved into my heart.

"Happy birthday!" shouted a bunch of people behind me.

Jeremy stood there by the car, his shoulders pointed down, his eyes on me. He was the only person here who knew this wasn't a gift.

I looked at my parents. They looked at me. They looked at me a lot.

I had let them think I was dead.

I had not called them when the world found out I wasn't.

They had not changed in appearance at all, except to get dustier and older. My father had always looked brittle; now he looked cancerous. I recognized the Windbreaker he wore. I knew those shoes of my mother's. There was nothing wrong with them except the unchanging constancy of their lives, a circle of grocery-office-Saturday-bed-linen-washing-Sunday-services-Tuesday-ratatouille-night-Thursday-church-meeting-rinse-repeat.

There was nothing wrong with them except that three years ago I'd decided that I'd rather die than turn out like them.

They were really nice people.

They had driven this car all the way out here for me.

I couldn't move, in case moving triggered emotional reunions on their part.

Magdalene, her voice loud and bright, said, "What a show *this* will be!"

What that meant was that I had been standing there too long, my expression too naked, and I had not had Cole St. Clair up for the cameras for who knew how long.

I didn't know what he would do, though. I didn't know what Cole St. Clair would do right now, faced with these people. Part of the reason I had made him was *because* he couldn't coexist with them. Because he was the opposite, everything they weren't. He was the alternative to shooting myself in the head.

It wasn't cruel, this transformation, as long as I never went back home.

And now: this.

I needn't have worried about a teary reunion. Both of my parents eyed the cameras timidly.

And this, finally, this was my reminder. It was still the show, after all. If they'd wanted a chance at the real me, they would have called first.

I plunged forward and seized my mother's elbow. A little cardigan-covered bird bone. "Welcome to television! Don't be shy! Let's do that old mother-son thing, shall we?"

I gave her a grand old hug, a big sloppy Cole-St.-Clair thing, and then I whirled her out of my arms in a dance move before heading for my father. He stared at me as I came around the car at him like I was a bear attacking. But I didn't hug him. I merely grabbed his hand. I shook it like a man as he stared at me, mouth agape. Then I used my other hand to form his hand into a long bro-shake with mine, complete with palm slap and fist bump at the end.

"What a glorious reunion this is," I said, to both them and to the partygoers who still watched. I tossed my father's limp hand away from mine. "What staggering timing. I, in fact, have just recorded a masterpiece in there. I think the two of you will agree that once you hear it played at ear-bleeding volumes, you're really left with no choice but to move your hips."

I did a little dance move to demonstrate. My gaze glanced off of Jeremy's — I couldn't take the look in his eyes — and kept going.

"I wasn't expecting this," my mother said, and gave a laugh-cough.

My father touched his Adam's apple. He was Dr. St. Clair, twice the punctuation and five times the schooling of his prodigal son, a professor version of me. "I thought it would be dinner someplace nice. . . ."

This was my idea of a nice dinner: sitting on the hood of a car eating a chili dog. This was what he meant: a chain steakhouse.

I couldn't take this.

"And instead," I said, "you found yourselves in Long Beach, at one of the more glorious parties of the night." I reached for Magdalene's hand and put it in my father's. Then I took my mother and dragged her lightly to Magdalene's other side. I placed her hand in Magdalene's. Half-crouching, dramatic and theatrical, I gestured to the interior of the warehouse. My fingers were spread wide, painting an image.

"Now," I intoned, "see that wonderland? In you shall go to frolic. This is the life! This is California! This is how the other half lives! Go! Go! Cameras! Behold their excitement!"

My parents gazed into the warehouse, looking for this bright future I'd promised.

And then, as they stood there, hands in Magdalene's, I got into the Mustang. It was still running. Their heads barely had time to turn.

I tore out of the parking lot, slamming the driver's-side door shut as I did. Everything behind me was left in billowing dust. All of it gone: the night and the stars and the song that I had breathed into being.

Chapter Thirty-Four

· COLE ·

I drove.

Part of me wanted to keep driving. Part of me wanted to stop.

I didn't know which was worse.

In the end, I couldn't focus on navigating anymore, so I just went back to the apartment. I was half afraid there would be cameras there, but the alley was dark, and so was the courtyard.

I climbed the stairs to my apartment and locked the door behind me. My fingers were starting to get cold. Everything in me felt shaky.

It took no effort at all to conjure my parents' faces. They probably thought I hated them.

I didn't hate them. I just never wanted to see them again. It wasn't the same thing.

My phone buzzed a message. Standing in the tiny dark living room, I looked at it. Jeremy: **?**

I wanted there to be a text from Isabel, but there wasn't.

I had told her the truth. I had *run* from my past, and where had it gotten me?

The same place I'd started.

Trust you?

I didn't know how to do this with my parents and without Isabel.

I didn't know *why* to do this with my parents and without Isabel.

I felt the room cameras on me, so I crossed the floor to the bathroom and closed the door behind me. I fisted my hands. Then I unfisted them and locked the door. Someone had taken the dismantled bedroom camera out of the sink. It was hard to remember caring about it.

There was something wrong with me.

The human body doesn't want to get hurt. We're programmed to feel squeamish at the sight of blood. Pain is a careful orchestration of chemical processes so that we keep our body alive. Studies have shown that people born with congenital analgesia — the inability to feel pain — bite off the tips of their tongues and scratch holes in their eyes and break bones. We are a wonder of checks and balances to keep on running.

The human body doesn't want to get hurt.

There was something wrong with me, because sometimes I didn't care. There was something wrong with me, because sometimes I wanted it.

We fear death; we fear the void; we scrabble to keep our pulses.

I was the void.

What are you afraid of? Nothing.

You are not doing this you are not doing this you are not doing this

But my eyes were already clawing over the bathroom for ways out.

Trust you?

I wasn't meant to live, probably. This was why I was wired this way. Biology formed me and then took a look and wondered what the hell it was thinking and put in a mental fail-safe.

In case of emergency pull cord.

I was crouching by the wall, breathing into my hands. Victor had told me once that he'd never considered suicide, not even for a second, not even at his darkest moments. *It's the only life we have,* he'd said.

Even when I was happy, I felt like I was always looking for the edges on life. The seams.

I was so perfectly born to die.

I looked at the cord for the bathroom blinds.

This is too much this is too big for what has happened you need to stop

I thought about the joy of recording the track earlier that day. I tried to drag it back to myself, but it was an academic exercise. Every chemical switch inside me was thrown to *get out get out get out*, and happiness wasn't even possible.

I cupped my hands over my ears, like the gesture of the headphones on them, and I listened in my mind to the song that I'd made, something that hadn't existed this morning.

My parents' *faces.*

I stood up.

I needed to . . . not feel. Just for a few minutes.

That would be all I was going to get anyway.

Wolf.

Clean, unbreakable, perfect. I had been all that, and here we were.

I went into the bedroom to get the things I'd need to trigger the shift. Not just a shift, but a wild shift, a howling shift, a shift that would break me. Not all of my wolf experiments had led me to easy places. I didn't want to go to an easy place now. The small, logical part of me thought the meticulous process would help. Remind me of all the reasons to stay human. Give me a chance to calm down. Remind me of all of the other ways I had learned to take this feeling down inside me.

But it only seemed to feed it. Even though I was moving quite slowly and methodically, time pushed and brushed past me, both the past and the future. With no effort at all, I summoned the memories of doing this, or something like it, countless times before.

Wolf.

My mind skirted to Sam back in Minnesota, who so hated the wolf. I could hear his voice telling me how I was scrubbing out everything about me, doing this. I was wasting everything good about me. How hateful I was to throw it all away. Victor had died as a wolf, longing to be a human, and I was giving it away for nothing.

I told myself that, and I told myself that again.

But this was a prerecorded session. I already knew how it ended.

Even though I was alone in the bathroom, it felt like there was someone or something else in there with me. A dark presence hovering in the corner, floating up by the ceiling. Feeding the dark inside me, or feeding off the dark inside me. All of us users and used.

I turned on the shower, and then I sat on the edge of the toilet, syringe in one hand, phone in the other. I dialed Isabel's number. I didn't know what I was going to say if she picked up.

I knew she wasn't picking up anyway.

Trust you?

It rang through to voicemail. For a few minutes, I watched the shower pour gallons of water down the drain. I thought about how outside it was a desert. Then I stabbed the needle into myself.

Pain reminded me it was working.

I leaned my forehead on the wall and waited for it to change me or kill me, and I didn't really care which. I did care which. I hoped it did both.

The thing I'd put in my veins scrabbled through my bloodstream to my brain. When it got there, it clawed and beat and gnawed at my hypothalamus, screaming the same message over and over:

Wolf

Wolf

Wolf

Pain snatched my thoughts away. My mind was a chemical fire, burning itself out. I crashed to the tile, shaking and sweating and retching. My thoughts immolated.

And then

It was light. Shining overhead, reflected in the ever-shifting, never-growing puddle. It was sound. Hissing water splattering the ground, soft and continuous. Scent: acid and fruit, sweet and rotten.

Wolf.

Chapter Thirty-Five

· ISABEL ·

I drove.

Part of me wanted to keep driving for the rest of my life. Part of me wanted to go to Cole.

I didn't know which was worse.

In the end, I found myself way up the coast, past Malibu. The road here was dark and snaky, on one side the rocky coastline and the wild sea and on the other the steep, scrubby mountain cliffs. The palm trees were gone, the people, the houses. As I drove up a random canyon road, I felt like I was driving straight up into the black night sky, or into the black night ocean. I had no idea what time it was. It was the end of the world.

I finally parked the SUV at one of the scenic pullovers. Down below, the crash of the surf made an uneven white line parallel to the shore. Everything else was dark.

I got out. Outside, the air was freezing. My knees were shaking, and so were my hands. I stood there with my arms wrapped around myself for a long minute, feeling myself tremble and wondering if an emotional shock reaction was possible when you had no emotions.

Probably it was time to admit to myself that I had emotions, and they'd betrayed me.

Then I opened up the back of the SUV, got out the tire iron, and closed the hatch again. I thought of that sick feeling in my stomach when I'd first seen Cole at the party. It was exactly the same, in retrospect, as the feeling that had crept inside me when my father's voice had gotten strange earlier. When I'd known he was about to tell me something I didn't want to hear.

I looked at the moon-white surface of the SUV. I tightened my grip on the tire iron.

And then I beat the hell out of the SUV.

The first dent wasn't the best. There wasn't anything surprising about swinging a tire iron at a vehicle and leaving a dent. That's what happens when you hit something metal with something else metal.

But the second hit. That was the one that sent a rush of feeling through me. It surprised me. I hadn't known there was going to be a second swing until it happened, or a third, or a fourth. Then I realized I was never going to stop hitting this car. I smashed the doors and the hood, and I cracked the big plastic safety bumpers.

There was nothing in my head except for the knowledge that I had to drive this thing tomorrow, so I didn't smash out the windows or the headlights or anything that might keep it off the road. I didn't want it broken.

I wanted it ugly.

The tire iron dug down through the white paint, straight to the bare metal. Its guts were dull and utilitarian under all the gloss.

Finally, when my palm was hot from the effort of clutching the tire iron, I realized how tired I was.

I felt empty. Like I didn't give a damn.

Which meant I was ready to go back home.

CHAPTER THIRTY-SIX

· COLE ·

"Mr. St. Clair?"

I didn't open my eyes, but I knew where I was. Well, I knew the kind of place I was. I recognized the feel of tile on my skin and the smell of bleach millimeters from my nose. The grit between my hipbone and the floor. I was on a bathroom floor. My ears hissed.

"Cole? Do you mind if I come in?"

It took me a moment longer to realize which bathroom in particular it was. I had to backtrack, narrowing my thoughts. Earth. North America. U.S. California. Los Angeles. Venice. Apartment. Hell.

"Cole?" The voice seemed to consider. "I'm coming in."

Over the hiss of my ears, I heard a doorknob jiggle. I opened my eyes, barely. The action took a lot of thought and seemed unimportant. The door was still closed. I wondered if I'd imagined the voice. I wondered if I'd imagined my own body. As difficult as the concept of opening my eyes had been, the idea of moving any of the rest of me was impossible. My mouth was the driest part of me, like my face had climbed in and coated it.

The door jumped. I was too dead to flinch.

It jumped again.

Then it burst open, its progress halted by my legs. A pair of men's black shoes stepped in front of me, accompanied by the scent of coffee. They were not new, but they were very clean.

The door shoved shut. The shoes were still in front of me.

I closed my eyes. I heard a rustle, then felt someone push fingers into my wrist, felt my breath hitting something close. A hand, checking for respirations. I could smell aftershave.

Leon let out a relieved sigh.

A moment later, the hiss stopped. It had never been my ears. It had always been the shower. I heard Leon's shoes squelching on the damp floor.

"Can you sit up?" he asked me. Then, without waiting for my reply, he answered, "Let's do that."

A towel wrapped around me and then my armpits jerked and then, just like that, I was painfully dragged and propped into the corner by the sink.

I closed my eyes again.

In the filmy background, I heard Leon moving and running water in the sink and stepping back and forth. He put a cup to my lips and carefully tipped. There was a kind pause as I sputtered and breathed the liquid instead of swallowing it, and then he gave me some more. I felt more alive at once.

I said, "What is that? What are you giving me?"

"It's water," Leon replied. "You were lying in it, but you weren't drinking it."

"How did you get here?" I asked. My voice sounded like paper looked. "Are you real?"

"You weren't picking up your phone," Leon replied. "And I thought you might be in trouble. . . . I saw the episode."

"It's up already?"

He gave me a funny look. "It's been up two days."

I blew out my breath. It smelled pretty bad. "Oh."

Leon retrieved a disposable coffee cup from the other room. He handed it to me, watching me closely to make sure I wasn't going to drop it. I sipped it as he dropped another towel onto the tile and began to push it around with his feet to mop up some of the water and blood.

"This is sweet," I said. It wasn't even coffee. It was sugar marinated in coffee. "Just how I like it."

Leon shrugged. "Kids these days."

Suddenly, I saw him in sharp focus, either because the phrase reminded me of when he'd brought me the energy drink in the studio, or because my system was prodded to life by the water in my dry mouth or the sugar in the coffee. Leon was dressed for work in his neat suit and clean black shoes. Morning sun through the bathroom window lit his impeccable form as he used a foot to push a towel around this filthy floor.

I was so grossly ashamed.

"Don't —" I said. "Don't do that. I'll get it. God."

Leon stopped. He put his hands in the pockets of his slacks.

"This is disgusting," I said, but I wasn't sure if I was talking about the floor or me or Leon seeing me like this. "This is not — not the side of me I wanted you to see, friend. This is not the grand future I had planned for our relationship."

He shrugged his shoulders, hands still in pockets. "Things don't always go like planned."

"They do for me."

"So you must have planned this, then." He said it gently.

I gulped the last of the coffee. Both my stomach and my heart stung. "I've lost all my credibility. I'll never be able to convince you to quit your job now."

Leon's eyes smiled, even though his mouth didn't. "Was that the idea?"

"That was the idea. Joy and happiness for you, Leon, in this sunlit paradise."

He took his phone from his pocket and stepped over the towel on the floor. Crouching beside me, he held his hand out for the empty coffee cup. He traded me for his phone.

"What am I doing?" I asked him.

"Looking."

I looked. He'd opened it to his photo gallery. At the top was a photo of me, carefree and joyful, flipping arrogant devil horns at him. There was the photo we took at Hollywood Forever Cemetery, the sky blazing behind crooked palm trees. The photo of us on the Ferris wheel at the Santa Monica Pier, the night I'd gone out with him after Isabel had left my apartment.

Those photos I'd expected. I didn't expect the others. There were photos of surfers running out to the water. People knotted in front of clubs. A crazy, camel-shaped planter with palm trees jutting from it. A fiery sky behind the L.A. skyline. A neon sign that said FROLIC ROOM. A peacock peering from behind a wall. A man in blue underwear running down the sidewalk. David Bowie's star on the Walk of Fame. A pagoda in Koreatown. Bubbly, amiable graffiti on the side of an old van. A self-portrait of himself reflected in the side of his car, smiling, even though you could see that he was alone.

He'd done what I'd said. He'd become a tourist in his own city.

"It wasn't about the job," he told me. "It was just about me." After a pause, he asked, "Why did you run away from your parents?"

I closed my eyes. I could so clearly remember the pair of them in front of the Mustang, and it still killed me. "Because I can't look at them." There was a long pause, and he didn't fill it. "I thought I was going to end up like them, back when I lived in New York. I thought that was what a grown-up looked like. I can't take that."

"Couldn't."

I opened my eyes. "What?"

"*Couldn't*, not *can't*. Because you're not like them, right? You aren't afraid of becoming that now."

But I sort of was. It wasn't that I was afraid of becoming *them* — it was more that I was afraid of becoming the Cole that I had been when I'd lived with them. The Cole who was so tired of the world. The me who realized there was no point to being here, where *here* meant *life*.

My stomach rumbled loud enough that we both heard it.

"I'm starving," I said.

Leon said, "You should get breakfast with your parents."

"I don't know how to talk to them."

He took his phone from me and straightened. "Like you're talking to me. But maybe with some pants on."

Chapter Thirty-Seven

· ISABEL ·

I went to .blush. I did my job. I sold a lot of leggings. Sierra reminded me of her upcoming party.

I went to class. I did my clinicals. I rolled over a lot of old people and cleaned up a lot of soiled beds.

I went home. My mother made an appointment for my SUV to go to the body shop. My aunt gifted me a bouquet of therapist business cards. I had been in therapy for years, though. Talk was cheap. I wanted both of them to scream at me for my SUV — my father would have. But he wasn't there.

Wouldn't ever be there.

Cole texted me. **Talk?**

I texted back. **No.**

He texted back. **Sex?**

I texted back. **No.**

He texted. **Anything?**

I didn't reply. He didn't text again.

Rinse and repeat. Job. Class. Home. Job. Class. Home.

I didn't text Cole, but I kept updating Virtual Cole. I'd have to see him in order to give his phone back, and I didn't think I could survive that. And I didn't have it in me to screw him over by holding his Internet presence hostage. And anyway, updating Virtual Cole was the only thing that I had to remind me that life had ever changed at all.

Chapter Thirty-Eight

· COLE ·

I called Grace right before I went into the diner. Actually, I called Sam, but Grace answered his phone.

"It's the end," I said. "I'm going to breakfast with my parents."

"I had the worst dream about you last night," Grace mused.

"Did I go around L.A. biting people? Because that already happened."

"No," she replied. "You came home."

I hadn't noticed until just that moment that my friendly neighborhood camera crew was sitting on the curb right around the corner. That meant my parents were already here.

I was not convinced I could do this, no matter what Leon said. The weather condition of my heart was murk.

Grace had been talking. She was still talking. She finished, "That's really all there is."

"Any advice?"

"Cole, I was just *giving* you advice."

"Say it again. The summary version. The abstract."

"Sam just told me to tell you that the most important thing is to not do what you did to them on the episode."

"That won't happen," I replied, "because I doubt they'll leave the keys in the car again. Wish me luck."

She did, but I didn't feel lucky. I went into the diner.

I spotted them immediately in one of the red vinyl booths. They looked like a strange album cover, a perfectly matched older couple perfectly mismatched with the lime green wall behind them. I had picked this diner as a meeting place because I thought it might be more their style, but it was possible my parents didn't match anything in this town.

They'd spotted me. They didn't wave. That was fair. I deserved that.

I stood at the head of the booth.

"Hello, jolly parents," I said. There was a very long pause. My mother dabbed her cheek with her napkin. "Can I join you?"

My father nodded.

The cameras settled across the way from us. My parents eyed them. In unison, they slid menus across the table to me.

As I sat, my father said, "We didn't order yet."

My mother asked, "What's good here?" which was much better than any of the other questions I was afraid she was going to ask, like "Where have you been?" or "Why didn't you call us?" or "Where is Victor?" or "Are you coming home?"

The problem was that I wanted to answer something like, *I'm unsure of this fine establishment's specialties, but I imagine that friendly staffer there will enlighten us!* and then whirl over to seize a busboy for a bit of dramatic theater. But something about how they'd opened the conversation — in the roles of my parents — seemed to block this option. It forced me to be their son. It forced me to be that other me. The old me.

"I haven't been here before," I replied. Meekly. Gutlessly. My voice was a stranger to me. They were dressed the same as the last time I'd seen them, or maybe all of their clothing looked the same. Put my older brother in the booth beside me, and the St. Clair family would be as it always had been. I didn't know why I had come. I couldn't do this.

"We saw where you were staying," my mother said. "It seems like a nice neighborhood."

Venice Beach was paradise on earth, the precise shape and color of my soul, but there was no way to explain it to them. Not in terms they would understand. They would ask how people survived without garages and why the sidewalks were so ill kept.

My parents shuffled their menus. I moved the saltshaker and the pepper shaker, and lined up sugar packets and sweetener packets according to color.

"It only says poached on this one," my father said to my mother in a low voice. "Do you think they will do this with sunny-side up?"

God, they even smelled like they always did. The same laundry detergent.

If I could just think of something to say in their language, maybe I could survive this.

The server came over. "Are you folks ready to order?"

She was bird-boned, like my mother, and about fifty. She was dressed like an old-fashioned fifties diner waitress, complete with apron. She held a little notepad and pencil. Her eyes looked tired of everything.

"What is the best thing?" I asked her. "Not just the best thing. The best-best thing. The thing that makes you tie that apron on in the morning each day and think, *That is why I am going to work today, to serve that thing to customers who have not yet had that thing and, oh, what a memorable day those unaware initiates are about to have?* That is the thing I would like to order. Whatever that is."

She just blinked at me. She blinked at me for so long that I took her notepad and pencil out of her hand. I wrote *THE AMAZING THING* on our ticket. I handed it back to her.

"I trust you," I added.

She blinked at me more. "What about your folks?"

"They trust you, too," I said. "Wait." I snatched the pad back and added *BUT NO CHOCOLATE*. I put $55 in the total box.

I handed back the pad and pencil.

My parents stared at me. The server stared at me. I stared back. I had nothing better to say, so I performed the Cole St. Clair smile.

She grinned abruptly, like she couldn't help it. "Okay," she said, in a totally different voice than before. "*Okay*, young man. You're on."

As she headed back to the counter, I turned back to my parents.

And here was the strange thing. I wasn't sure if the server had been enchanted, or if Grace's advice had worked a spell, or if it was just that somehow I had finally drawn the logical line between Leon, the server, my parents, and everyone else in the world.

Because in just the amount of time it had taken to place my order, my parents had transformed. Suddenly, instead of my parents, I just saw two people in their late fifties, tourists in this glittering, strange place, tired from sleeping in an unfamiliar hotel room, eager to get back to routine. Their eyes were the same brand of weary as the server's. Life had not gone as planned, but they muddled through.

There was nothing terrible about them. They had no particular power over me. No more than anyone else.

It had never been them. It had always been me.

This realization was like a word I had to be taught every time I heard it. The definition never seemed to sink in.

They were just ordinary people.

I said, "How was the drive here?"

It was like they had been waiting all week for me to ask them. The story poured out of them. It took a long time, and it was really boring, and it didn't include any of the details I would have included, and *did* include a lot of the details I wouldn't have. And in the middle of it, the server brought us all passion fruit iced tea, and she gave my mother some fancy crepes, and she gave my father an omelet with avocados, and she gave me a waffle with a Cole St. Clair smile drawn on it with whipped cream.

None of it was life changing; we didn't talk about a single important thing. But none of it was terrible, either, unless boring counted. We had nothing in common, and at the end of this meal, we'd go our separate ways — me one way, my parents another, the server a third.

It used to matter so much. It used to seem like such a struggle to not turn into my father. But now, sitting here, it seemed impossible that that could've ever happened. I had wasted so much time on this. I kept finding out that the monster I'd been fighting was only me.

When we were done eating, I paid cash at the counter.

The server asked, "How was the food?"

"It was an amazing thing," I said. "You chose excellently. Tomorrow you should wield that pad with the confidence of a mental giant."

She smiled behind her hand at me. I wanted to thank her for the gloomy realization that in the end, I was my worst enemy, but I couldn't think of a good way to say it. So I just gave her another Cole St. Clair smile and returned to the table.

"This was nice," my mother said. "This was a cute find."

They weren't going to ask if I'd just tried to kill myself. They weren't going to ask about Victor. They weren't going to ask about anything unpleasant. But I didn't know why I was surprised. They never had before.

My father had folded his napkin into twelve geometric shapes. "We had better call a cab if we want to make it to the airport in enough time. Do you know, Cole, if cabs come here?"

"Oh," I said, taking out the keys to the Mustang, "I can take you. I seem to have a sports car."

CHAPTER THIRTY-NINE

· ISABEL ·

COLE: i survived my parents it's your turn to text me

ME:

COLE: here's my number in case you forgot it

ME:

COLE: please

ME:

COLE: isabel please

ME:

COLE:

Chapter Forty

· COLE ·

After I failed to do anything more interesting than putting on pants for several days in a row, Baby called me. "Time's up, Cole. What are you doing today?"

I was too devoid of enthusiasm to be creative. I flipped open the little notebook to her original list. "Block party."

"Great."

Yes. Great. Block party. Fine. I could throw that together as soon as I cleaned up some of the shit I'd broken in the bathroom when I shifted several nights before. I would have to get the word out via Virtual Cole. I had been desperately trying to avoid texting Isabel until she texted me, but I couldn't wait any longer.

Can you arrange for a colebot to win a block party today

I rewrote the text ten times before I sent it. It wasn't my strongest work, but it had to sound neither bitter nor needy. Any punctuation I added pushed it toward one or the other, so in the end I went with the good old absence of grammar to indicate indifference.

Isabel immediately texted back: **Give me 30 minutes.**

Her punctuation implied that I shouldn't think this meant we weren't fighting. Twenty-nine minutes later she texted me the winner's name and address.

Oh, young love.

Seven minutes after that, I was done cleaning the bathroom, and nine minutes after that, T had arrived with the cameras, and fifteen minutes after that, Jeremy had arrived with his pickup truck.

When you're in a band, you spend the first four hundred thousand years of your career dragging around your own crap. Your speakers, speaker stands, mixing head, mics, pickups, power cables, mic cables, speaker cables, instruments, the everything. You forget something, you're screwed. You break something, you're screwed. You don't have a long enough extension cord? Screwed.

Once you hit it big, though —

You're packing your shit into a late-model Mustang and a pickup truck and hoping you didn't forget anything.

I was living the dream, for sure.

"I'd carry something," T told me apologetically, his camera on his shoulder, "but I've got the, you know."

"Recording device," I replied, putting my synthesizer in Leyla's lap. She didn't complain, because she was fine with everything that came through the threads of fate and whatnot. This is what I thought: Fate was a lousy lay, and I was over her. I told T, "Yeah. It's cool. Get this side. This side. It's my famous side."

Then Jeremy and I drove in tandem to West Adams.

All of the houses in this neighborhood were older, the same age as the ones in my neighborhood back in Phoenix, NY. But the West Adams houses felt exotic because they were pink and lime green, and stucco and tile-roofed, and anchored by filigree metal railings. I wondered how I would have been different if I'd grown up in one of these instead.

Shayla, the L.A.-area fan who had won (apparently, Isabel had asked fans to identify which album's liner notes featured a photo of the back of my head), was supersonic with excitement by the time we got to her house.

So were the two hundred people already there. Virtual Cole had a pretty staggering reach.

The gathered fans had pretty much already taken over every street-side parking opportunity ever, so we had to chuck our stuff out into the driveway and then decide which of us was going to go find parking and walk back.

This felt familiar, too.

"Ohmygodohmygod," said Shayla. "CanIhugyou?"

I allowed it. I could feel her quivering as she did. When she stepped back, I smiled at her, and a slow smile spread across her face, bigger and bigger.

Sometimes, a smile goes a long way.

This was one of those sometimes. I needed a smile, a lot, and she had a great one. Not in a sexy way, but in a way full of nonjudgmental enthusiasm.

My brain was shutting off, the complicated part, and the simpler part of my brain, the concert part, was kicking in. It's hard to explain it. It's not nerves. It is something else.

The crowd jostled behind me, buzzed and eager. It was feeding me, evening out the ridges in my spiky, cluttered thoughts. I'd forgotten about this, somehow, this part of gigging. I'd forgotten its hectic erasure of emotions. Here there was no room for anything besides Cole St. Clair, singer, performer, consumed.

I was grateful for it. I didn't want my thoughts. Not right now.

Isabel —

Jeremy appeared at my elbow, his long hair tucked behind his ears and a pair of blue-tinted sunglasses balanced low on his nose. He looked like John Lennon if John Lennon had been blond and born just outside Syracuse, New York. "Cole. What's the way?"

"Music," I said. It was all I was thinking about just then. These people wanted to hear us play, and I wanted to play for them.

"That's it?"

"Loud," I said.

Jeremy scratched his vaguely beard-y face. His hair was light enough that it was hard to tell if he was actually growing facial hair or not. "Old school."

I looked at the gathered crowd. "This is kind of old school."

So we played music.

In a lot of ways, a block party takes a lot more work than a concert with a stage. At a big concert, you have a stage, you have lights, you have a *way*, and half the job of setting a mood is done for you. It's a show before you ever step up to a microphone. But a block party — you're just a bunch of kids in someone's front lawn. There's no difference between you and the audience except you hold a bass guitar or clutch a mic. Every bit of performance has to be won. Carved out of normalcy and chaos. You have to sing louder, jump higher, be crazier than anyone in the crowd.

This was the first lesson: Look like you are supposed to be there.

Fame follows the expectation of fame.

This was the second lesson: Never rush an entrance.

Jeremy took his time building us a tempo, stepping us up into a song, the bass leading into the music, not looking over its shoulder to make sure the others were coming. Leyla — damn her, I wanted Victor, I wanted Victor, I wanted Victor — came in then, *tap-tap-tap-tap-tap-tap* — and I let it go and let it go and let it go.

The tension built and built and built. And then, as I did a little twist with my hand so they were paying attention, I hit a single note on my synth:

BOOM.

The crowd went wild. And when I dragged the mic closer and sang the first word into it —

In the beginning, there was the dark and there was the buzz.

No, let me start over.

In the beginning, there was the suburbs and the days that looked the same stacked on each other's backs. Then there was me, and the angels fell.

No, let me start over again.

In the beginning, there was me on a high school stage with Jeremy and Victor, and I felt like I'd never known what I'd been made for before that moment. It was not one listener or two or twenty or fifty. There was no magic number. It was this: Me. Them. It was the drums dropping out for my keyboard to tumble up an ascending bridge. It was the heads tilted back. It was the tug and push and pull and jerk of the bass. It was whatever you plugged into the equation to equal an electrical current between us and the audience. Sometimes it took one thousand people. Sometimes it took two.

In West Adams on that summer afternoon, I crooned and screamed the lyrics at them, and they howled and screamed them back at me. Jeremy's bass picked relentlessly up the scale. Leyla, face sheened with sweat, thundered in the background.

We were the living, the reborn.

People kept coming. The noise of us and the noise of them kept bringing them in, closer, closer, more and more.

This is why I did it, this is why I keep doing it, this is why I couldn't stop.

Suddenly, in the midst of this perfection, there was the scratch of a random guitar chord. Guitar? Guitar.

You have got to be kidding me.

Some pale young creature had erupted from the crowd with his guitar. He leaped up and down beside Leyla's kit, grinding away on his instrument like the world was about to end. All enthusiasm, no malice.

At a real concert, we had security and stage dudes who took care of this. Our job as the band was merely to keep the show going as the disruption was removed.

Here there was only us.

I left Jeremy thrubbing away on the bass and Leyla holding

down the beat. My mic still in one hand, I used the other to grab the guy's arms to stop the guitaring. And then I gripped him to me and danced him forcibly to the crowd. I wrapped my arm around him to hold the mic to my mouth.

"Take him!" I shouted gladly to the crowd. "He is one of yours!"

I released him. Arms seized him like zombies. He was smiling blissfully up at the sky as they took him. I was face-to-face with the others now. Us and them, and the them was right there.

And I saw a face from the past.

It was impossible; it was Victor's eyes, Victor's eyebrows. My stomach was falling from a very great height.

It wasn't Victor. It was his sister, Angie.

I hadn't even begun to parse what this might mean when she hit me.

It wasn't the greatest punch, but it landed pretty well — I felt my teeth cut into my lip. My mouth felt warm. Adrenaline hurried to attend to my needs. A wolf stretched and curled inside me.

Angie snatched the microphone from me, and then she hit me with it. *That* I felt. It hit my cheekbone solidly, and then, as one hand went up, instinct, she smashed it into the back of my head.

Skill? Skill isn't what hurts people. A lack of mercy is.

I deserved to be hit, too. I deserved everything she was giving me.

I killed him, I killed him, I killed him

"You asshole!" Angie shouted at me, and she wasn't wrong, even taking Victor out of the equation. She punched me again with the microphone.

T came in close, but not to help: to film.

Angie hurled her entire body at me. She wasn't a very large person, but justice and physics were on her side. We careened back through Leyla's kit, both of us falling. Above me was blue sky and the edge of Shayla's roof and at least two cameras and now her face blocking everything —

She still smelled like the same shampoo she'd used when I'd dated her, back when Victor was alive, and I had never hated myself as I did in that moment, not in the darkest and most disgusting holes I had lowered myself into on any of my tours.

"Angie," Jeremy said, as urgent as I'd ever heard him. "Angie, come on."

My back stung something fierce, like I'd been sliced in two with a cymbal. I tasted blood. She needed to hit me harder, because I could still feel everything.

I couldn't stop seeing Victor's face mirrored in Angie's. What I'd done to both of them would never go away.

"Angie," Jeremy said again, out of my view. "Think about what you're doing. This is TV. This is your record, forever. This isn't the way."

Leyla loomed over me. She gripped my hand and pulled me up. She didn't say: *This is the future growing the seeds you sowed in the past.* She asked, "Are you okay, man?"

I stood there in the middle of Shayla's flat lawn, and suddenly there was no stage. It was just a bunch of drunk people standing in front of an old house. It was an ex-girlfriend looking defeated, a bloody microphone hanging in one of her hands. I'd scuffed the hell out of my patch of grass by jumping up and down while I sang. I looked at it, and at Angie, and then at

Shayla. My face still felt warm, and I suspected from both that and the way she was looking at me that I was bleeding a lot. I'd stopped feeling anything, though.

"Sorry I wrecked your lawn," I said. "Tell the next band to put down a rug or some other shit."

She clutched her hands together. "Should we call the cops? 911?"

Angie just stared at me. The microphone hung in her hand. She said, "You ruined him."

Then she dropped the mic and walked into the crowd.

It seemed obvious that this represented the end of the set, but the thought of taking all this stuff down and finding a way to put it back in the Mustang suddenly seemed like a huge amount of trouble. Finding the Mustang, period, seemed like an enormous quest. There is a wave that leads you to a gig, but after it's crashed you onto the shore of the show, there's no similar wave that takes you away, especially after your knees are buckling and you can feel every one of your teeth loose in your head. After you can see nothing but your dead drummer and every girl you ever slept with and hated yourself for in the morning.

Shayla was still going on about the cops, but I didn't know what good they would do unless they were going to retrieve the car. I could hear my heartbeat in my forehead or maybe my temple. Jeremy's voice went on, smooth and easy, echoed by Leyla.

I should've thought of a way to wrap up this episode neatly, but I guessed they would probably edit that punch into something glorious.

T's camera eyed me. I told it, "That's a wrap."

It was the best I could do. Hills and valleys. My mind curled up in the shadow of mountains I'd climbed and then plummeted from.

Jeremy took my arm. "Cole," he said, "come on, man." He looked at T. "You've got enough on there. Turn it off."

Chapter Forty-One

· COLE ·

Jeremy drove his old pickup truck while I sat in the passenger's seat, leaning my head against the door. We didn't speak. I was hoarse anyway.

He lived in a house out in the Hollywood Hills. Even though it was not far geographically from the city, it seemed like a different state. The narrow streets snaked up the steep hills, crowded with mailboxes, yucca plants, orange trees, dusty pickup trucks, and BMWs. The houses were mismatched shabby contemporaries from the twenties, one-hundred-year-old denizens of an older Los Angeles.

The streets kept getting narrower and steeper, the turns becoming more and more improbable, until finally we came to the place Jeremy shared with his girlfriend. The light green house was low-slung and lattice-covered. A eucalyptus tree grew beside it, appearing at one with the house, which seemed appropriate for Jeremy. A dusty and very busted Mustang from several decades before mine was parked half-in, half-out of a metal carport.

Jeremy parked on the street. "I think you should leave your work phone in here."

I stared at him, not understanding. Then I said, "Isabel has it."

Jeremy frowned. Mentally, he catalogued my online presence over the past several weeks.

"Yes," he said simply. He pulled up the parking brake and put it in gear. "Well, leave anything else having to do with the show in the car, too."

We climbed crooked concrete stairs, me slower than him. Inside, the house was everything I would have expected from Jeremy: modest, airy, and very spare. He led me into a galley kitchen full of ugly, pristine '70s appliances, and I leaned on the doorjamb and felt sorry for myself while he rummaged in drawers for a dish towel.

"Hold still," he said. I rested my cheek on the counter while he dabbed at the side of my face. The towel came up covered with dirt and grime.

"Jesus Christ! Jeremy! Cole? St. Clair?"

This was how I found out that Jeremy's girlfriend was the ukulele player for a band that had opened for us two years before. She stood in the doorway to the kitchen in a bra and shorts. Probably some girls would've been bothered by suddenly discovering guests while in this condition, but everything about her posture indicated she was not one of them. The last time I had seen her we had been in Portland doing a benefit concert for orphans.

"Hi, Star," I mumbled.

Star looked at Jeremy. "Did *you* do that to him?"

Jeremy probed my forehead with his fingers. "Do you know if we have a first-aid kit?"

Star joined him and bent over me. She smelled like patchouli, sweet and dreamy. I could see her bare legs and Jeremy's bare legs. The way they stood together was so comfortable, so unaffected, that I suddenly felt incredibly shitty about all of my life choices. I wanted — I wanted — I must've hit my head harder than I thought.

I wanted Isabel, but she was such an impossible thing to want.

Star touched my hair, very gingerly. "Maybe he should go to the hospital, Germ."

I closed my eyes. I would have rather died on this counter.

"He needs to be someplace quiet," Jeremy said. "We've had a bad day."

They moved away from me, into the other room, and I heard their murmured voices. In my head, their voices were like this house, settled and modest and familiar. I heard them say *he* a lot, and knew they were talking about me, but I didn't care. People were always talking about me.

"I need a toilet," I told Jeremy, and they both gestured around a corner.

In the bathroom I locked the door and turned on the light and the fan, and I leaned on the stand sink and rocked back and forth. There was no mirror, and so I kept seeing Angie's face and Victor's face and remembering every conversation Victor and I had ever conducted about drugs or wolves or suicide. I got a needle from one of my pants pockets and stripped and curled up beneath the sink and stabbed the point under my skin.

I was gone for five minutes. It wasn't long enough to do anything but tamp down the worst of the jitters and maybe heal the bruise on my head a little. I hadn't broken anything and the door was still locked and Jeremy wasn't pounding on the other side of it so I couldn't have been loud.

I got dressed and flushed the toilet as if I'd used it and then washed my hands.

I felt better. Or different. I'd been temporarily reset.

Outside, Jeremy stood pensively in the kitchen. He sighed when I walked in and then he said, "She's going to get some Neosporin and some Korean barbecue. You still aren't a vegetarian, right? Yeah, I didn't think so."

He gave me a glass of water, a clean dish towel with a bag of frozen edamame beans in it to hold to my head, and we wandered through his house, looking at his lack of furniture and material goods and plethora of bamboo mats and potted plants. Probably it would have been insufferable if he hadn't also had a very comfortable-looking sofa and an orange bust of Beethoven and all of the wood-sided old speakers he'd brought to the very first episode.

"I like this place," I told him, because the way he took his shoes off and walked around barefoot and proud through the house made me think he'd like to hear me say it.

"I do, too," he said.

"You're dating Star," I said.

"I am."

"She got hot. How long's that been going on?"

"Two years."

"Wow."

"You were gone a long time, Cole."

I abandoned the bag of beans in the kitchen sink and we headed back outside and downstairs to wait for Star. As we stood by the lattice overgrown with red roses, he explained how he'd bought this house with his last NARKOTIKA advance, and now he gave the money to Star to pay bills and make sure the taxes were sorted out and he worked band gigs when she said they needed more to keep things on the level.

"She takes all your money?" I asked. A hummingbird zoomed by my head.

He looked at me. "I *give* it to her."

Basically, what was happening was this: I had gone away for almost two years, and when I came back, Jeremy had grown up and gotten a house and gotten happy — no, he'd always been happy, now he was just happy and with someone — and I had instead come back and become myself as I always was.

My face throbbed, or my heart did. I was so tired of being alone, but I was always alone, even with people around me. And I was so tired of being surrounded, but I was always surrounded, even when I was by myself. There was so much talk about how everyone wanted to be goddamned special. I was so tired of being the only one of my kind.

"I don't think I can do this," I said.

Jeremy didn't say *what?* He just rubbed the edge of the dusty, busted Mustang where it poked out into the evening sun. The hummingbird I'd seen earlier zoomed by again. It paused by the roses, but they weren't what it was looking for.

"I don't think I can go back out on the road. I don't think I can take it."

He didn't answer right away. He climbed onto the hood of the old Mustang and sat on it cross-legged. The bottoms of his bare feet were very dirty and he wore a hemp anklet, which he plucked at. "Are we talking about tour, really?"

"What else would I be talking about?"

He said, "Is it really going on the road you can't do? Or is it being you?"

I looked at the grass at the edge of the tiny, sun-bitten yard. Tire prints marked the gravel and dirt. Star had taken the pickup with my phone in it. Possibly not taken. Possibly Jeremy had given her the keys.

"Cole, I think we have to talk about this."

"You don't want to know, Jeremy. You really don't."

"I think I already do, though."

I stared off down the dusky street. Way, way down the street, a little boy was tooling around on a faded blue bicycle. What a safe place this neighborhood seemed like. It was somehow more like California than the rest of L.A. More like the land itself. Like the dry stucco and faded wood houses and the dust-covered cars had slowly been pushed up from the dry landscape by generations of heaving quakes. It wasn't that I liked it *better* than the rest of Los Angeles. It was just that it seemed like it required less work to keep it looking like this. It seemed like a place that wouldn't notice you as much if you had a day off or got old. It seemed like a place where it might get dark at night.

Jeremy said, "Do you know what makes it bad? It's that you do it alone. It's that you lock yourself in a bathroom. It's not the thing itself. It's that you make it secret. It's that you only do it when you're upset."

I didn't move. I just kept staring at the little boy making uneven circles at the end of his short driveway. I felt as if the world was being crumpled like paper around me. Even if I could figure out how to open the sheet back up again, it would always be wrinkled.

"There are other ways to be unhappy, Cole. There are better ways to cope than just pulling the plug on your brain."

My voice was rougher than I expected it to be. "I've been trying."

"No, you've been happy. You haven't had to try until now."

I didn't answer. There was no point arguing. He knew me as well as I knew myself. He'd played bass for my thoughts for three albums.

"Victor's dead," I said.

"I know. I guessed."

"It's my fault. The whole thing. I got him into it."

"Victor got himself into it," Jeremy said. "We were all kids from New York. I didn't follow you down any rabbit holes. Victor would've gone without you."

I didn't believe that. I was very persuasive.

"How do you do it?" I asked.

"I just live, Cole. I don't go away in my head. I deal with the crap as it happens, and then it's gone. When you don't think about it, it lives forever."

I closed my eyes. I could still hear the little boy riding his bicycle down the street. It made me think about the boy on the roof, the one who had crashed his plane because it wasn't about the landing, it was about the flying.

"I always thought you'd be the one who died," Jeremy said. "I kept thinking one day I'd get the call while I was sleeping. Or I'd come to get you in your room before the show and I'd be too late. Or I —"

He stopped, and when I turned to look at him, still cross-legged on the hood of the Mustang, his eyes were shiny. He blinked, and two tears shot down his face, fast and shiny as mercury.

It was possibly the worst and best that I'd felt in my life. I didn't know what to say. Sorry? I hadn't meant to hurt anybody else?

"Nobody told me it would be this hard," I said.

"Why is it always harder for you?"

I shook my head. I didn't even know if it really was harder for me, if I was just a flawed model. I wiped my nose with my arm and pointed to the Mustang beneath Jeremy.

"That's a thing," I said.

"Yeah," Jeremy said, his voice much different. "Yeah, it conveyed with the house. It came with a trash compactor, too, but Star broke it."

We both sighed.

"There she is," said Jeremy as his pickup truck appeared at the bottom of the hill. It stopped beside the little boy, and the kid came over to talk to Star through the driver's window. I saw her long brown arm hanging out of the side of the truck, bracelets hanging around her wristbone, and I saw her hair hanging in hanks on either side of her face, and the kid on his busted bike keeled over talking to her with his hair all scruffed up.

And suddenly I was just *eaten* by nostalgia, for a past that wasn't mine.

I just wanted to be happy. I just wanted to *make* something.

"You have to take it off the table," Jeremy said, finally. "It's always going to be an option, otherwise. You're going to have to give it up and mean it, or it'll always be your solution when things go bad."

The pickup truck pulled up beside us. Star put it in park and leaned across to gaze at me through the open passenger window. She grinned easily at me.

"Did you choose life while I was gone?"

I said, "Sure."

Jeremy asked, "Did you mean it?"

It hurt, but sort of in a good way, to look him in the face. "Yes."

CHAPTER FORTY-TWO

· ISABEL ·

That night, I arrived at Sierra's house in the canyons with my shivered-ice eyes and my slaughter lips.

Party time.

I was in a dress that was white vinyl or leather — I couldn't tell the difference; could anyone else? If they bothered to analyze it, it meant I was wearing it wrong, anyway. I was also wearing white sandals with enormous white heels. The only color to my wardrobe was my horror lips. No one could say I hadn't warned them.

I used to wonder what partying was really like. When I was eleven or twelve. Everyone in movies seemed so eager to go party. All the television shows were girls wondering if they were going to be invited to this or that party, talking like there were different levels and qualities of party. I couldn't imagine what was luring them to these places, but the desperation to get there promised that it was something good.

Now I'd been to more than my fair share of parties. And it turned out that the TV parties had not been lies. They boasted most of the features of real parties: booze, making out, music that sounded better on your own speakers. Maybe some drugs or drinking games or pool or witty banter. Possibly witty banter should have been lumped in with drinking games or with making out.

Maybe I was always too sober at these things.

The house was located in the Hollywood Hills, in a high-altitude fancy neighborhood that overlooked the lights of other, slightly less fancy neighborhoods. It was an enormous white, gated compound, a sort of mesa of smoothed concrete and windows. Tastefully hidden floodlights guided me out of the taxi to the courtyard. Because it was Sierra's house and Sierra's party, the music was dreamy shoegaze. It sounded like a cross between a spilled water glass and a slow-motion electronic lynching. The place was already full of people.

God, I hated them all.

I stalked in. The irregular beat of the music and the mass of people made it feel like the ground was moving. Heads might have turned. I couldn't tell. Being me meant that I couldn't do more than a dismissive sweep of my eyes over any given person.

Part of the problem with parties was that I couldn't even tell what the goal was, so I never knew when I was done. I searched for Sierra. At least if she saw me, I got credit for coming.

I walked by the big pool. It was full of splashing nymphs and was lit with color-changing lights. Pink, purple, green. A boy, half-in, half-out of the pool, grabbed my ankle with his wet hand.

"Come in," he said.

I looked down at him. He wore glittery eyeliner. I wondered what brand of eyeliner it was that it didn't wash off in the pool water. His wet hand on my ankle reminded me of Cole doing something very similar months and months before.

I said, very coolly, "I don't like to get wet."

I expected the boy to protest, but he just looked abashed and then slid under the water along with any respect I might have had for him.

In the middle of the pool, a girl floated on her back in slow, lazy circles while a guy paddled lazily beside her and kissed her hand. I wondered if there was ever a world where I might have turned out like them. I wondered if that was the person I might have been if we had never moved from California; if my brother had never died; if we had not moved away from Cole; if my parents had never gotten separated.

As I stepped away from the pool and onto the infinite tiled balcony that surrounded the house, someone wearing a green glowstick around his neck offered me a drink. It was swirled in two different neon colors, seeming at once like something I wanted to put in my mouth and something nature didn't mean for me to ingest.

I shook my head. Once, my brother had said that alcohol made you someone else — I definitely didn't want that. What if the someone else was worse than what I already was? And another time, my friend Mackenzie had said it just made you more of who you already were.

The world didn't need that.

I trailed my fingers along the metal balcony as I walked. The lights inside the house were off and everyone in the house wore glowsticks or Christmas lights or other half costumes that luminesced. I didn't want to go in, but it was undoubtedly where Sierra would be. She was such a child. Everything here, really, was like a child's fantasy world brought to life, made concrete.

But this was just a bunch of grown-ups in dress-up and so much pointless glitter.

I just hated —

Why couldn't this glitter rub off on me?

Hands on my arm. It was Sierra. She'd found me, after all. She looked alien with glow-in-the-dark eyelashes and phosphorescing dots drawn down her nose and cheekbones. Her hair was braided through with fiber optics. She wasn't a woman; she was an installation. All of her friends were similarly glow-in-the-dark. Sierra grabbed my arm. "Treasure! I was hoping you would come. Get a drink, get a boy, get a dream, everything's lovely!" Her pupils were black and dazzling with two little reflections of neon pink and green. She air-kissed my cheek.

In response, I parted my lips and blinked, my lashes lingering on my cheek. I'd done that expression in the mirror before, lots. You could do it ever so much slower than you thought you should, and it only made you look more cynical.

Sierra was delighted. She introduced me to her friends and plucked at my dress, her hand right on my breast, and then she threw her head back so we could all see how she had the longest neck.

She said, "Here, you need some —"

From somewhere, she produced more of the glow-in-the-dark makeup.

"Close," she ordered.

I closed my eyes. I felt her swipe my eyelids, my lips.

"Open." Sierra smiled toothily at me. "Now you're one of us."

That would never be true.

"Go," Sierra told me, waving her hand. "Play. Then come back and tell me all the tales of the fabulous places you have been!"

"Right," I replied. "Off to play right now. Ta."

It wasn't that I had been dismissed, but I felt dismissed. Sierra really did think I was going to flit off with my newly fluorescent face and meet her cool friends. This was a party of children, and children loved other children.

Maybe I didn't even know how this was done.

I made my way through a dark living room (a pale sofa was smeared gently with glow-in-the-dark paint) to a dark kitchen (the counter was spattered with luminescence) and then a dark somewhere else (no glowing besides a glass coffee table imperfectly reflecting my face). The music was coming from everywhere. The air smelled like oranges and pretzels and neon pink.

As I wandered slowly through conversations between people who had just met, I thought about how L.A. was a place to not be alone. Every place was a place to not be alone, but L.A. was a city that gloried in connections, that eased them and facilitated them. It was a city that made it more obvious how goddamn impossible it was for you to make connections if you couldn't make them in L.A. This was a place for smiling at strangers and holding hands and kissing strangers, and if you weren't doing those things it was because you did not smile and you did not hold hands and you did not kiss. The strangers part was irrelevant.

How long had I been here?

"Isabel!"

It was Mark, Sierra's Mark. He was in a group of guys that all kind of looked like him, pretty and harmless and tan and cheerful. They were visible because they stood beside a wall of windows. Behind them, the ground sloped off and L.A. moved restlessly.

"You guys aren't glowing in the dark," I said.

"We're bright enough," Mark replied. His friends laughed. I didn't. "You want a drink?"

"Something not glowing?" I asked. "Does plain water exist in this place?"

"Water!" said one of his friends. His goatee was immaculate. "Here? That's not kosher, man."

"I think it is probably the only kosher thing here," I replied testily. "Do you actually know anything about Jewish people?"

"I'm circumcised," he replied. "That's Jewish, right? Oh, wait, Jesus, are you Jewish?"

I looked at him. I did the slow blink. I parted my lips. He watched. I said, "I thought you were getting me some water."

He scrambled off to find it. Mark laughed in admiration. "Well done."

I narrowed my eyes in acknowledgment. Really, the secret was to say pretty much nothing at all, and when you did open your mouth, say something awful. Then they all did what you wanted.

Mark hurried to fill the silence. "Grubb here and I were just talking about, like, this guy who landed a fighter jet after the wing had fallen off. Apparently, it fell, like, right off and he landed it anyway."

Grubb said, slow as lava, "Isn't that the craziest thing you've ever heard?"

I said, "Crazy."

Mark touched his neck and his chin, but he was looking at my neck and my chin. "Where is Lars with your drink? He's taking forever."

"Just as well. I wouldn't trust him with anything someone else poured anyway," I said. I didn't look away from Mark's eyes. It wasn't that I wanted to flirt with him, or that I wanted him, I just wanted to see what I could do. "Might have glow-worms in it."

Mark's teeth grazed his bottom lip as if he were thinking about the water, but I didn't think it was a beverage he was imagining. My heart beat a little faster with the power of it. It was a tease, but what could it hurt? I just wanted to know. I wanted to know that if I wanted someone else, could I get him, and how much effort would it take? Was it as easy as just being there, saying nothing, letting them imagine who you really were?

"Look, let's go find you one," Mark said. "You can watch me pour it. No glowworms."

My palms were suddenly sweaty. This wasn't actually a tease. Not anymore. This was a real thing.

I wondered how Cole felt when he slept with a girl on tour. Was it this? The game. The chase. The kick to the ego, the warmth in my guts, the knowledge that my lips wanted to be kissed and I wanted someone to unzip this dress and see how good I looked in my bra.

I could tell him I'd get the drink myself. I could wait for Lars, although there wasn't a chance in the world Lars was going to bring something nonalcoholic, because I knew guys, even if I didn't know him.

I just wanted something to happen. I just wanted to stop walking around this party alone, waiting for . . . I didn't even know. When I would know I was done. When I would know I had parti*ed*, past tense.

I said, "Let's go find something."

"Be right back, man," Mark told Grubb.

Right back. Right back. Because this was nothing.

I followed Mark. To my surprise, he really did lead me to the bar, where he drew a glass of water. He offered it to me, his gaze holding mine. He waited. My heart was jerking. I wanted to accomplish something, anything, even if that something was making out with Mark.

I said, "Where am I going to drink this?"

It was all Mark needed. He said, "Come on, I'll show you something."

Something turned out to be a circular-walled concrete observatory at the end of one of the stretching balconies. It turned out to be a little bedroom inside, with a curving custom mirror on one wall and a chic red mattress just inches from the floor, all lit by skylights that let in the floodlights. It turned out to be Mark closing the door behind us and taking my glass from me and setting it on a low end table.

Then he grasped either side of my waist on the vinyl-or-leather dress and kissed me.

It was probably vinyl. There was no way it was real leather at the price I'd paid for it. But on the other hand, I'd gotten it at the secondhand shop. So it could have been someone's expensive castoff.

We were still kissing. He was as fierce and urgent about it as Cole had been. It didn't matter that Mark didn't really know me. He still approached my mouth as if it were limited edition, going out of style, get it now before it's all gone. It was somehow freeing and depressing to know that love didn't seem to have anything to do with passion.

He gripped my hips, hard, and it didn't feel disagreeable. So this was what it was like to be an object. This was what it was like to objectify. If he had no name, how did it change things? If he had no face? If he was only his hands or only his pelvis pressed up against mine —

He pulled back, just for a second.

"Don't say anything," I said.

He laughed under his breath.

"No, seriously. Shut up."

He shut up.

There was nothing unpleasant, physically, about making out with this person. In fact, the opposite, if I was reductive. My mouth parted beneath his. My belly pressed into his abs. His fingers teased down the zipper on the front of my dress, and my breath skipped when he kissed the edge of my breast. I felt like someone else. From the outside, I thought we probably were a very pretty couple. This seemed like a very grown-up, L.A. moment to have. Two pretty people kissing in an observatory built to study people, groping beside a bed meant for things beside sleep. I knew he would take off my dress if I let him, and I didn't see why not. It probably wouldn't be *bad*, even if it wasn't good. It would be a chic and distinct story, anyway.

His shirt had tugged up. He was ripped and not offensive in any way. This was fine. I was fine.

Beneath his right palm, the material of my dress had made uneven waves. Surely vinyl wouldn't move like that? I really didn't know. Now I felt like I was going to have to look this up online.

He unzipped my dress straight down to my belly button.

So, I guessed this was happening. I kept waiting to feel half naked.

Mark leaned back.

"God," he said, "you are beautiful."

His voice sounded precisely like it did when he walked into the back room in the evenings to do paperwork. Precisely like it had when he'd asked me if I knew Cole. Which was to say, precisely like Mark, because he *was* Mark. What was the *point* to him even saying that? Possibly he'd misunderstood what this was all about.

I said, "I told you to shut up."

He laughed.

I didn't. I slapped his hand away and tugged up my zipper. "We're done here."

"What?" he said. "Really?"

"Yes, really."

I expected him to protest, but he just ran a hand through his hair. His lips were smeary neon. From me. That was from my lips. Finally, he said, "Well, damn."

Part of me wanted to tell him, *No, really, let's still go through with it.* Because now I was just stuck with this bad taste in my mouth, and a dim feeling of hating him or hating me or hating everything.

"It was probably a bad idea anyway," Mark said. "I'm not drunk enough."

The more he spoke, and the longer it had been since he'd touched me, the more the truth was sinking in: I had almost slept with my boss's husband. I had made out with my boss's husband at a party. I was that girl.

"You should go," I told him. My voice was this side of the crypt, but only barely. "Sierra's looking for you."

When he looked at me, his expression was confused for a second, and then it turned to something like pity. He laughed, but it wasn't a funny laugh, and it was at me or him. I felt naive and stupid. "No. She's not."

I leveled my gaze on him, blue eyes cold-dead behind their mask, and waited until the uncertainty crept back into his eyes. Then I said, "I have to fix my lips."

By the time I had fetched my purse, he was gone, the door barely cracked. I stood in front of the mirror and observed my neon-smeared lips. I cleaned them up and carefully drew my cool pink lips back on and readjusted my hair around my face and tugged the zipper of my dress until I looked the same as I had before.

Then I took my phone out of my purse. I redid my eyeliner,

careful not to smudge the neon blue Sierra had put on my eyelids.

I took a breath.

I dialed Cole's number.

"Are you sober?" I asked.

"Oh, come *on*. That's what you —"

"Cole. Are you?"

A pause to convey irritation. "Yeah."

I kept my voice very even, but it took a lot of effort. "Please come get me."

CHAPTER FORTY-THREE

· COLE ·

When I got to the party, I had to park way down the street, and then after I got in, it took me a while to find Isabel. Inside the house, the lights were out and black lights were wired up to make all of the girls glow in the UV. Outside, it was all glitter and experimental dancing because they were that sort of people. I was recognized, because it was that sort of party, but no one cared, because it was that sort of party. The music made me want to punch a hippie.

Isabel stood by the pool in a group of people who moved their arms with the enthusiasm and gracelessness of the inebriated. She was posed. One shoulder down, chin up. Her eye makeup was black and thick except for a line of neon blue that matched her eyes. Her mouth was a glass creation, still and chiseled. She wore a white leather dress that made her look one thousand times more sophisticated than most humans. Surrounded by all this glitter, in this noise and silliness, in a world that I clumsily and loudly inhabited, she was beautiful.

The guys in the group gazed at her with fearful awe. They looked at the face she wore right now and saw a stunning ice queen. Something to be thawed.

All I could see was how sad she was.

As I got closer, I heard their voices. The others were hysterical and loud. Isabel's voice, lower, sounded bored and over it.

I walked up behind her. They saw me before she did. "Hi, princess," I said, loud enough for them to hear me. "The world called. They want you back."

She turned to me and her face, just in the split second when she saw me — I was murdered by it. Not because it was cruel, but the opposite. For one fraction of another fraction of a second, I saw naked relief on her face. Then it was gone behind the mask. But I still had it inside me.

"What, are you going?" asked one of the other girls. She was blond and blue-eyed like Isabel, but slightly older and several degrees softer looking.

Isabel's hand was between her leg and mine. Without any fanfare, I threaded my fingers through hers. "Yes, yes. I'm very needy. Don't tell anyone." I flashed a smile at her, a needy one, and the girl's eyebrows shot up.

"I'll see you on Thursday," Isabel said. How easily she hid her misery in plain sight. I didn't think I'd ever seen her so upset. She might have said something else. I didn't know. I was leading her away, out of there, through the people, through the gate, down the road, toward the Mustang. We were out of neon and into the dark, but I didn't let go of her hand.

We got to the car.

"I want to drive," she said.

I did not want to give her the keys. Wordlessly, I handed them over.

She drove too fast, and she braked too late, but the thing about Isabel Culpeper was that she always managed to pull herself up before she went over the edge.

"Whose party was that?" I asked.

Isabel's mouth went thin. She didn't look away from the road. "My boss."

She floored the Mustang away from a light. We were going to die. I was ceaselessly turned on.

"Where are we going?"

"I don't know," she said.

The engine snarled away in the silence. I didn't think I'd ever been in a car without the radio turned on before. It felt like the end of the world.

"Why can't I do it?" she asked, suddenly angry. We screamed around a turn. It was possible this night would end with the car getting impounded, but it seemed like a bad idea to tell her.

"Do what?"

"Just forget about everything. Just go somewhere and get *smashed* and pretend like there are no problems or consequences. I know why. Because there are still problems and consequences. And going and — and — *partying* doesn't make them go away. I feel like I'm the only sane person in the world. I don't get why this whole world runs on *stupidity*."

Her voice was getting flatter instead of louder. "You do it. I saw you drunk. And I know you became a wolf again. I can smell it. I'm not an idiot."

I didn't answer for a long time. I knew it maddened her

more, but I didn't know what to say. It was too raw that she hadn't trusted me, and too raw that, in the end, I hadn't been trustworthy after all.

I had been sober, but I had also been a wolf, and that was worse.

Isabel didn't look away from the road. She tore around another turn. "Be *afraid*. Why aren't you ever afraid?"

"What do you want me to be afraid of?"

The tires scuffed as we scudded to a noisy, bouncing stop at an unoccupied red light.

"Dying. Failure. Anything."

I'm afraid you won't pick up the phone.

I said, "Where are we going, Isabel?"

I sort of meant right then, but I also sort of meant more.

She repeated, "I don't know."

"Do you want to go home?"

She didn't answer. That was a no. That was good. I didn't want to take her home.

"Do you want to go to my place?"

"I don't want to be on camera."

That, at least, I knew how to take care of.

CHAPTER FORTY-FOUR

· ISABEL ·

Cole didn't quite take me home. He directed me to park the Mustang behind his place, but when we got out, he led the way away from the gate and toward the house next door.

"It's empty," he told me. "It's a rental. I checked it out the other day."

Inside, it was dark in a way that Sierra's house hadn't been. It was dark in a way that was dusky and imperfect, comforting in its realness. The furniture was shabby chic, sparse and pleasant and inexpensive in the way of rental furniture.

Cole gave me a tour, throwing open doors, barely looking inside each. "Bedroom. Kitchen. Mudroom. Half bath. Stair to roof deck. Bedroom. Hallway to side yard."

Then he led me through a tiny sitting area to a sliding door hidden by a bamboo shade. He threw his shoulder against it until it gave way. On the other side, impossibly, was a miniature garden world. I couldn't understand it until I stepped through the door. A white sofa sat in the middle of it; just ten feet away was another sliding door to the rest of the house. In between, in this small room, the walls climbed and sprouted and unfolded tropical leaves of all shapes and sizes. Oranges studded one tree, lemons another. Ferns crowded densely at the bases of small palms. Mysterious flowers like exotic birds revealed themselves only slowly, only on a second look. The air smelled like growing things and beautiful things, things people put in bottles and rubbed behind their ears.

Cole put his hand around my hair and used it to pull my head back until I was gazing straight up. I saw what he was directing my attention to: the ceiling, far overhead, peaked and made of glass. This was a greenhouse. No, what was the proper word? A conservatory.

The walls of plants and the night eliminated any road or party noise. We were in the middle of nowhere. Back in Minnesota again. No, farther than that, stranger than that. Someplace no one else had ever been.

Cole walked to the couch and threw himself onto it as if he had seen the entire world and was bored with it. After a moment, he sighed deeply enough that I saw it instead of heard it, the great lift of his chest and then the release.

I set my purse beside the couch and sat on the other end of the sofa. Throwing my legs across his, I leaned back on the sofa arm and released a sigh of my own. Cole rested his arms on top of my legs and blinked at the wall opposite. There was something threadbare about his expression.

We sat like that for several gray-green minutes, the fronds of palms and ferns barely moving. Beside me, a lustrous trumpet flower hung like a waiting silent bell. We didn't say anything.

Cole kept looking at the wall, and I kept looking at him and at the orange tree on the other side of him.

Cole moved his hand, brushing his fingers over the knob of my anklebone.

I breathed in.

His fingers lingered, playing over my skin, nearly tickling. With them, he described the shape of my ankle, the edge of my sandal: a sculptor's hands.

I looked at him. He looked back.

Carefully, he unbuckled the strap of my sandal. The heel hit the floor first. He slid his hand over my foot, my ankle, up my calf. Goose bumps trailed after his fingers.

I breathed out.

The second sandal joined the first. Again he ran his palms up my leg. I was caught in the way that he touched me. It was as if his fingers found me beautiful. As if I were a lovely thing. As if it were a privilege just to trace his fingertips across my body.

I didn't move. He didn't know how only hours before, back at the party, I'd let someone else touch me, and had touched him back.

But —

Cole stretched forward to meet my lips. This kiss — his mouth was hungry, wanting. But still his hands were on my back and pressed against my hip, and still his touch was a silent shout: *I love you.*

How stupid I'd been to think I couldn't tell the difference between this kiss and Mark's kiss. How ridiculous to reduce

Cole to his mess and his loudness, to be so furious with him that I erased the other true parts. What was I with the kindness scrubbed from the record?

Eyeliner in a white dress.

We were so little, when you took away all our sins.

As I linked my arms around his neck, I was crying.

What an idiot I was. This perfect moment, this perfect kiss, and I was crying. There was so much *wrong* with me. I was so incredibly messed up that I couldn't cry when everything was wrong and I couldn't not when everything was fine.

Our lips were salty with it. Cole didn't stop or pause, but his hands crept up my back to hold me tighter. After a moment, he pressed his forehead against mine and I put my hands on his face and we just stayed like that, breathing each other's breaths. It was so much *us* and so little *him and me*. Us, us, us. The opposite of lonely was this.

Cole said, "You're the only good thing I've ever done in my life."

I replied, "I'm sorry I'm such a wreck."

He kissed me again. My mouth, my throat, under my ear.

He hesitated. Pulling back, he said, "Tell me this means something to you."

It was a strange thing to be asked. It seemed like it should have been the other way around. He was the one who had been the touring rock star with countless girls on countless nights. He was the one with the cavalier smile and the easy laugh.

But that wasn't the truth. Not really. Not now. Now the truth was that I was the one with the heart of metal. I was the one always walking away.

A tear dripped off my chin and onto my leg. It was gray with my eyeliner.

I said, "Don't let me leave you."

Then, in our secret bit of Los Angeles, we kissed and slid from our clothing. His hands adored my body and my mouth explored his and in the end it was this: us us us.

Chapter Forty-Five

· COLE ·

This place, this place. Dry Venice, invented Eden, glowing New Age hipster palace where people come to believe in fate and destiny and karma and all of the things that are only true here and only if you make them true.

I was dead in Los Angeles once.

Chapter Forty-Six

· ISABEL ·

I opened my eyes and didn't know where I was. And then, even after waking more fully, I suddenly *knew*, but I didn't understand. My brain was a tangle of images and sensations. My own bare legs on top of a comforter, a streetlight moon outside a cracked window, a spidery shadow cast on the wall from a pitcher of dried baby's breath. Cole's stubbled chin in the curve of my breastbone, his side, tan and even and endless, his belly button, his hips, his legs, one of his ankles hooked over one of mine, one of his hands carelessly sprawled up against my neck, the other curled in the silky space below my breasts.

My mind took the images, finally, and put them all together into thoughts and memory. Finally, I understood: I was so, so naked.

We were in one of the bedrooms of the rental. Drunk with each other, existing in a sweaty place outside of logic, we'd stumbled in here last night and fallen asleep on top of the comforter here. Now it was some ungodly time of the morning and —

What was I even doing? Who was this other person? What was I thinking?

I extricated myself from Cole and found my clothing on the floor. I reached past it to where my phone was tucked into my purse. Two A.M. My mother would still be at work; she wouldn't be worried. But of course Sofia had been watching and waiting with sleepless owl eyes, anxious for my welfare. I had four missed calls from her.

"Hey," Cole said. He looked young and uncomplicated and half asleep. He lifted just his fingers from the comforter in my direction. Sleepily, he said again, "Hey."

I was suddenly petrified that he would say a name other than mine. I knew in a bruising, truthful way that if he said another girl's name right now, it would break my heart.

"Isabel," he said, "what are you doing?"

I didn't know. I felt unsteady on my legs. I started putting on clothing.

"I have to go," I said. My voice sounded a lot more awake than his in this room. In the light from the streetlight, I could clearly see the dresser, the mirror, the glass sculpture in the corner of the room. It seemed like it was never dark in any place in this city. I longed suddenly and fiercely for actual night, for a perfect blackness to hide me more completely.

"No," he replied simply. He lifted his entire arm now, and stretched it toward me. "Stay."

"I can't. People are — no one knows where I am. I need to go."

"They'll be okay till morning. Come back. Come sleep."

"I'm not going to sleep. I need to —" I couldn't seem to

work out how to get my dress back on. No part of it was right side out. It was all wrong sides, and my fingers were clumsy.

Cole pushed himself up on an elbow to watch me struggle angrily with the garment. Finally, I aggressively zipped it; the zipper wasn't even. Who was going to see it this time of night anyway? No one. I couldn't remember where I'd put my car keys. Maybe they were still out in the conservatory. I couldn't find them on the side table or in my purse or on the floor or — no, no, I'd come in Cole's car, I needed a cab, I'd have to call one, I couldn't even think of —

"Isabel," Cole said from right behind me. He took my elbows and turned me around to him. I resisted, body stiff. I couldn't look him in the eye. "If you have to go, I'll drive you. You're out of your mind."

"Please let go," I said, and it was the meanest thing I'd ever said, and I didn't even want what I was asking for.

He let go. I expected his face to be blank, the real Cole gone someplace where I couldn't poke at him, but he was still there. "Don't do this to me."

The emphasis, somehow, was on the word *me*. That he didn't expect me to be able to stop from doing the *this*, whatever it was, but I could at least stop aiming it at him.

I wanted my hands to stop shaking. I wanted my brain to regain control of my body.

"I have to go," I said. "I'm going to go. Don't be an asshole about it."

I didn't even know what I was saying. I just knew that I was going. I had everything together. I would call a cab. I would walk to Abbot Kinney and get into it.

Cole's voice was raw. "Fine, Isabel. Just — I get it. You get to call the shots. Call me when it's good for you, right? It doesn't matter what I need. It doesn't matter how much I . . . I get it. Whatever. I'll play your game."

I didn't reply. I was already gone.

Chapter Forty-Seven

· COLE ·

light on
which one looks good today
Maybe me
Maybe not
do i match your shoes
your hair
your face
Maybe me
Maybe not
back on the rack
stretched but not worn
i am the used

CHAPTER FORTY-EIGHT

· COLE ·

I wrote the album.

I had nothing else to do.

The L.A. sky turned overcast and smoggy. Everything looked different without the brilliant sun and saturated colors. The houses were flatter, the cracks in the streets deeper, the palms drier. It didn't feel like the L.A. I loved was gone, just like it was hiding or sleeping or had been knocked out and lay in a ditch waiting for me to find it.

I was tired of waiting. Of making. Of doing. I wanted some closure, an ending, a feeling I had gotten somewhere.

I wanted Isabel to call me and tell me she had been wrong, that she wanted me, that she loved me.

I called Leon. "Comrade. Do you want to get lunch with a famous person?"

"I wish I could," he said kindly. "But I have pickups until midnight today."

That was one thousand years from now. L.A. could be dead by then. I said, "Tomorrow, then. Chili dogs. Put it in your datebook. This time I get to drive."

I got in the Mustang and drove. I didn't know where I was going, but it took me to Santa Monica. I knew Isabel was here, but the car didn't know she didn't want to see me. I drove into a massive parking garage and sat there. I wanted to shoot up. I touched my skin where I would inject the wolf. I could almost feel it. I wondered if it was possible to invoke the shift without a needle or a temperature change, like that time I'd smelled of wolf when the topless girls came over.

I'd told Jeremy I was taking it off the table.

It was off the table. I'd meant it. It was just harder to really mean it than I'd expected. No. Not really. I knew it was going to be hard.

Withdrawal was never easy.

Isabel was just blocks away. I was tired of checking my phone for messages.

The car was getting stuffy. I opened the door and sat there in the dim blue parking garage and touched my wrist and the inside of my elbow and thought about disappearing.

I heard my name.

"Cole? Cole?"

I turned my head. It was a smallish sort of guy with a biggish nose and sort of greasy auburn curls, standing just outside the car. He was probably my age. His face had a religious cast to it. A familiar, glowing expression.

This was a fan.

I made sure I had my Cole St. Clair face on. I didn't have a pen to sign anything, but maybe he'd brought one.

"Hey," I said, climbing reluctantly from the car. I shut the door. "What's up?"

He mouthed *what's up* in a wondering, amazed way. "I'm, uh, I'm sort of, I don't know what to say. I'm sorry, I'm, uh, awkward, you're just, I'm . . ."

"That's okay, slick," I told him. "Take your time."

"I'm not a stalker, I swear, I totally am not," he said.

This was never the best way to start a conversation, but I'd heard it before. I just waited.

"I saw you come in here, I've been watching the show, I'm a huge fan of NARKOTIKA. I have, like, all of your albums, twice, and I buy them all the time to recommend them to, like, everyone I know."

There was absolutely nothing wrong with what he was saying, but for some reason, I felt a little buzz in my throat when he said *NARKOTIKA*. A sort of claustrophobic squeeze. I had had this conversation, or one a lot like it, on tour. It felt like I was living a memory instead of a minute I was really in. Like I had dreamed two years and now I was waking up and I had never left my old life behind.

"That's awesome," I told him. "Always great to meet a fan."

"Wait," he said. "Wait, it's not just that. When you disappeared, Cole . . ."

My ears felt a little ring-y.

"When you disappeared, I was having a rough time, too," he said. He pulled up his sleeves. In the crooked blue shadows of the stairwell, his arms were a mess of scars. Track marks and cutting. But old. Old scars. "But when I heard on the radio that you were in rehab, I thought, *I can do it, too.* And I did. I totally did, because of you. Because if you could come back from that, back from the dead, I could do it, too. You changed my life. That song you guys had, *I put the coffin inside/you don't need to bury me,* I know it's about, about rebirth. . . ."

"Coffinbone" wasn't about rebirth. It was about wanting to die. All of the songs back then were about wanting to die. My chest felt small.

"When I heard you were in town recording, I knew the time was right for this. And when I saw you drive in here, I knew this was my, this was my chance to tell you thanks. And show you — sorry, it's still a little raw." The guy half turned, jacking up his shirt. The skin of his back was red and angry with the irritation of a brand-new tattoo.

In cursive it said, *I put the coffin inside/you don't need to bury me.* And then a date. The date he got out of rehab or went in or something. Probably he wanted me to ask. But I didn't.

There was nothing wrong with any of it except that he'd taken a quote about wanting to die every second of every day and tattooed it on his body because he didn't understand. There was nothing really wrong with that, either, because it meant what he wanted it to mean.

But I knew what it had meant in the beginning, and the permanence of it, of marking his body forever with my desire to die, made my stomach churn sickly. The feeling didn't go away when he pulled down his shirt.

"That's amazing, man," I told him. "Good for you. Give me a — give me a fist bump."

He shivered and wiped his left eye and then gave me the

most timid fist bump known to man. He looked like he might fall down.

"I just wanted to tell you," he said again, "what an inspiration you are. I don't want to stop you from your, whatever. Oh, gosh, this is the best day of my life."

I summoned a little wave for him as I turned away. As I headed down the stairs, the metal echoed and rattled beneath me. My legs felt wobbly, and my pulse had suddenly begun to race.

He'd done everything right. He hadn't detained me. Hadn't asked me to sign his face or his dick. Just said his piece and then gone on his way. Cleaned himself up and unfairly credited me with the burden of his recovery.

But my recovery was such a fragile thing. What happened if you hung your cure on someone else's, and they turned out to be still sick? I wished for the sailing optimism of my first days here. My bulletproof confidence.

By the time I got to .blush., my skin was clammy. I could feel my heart tripping. My mind said: anxiety attack. My body just screamed. Every piece of my skin was sending a thousand messages a second to my brain. *Run. Fight. Get the hell out of here.*

There was nothing to be afraid of. Nothing to be anxious over. But then I would turn over the image of that tattoo like a shovel turning over grave dirt. And my stomach would churn. It felt as if the temperature were plummeting.

It's not cold out here, I told myself. Even overcast, it wasn't cold. I looked out at the street and imagined blistering sun brilliant on the car mirrors, white light searing the sides of the buildings. But my brain howled the cold at me. My arms were goose bumps with the fake cold.

I had known all along that the more times I forced the shift, the more likely I was to shift accidentally. I had been playing this game for weeks now.

No.

I called Isabel. My fingers were already shaking enough to make hitting the buttons difficult.

Her voice was another cool thing in the whitewashed day. "Culpep —"

"Is the store empty?"

"Cole, this isn't —"

"Is it empty?" She had to say yes, because I was already there, my face reflected in the black-ice mirror of the door, my hand on the door handle. I needed to put my head between my legs, to breathe into a damn paper bag, to shut myself in a room far away from the clouds and the world. I needed to get off the street.

"Yeah. Hey, what is —"

"I'm sorry," I said, and I hung up. I threw my phone, wallet, and keys into the potted plant by the front door.

This isn't happening.

But it was.

The second I pushed open the door to .blush., the second the air-conditioning hit my already cool skin, it was over.

Isabel stood in between tables of clothing, staring at me. Her face looked bizarre somehow, like I couldn't understand the angles of it.

My stomach seized. My skin was ragged. My breath was in

pieces. I couldn't tell her what was happening. But she didn't need to be told.

She shut her eyes, just for a second. She opened them. She said, "No. Cole, I can't.—"

But I was already a wolf.

CHAPTER FORTY-NINE

· ISABEL ·

Just like that, it had happened.

This was how to deal with disaster: Isolate the worst part of the problem. Identify a solution. Tune out every bit of noise.

Here was the disaster: Cole St. Clair was a wolf in the middle of Santa Monica, trapped in my place of work, a business I had just been setting up for a private showing Sierra had this evening. It would have been bad any other time, but now, it meant that a wolf stood in the front of a store currently lit by one hundred candles.

Isolate the worst part of the problem.

Cole St. Clair.

Identify a solution.

It was enough to make me want to give up.

There he was, in the flesh, everything I'd been afraid of. It was not a monster. It just wasn't Cole.

It was every wolf I'd left behind in Minnesota. It was every hurtling, grief-saturated memory that galloped into my mind. It was every tear I hadn't cried since I'd moved.

The wolf didn't move. Its ears swiveled slowly toward me and away, back toward the street noise. The hackles of its lovely coat were scuffed up into feral suspicion. As before, just as I remembered, the eyes were still Cole's: brilliant green and intense. But everything that made him Cole was stripped from them, replaced with instinct and image.

He was poised for flight, but there was nowhere to go.

I should have never let him back into my life.

The wonder of Sierra's creations was that he didn't look out of place here, as long as he didn't move. He looked stuffed and intentional. I had seen plenty of stuffed animals in my time. Thanks, Dad.

That spurred my brain into movement.

Think, Isabel.

I took in the scene: wolf, pile of clothing, candles.

Isolate the worst part of the problem.

The candles weren't a problem yet. Discovery wasn't a problem yet. Those were only possibilities.

The problem was the wolf. And if I thought about it, I knew the answer to this. I knew enough about the science to know that his body defaulted to human in this weather. The wolves back in Minnesota shifted into wolves in the winter, but this store was only a temporary winter. I didn't know why the air-conditioning had made him shift now of all times, but I had seen its effect on him right in front of me.

Identify a solution.

I glanced toward the wall opposite, where the thermostat was.

Heat.

I glanced up at the clock on the wall. Fifteen minutes until Sierra was supposed to get here to start setting up the champagne. My heart was thumping.

Damn you, Cole, damn you —

I took a step, just to see what would happen.

The wolf's head jerked to follow the motion. There was nothing overtly aggressive about the move, but still, everything in the wolf's posture suddenly looked dangerous. I saw the knot of shoulder muscles beneath the fur. I heard the thin, barely there scrape of nails on concrete as his paws tensed. I saw the dead-white canine as he silently lifted his lip and then dropped it again.

A warning.

As a wolf, Cole didn't know me. He wouldn't go out of his way to rip my throat out. But if I threatened him, nothing would stop him, either.

I cut my eyes away from him. Staring would only be seen as a challenge. I took another step. Then another. I wasn't getting any closer to him. No threat.

The wolf turned, swift and sinuous, and left a noseprint on the inside of the glass door before turning back. Low to the ground, wary, he moved farther into the store.

As long as he didn't come over here — I had made it to the thermostat. I flicked on the heat and turned it all the way up.

On the other side of the store, the wolf caught a sudden glimpse of himself in one of the decorative mirrors that leaned against the walls. He jerked back, surprised.

His haunch hit one of the tables. Three tall candles sat on the topmost part of it, above a display of taupe tops with seagrass woven sleeves.

In the mirror, I saw the reflection of the lit candles wobble. I held my breath.

The candles tumbled.

For one brief moment, as one of the candles fell and went out, I thought it would be okay. And then the other two hit. One of them rolled off to the side and sputtered. The third landed on a top, and it caught. The fire bit into the sea grass.

Damn you, Sierra —

The reflection of the growing flame caught the wolf's attention. Even lower to the ground, he slunk away, fast, but there was still nowhere to go. He was trying to look brave and aggressive, but this world was small and unfamiliar and fiery, and he couldn't bluster himself out of this trap.

It was starting to get hot in here. *Come on, Cole. Come on.*

The burning display began to release uneven smoke in opaque clouds. In two seconds, the fire alarm was going to go off.

All I needed was for the fire department to show up and call the cops to shoot this wolf.

Isolate the worst part of the problem.

I took my chances. I grabbed a vegan leather jacket from the wall and bolted across to the burning display. I beat the flames. I didn't know what vegan leather was, but it melted.

As I hit the flames again and again, the wolf shot away from me, back toward the front of the store. His eyes were locked on me. Making sure I wasn't a threat. Or maybe looking at the fire, making sure it wasn't a threat. In any case, he didn't see the frontmost display in time. He barreled right into it. This one was lit with low, stubby candles that wouldn't tip. But he crashed right into it. I smelled a quick flash of singed fur.

Overhead, the fire alarm went off. Loud and pure and continuous.

And he broke.

The wolf clawed up the table opposite, dashing candles every which way. Everywhere, I saw flames catching and holding. The tables of shirts, the racks of leggings, Cole's piled clothing. Even Sierra's plants gave themselves up, dried leaves curling first, and then the others wicking the fire hungrily. It was as if this entire place had been rigged as a bomb.

I dashed to the back counter and got my bottle of water. I soaked the edge of one display. It was such a useless gesture. In the back room — was there something larger? When was the fire department going to get here? Did I just let the wolf out into the street?

I couldn't think. The fire alarm screamed at me to get out.

Cole had pressed himself into a corner, ears flat back against his head, shaking.

"How can this not be hot enough for you?" I snarled.

But it was hot enough. Because he was shaking with the shift. Now his paws had become fingers, and they clutched the wall and scrabbled on the concrete, and his head was bent, shuddering, and then it was Cole, the boy, the monster. Naked and human, curled in the corner.

I hurt. Everything in my heart hurt so bad, seeing him, smelling the wolf, watching everything get absolutely destroyed.

His eyes were wide. Flames flickered in the shine of them.

"God," he said.

The flames came no closer because of the concrete floor and walls. The only thing in here for the fire to eat was everything Sierra had made and everything I'd grown.

I heard sirens in the distance. Fire. Police. Cameras. Proof.

"You can't be here," I told him, more furious than I could imagine, though I didn't know yet what, exactly, I was furious at. I hurriedly kicked off my boots and peeled off my leggings from under my long tunic. I threw them at him. "Put those on. Get out. Go out the back."

The windows out front were suddenly filled with the dark red of the fire truck.

"But —"

My stomach felt sick with the ruin of all of it. In five minutes, Sierra was going to pull up. Nothing felt real. Or else, this was real, and nothing else had ever been.

I screamed, *"Get out of my life."*

Cole shook his head like *he* was angry, and then he jerked on my favorite leggings. The front door came open, a suited fireman framed by it.

"Are you alone?" shouted the fireman.

I glanced over to the corner. Cole was gone.

When something caught on fire, you could say *It went up in flames* or *It all burned down*. Up and down at once. Everywhere. It was all just destroyed.

I said, "Yeah."

Chapter Fifty

· COLE ·

This is what they don't tell you about being a werewolf.

They don't tell you you'll have to run from a burning building wearing a pair of too-tight rainbow-skull-printed leggings to avoid being implicated in arson. They don't tell you that when you run to your car, you'll remember you threw your car keys into a potted plant in front of the building you just burned down and that you'll have to return to the scene of the crime with as much discretion as a three-fourths grown man in a pair of very shiny leggings can manage before the personal effects can be found by someone who might rename them "evidence."

They don't tell you that when you kneel with grace and dignity to retrieve the keys, you'll rip the seam of the shimmery leggings right up from the ankle to what God gave you.

They'd probably tell you that being naked in public was illegal, if you asked.

But they don't tell you how tiring it is to run from cops when you've just been two species in quick succession and then had to run to your car and then back again.

They don't tell you how this long-haired guy will try to give you his number as you're running and flapping and bouncing your way back to the parking lot in the most circuitous way possible, so as to not lead the cops back to your Mustang, which by now you wish had died in the last fire you set.

They don't tell you how many people are going to get photos of Cole St. Clair, three-fourths naked, running around Santa Monica.

They don't tell you how hot black cloth seats get after the sun's come out and you sit in them and you're wearing nothing or next to it.

They don't tell you how even though you won't remember a thing from when you were a wolf, you'll remember the look on your now-ex-girlfriend's face right before and right after for the rest of your life.

They don't tell you anything. No, that's not true.

They tell you, *Come on, be a wolf. You've been looking for something for a while, and this, boy, is what you were looking for.*

CHAPTER FIFTY-ONE

· COLE ·

F♮ LIVE: *Today on the wire we have young Cole St. Clair, former lead singer of NARKOTIKA. We had him on the show five weeks ago, just after he signed on with Baby North of SharpT33th.com. Did I hear a collective gasp? No worries, he's survived, it seems. You're just about done with the album, right?*

COLE ST. CLAIR: *Da.*

F♮ LIVE: *How would you rate the experience on a scale of one to ten?*

COLE ST. CLAIR: *Somewhere between an* F *and a hydra.*

F♮ LIVE: *That's the kind of math I expect from rock stars. You told me before we started rolling that you had just one track left to record. Then what?*

COLE ST. CLAIR: *You tell me.*

F♮ LIVE: *How world-weary you sound! How did you find L.A.? You staying with us?*

COLE ST. CLAIR: *I love L.A., but I broke her things. I don't think it's going to work out.*

F♮ LIVE: *You broke a lot fewer things than most of us expected.*

COLE ST. CLAIR: *What can I say, I'm a changed man. We gonna listen to that teaser track now?*

F♮ LIVE: *You East Coasters are always in a hurry.*

COLE ST. CLAIR: *I don't think I'm really an East Coaster. I'm — what's that term? Currently without country.*

F♮ LIVE: *L.A. still wants you, boy.*

COLE ST. CLAIR: *Martin, if only that were true.*

Chapter Fifty-Two

· ISABEL ·

I knew that at some point soon, I was going to have to return Virtual Cole to Cole. I knew from both it and the radio and the calendar that he was nearly done with the album, and by extension, the show. And by further extension, Los Angeles.

By further, further extension, me.

Only that wasn't true. I'd been done with him first.

Maybe I'd just leave his phone at the apartment gate. Then it would finally be over, really and truly. No loose ends.

The only problem in all of this was how much I missed him.

It never went away. It never got any less. I kept thinking that if I just kept myself busy, finished this class, applied for colleges, researched futures that took me away, I would stop missing him for at least one minute of one day.

But everything in this goddamn city reminded me of him.

Sierra called me a few days after the fire. "Sweetness? I'm so sorry I yelled at you."

In her defense, she had found me standing in the smoldering remains of her business. "I think shouting was appropriate."

"Not at you, lovely. I know that now. I'm so terribly sorry I blamed you."

It also turned out that she was sorry that she had gotten busted for ordering an employee to violate fire code with all of the candles and none of the fire extinguishers. Turns out she was hoping I wouldn't sue her.

"How long until you reopen?" I asked. I didn't want to have to apply for a new job. I wanted to go back to not giving a damn.

"All of the Fall line is gone," Sierra said. "I have to make it all from scratch. I don't know if the energy is balanced in that place anymore. I don't know. I have to make some tough decisions."

"I'm so sorry," I said. I was surprised to hear myself say it. I was more surprised to hear myself mean it.

"Oh, I was in such a rut, gorgeous. This is good for me! All of my old ideas are gone and a new Sierra emerges! Do come to the next party. I am still sorry about yelling. I won't yell again. Ah! I have to run. Ta, lovely. Ta."

I hung up. Thinking of her party made me think of Mark, which made me think of Cole.

I missed him. I missed him all the time.

The only thing that made it a little better was the foyer of the House of Ruin. My mother had already replaced all of the marriage and wedding shots that had hung there. The photos of her and my father had become photos of me and her, looking identical and sisterly. Or just her, grinning at the camera with her medical school diploma in her hands. Only, she should have known better with that last photo. Because even though my father's face wasn't in it, he still technically was. That grin she wore had been for him as he snapped the picture.

It didn't matter for my purposes, though. Because all I needed out of the wall was the absolute reminder that 50 percent of all American marriages ended in divorce, and the rest of them were on their way there.

I would stop loving Cole. That was just the fact of it. This wall was proof that one day, I would stop caring.

I closed my eyes. Not all the way. If I sealed the lids, it would break the surface tension, and then these tears would escape.

"Isabel, you should come with," Sofia told my back.

My eyes flew open, wide as they would go. I didn't turn around.

"With? With who?"

"Dad and me," she said. "We're going —"

"No, I'm busy." I could feel her still standing right there, so I added, "Thanks for asking."

She didn't move. I didn't have to turn to know that she was working her courage up to say something. I wanted to tell her to spit it out, but I didn't have any energy left over to be mean.

"You're not busy," Sofia said bravely. "I've been watching. Something's wrong. You don't — you don't have to talk about it, but I think you should come with us."

I couldn't believe that I'd been so bad at hiding my feelings. I couldn't believe, either, that I had somehow lost enough of my prickly exterior to make Sofia think it was acceptable to call me on it.

"Say yes," Sofia said. "I won't pester you."

"You *are* pestering me!" I spun. She didn't look chastened, though her hands were folded in front of her.

"It's really nice outside," she added. "I'm bringing my erhu. We're going to go sit on the beach."

She unfolded her hands, and then she took one of mine. Her fingers were very soft and warm, like she had no bones. What the hell. It couldn't make me feel worse, surely. When Sofia gave a gentle tug, I didn't resist. At least until I got to the door.

"Wait, my boots." I also meant *my hair. And face. And clothing. And heart.* So many things really needed to be put in order before I left the house.

"We're going to the *beach*," Sofia said. She let go of my hand and swiped up a pair of my mother's flip-flops from the pile of shoes by the wall. She dumped them into my grip and went to get her erhu.

Unbelievably, I ended up driving her to the beach in flip-flops and gym pants and a tank top, with my hair like a homeless person's. I parked at the edge of the lot, where a bunch of sweatily buff boys played volleyball. My uncle (ex-uncle?) Paolo was already there, still in his EMT uniform, which reminded me horribly of the cops in the bass-player episode of Cole's show. He ruffled Sofia's hair like a kid's (she smiled blissfully) and draped his arm over Sofia's shoulder. "I was going to bring cupcakes. But then I thought, no, Sofia is going to make something that'll make whatever you bring look like crap! So I brought booze instead!"

He didn't mean actual booze, of course, just local root beer, the outsides of the bottles moist with condensation. Sofia was delighted, as she had, of course, made bakery-perfect cupcakes. I was impressed with Paolo's knowledge of his daughter.

They were so keenly cheerful in each other's presence that I felt like a third wheel as I helped carry things out to an empty spot on the beach. Sofia spread a blanket and her father pulled out a pile of do-it-yourself magazines that he'd collected for her. I really wanted to see calculation in it, some sense that he'd done all of this to make up for abandoning her with Lauren, but I couldn't. Because he was clearly just an overworked and over-tired EMT who was genuinely happy to steal the time to see his daughter, who he knew really well.

There was only one person who knew me that well.

It would be better after he left town. When I didn't know exactly where he was. I needed to get rid of Virtual Cole. I'd drop it off tonight. I knew he was going to the studio to finish the album. I'd leave it on his car.

I couldn't let myself think about it too hard.

Sofia and her father chattered back and forth, both of them talking wildly with their hands, and then Sofia took out her erhu and played. You could hear it up and down the beach, but no one cared. This was L.A. They'd heard everything.

I lay back on my elbows, eyes closed to the sky, my scalp tickling because my hair kept brushing the sand behind me. My bare feet were off the blanket into the sand, and I dug my toes in.

In my head, Cole kept dropping his head onto my shoulder in the cemetery. He kept becoming a wolf. He kept building everything up and burning it down.

Just think of going to class, Isabel. I told myself. *Getting a degree. Becoming a doctor. This is life.*

I wondered how long it would be before my father came to visit and take me to the beach before returning to his San Diego life.

Sofia stopped playing.

My uncle asked me, "Do you want to talk about it?"

This was because I was crying. I sat up and pulled up my knees and drew them closer and closer until I was crying into them.

Life *sucked*.

Sofia put her hand on my back, which normally I wouldn't have ever tolerated, but I was just too done to protest.

"It'll get easier," Paolo said.

But I *knew* that. That was the worst part. The worst part was that eventually you forgot about the people you loved. The dead ones and the ones who raised you and the ones you wanted to be with at the end of the day.

I had learned before my CNA class that the body produced three kinds of tears, each with a unique chemical makeup. One of them was generated regularly to keep your eyes moist. The second sprang to life when the eye got something in it, like debris, lubricating and washing out the intruder. The third happened when sadness built up inside you. The chemicals produced through depression were carried out of the body through these tears. You were crying your sadness out.

So I knew there was a scientific reason why I felt better after I cried.

But knowing that didn't take away the fact that I did feel a little better.

Finally, I lifted my head just enough to rest my cheek on my knees. I asked my uncle, "Do you still love Aunt Lauren?"

I waited for Sofia's hand to tense on my back, but it didn't.

Paolo made a rueful face. "I like her. She's a nice woman."

"Then what happened?"

He thought about it. I thought about how my face probably looked like a battlefield. Sofia gathered my hair into a ponytail and then released it again.

Finally, he said, "We weren't friends, I guess. It was just love. Infatuation. So we didn't really do things together unless it was a date night. We needed an excuse. And after a while, we just didn't bother making excuses anymore. We had other friends. We didn't really grow apart. We just weren't ever together. It was a failure of friendship."

I thought about me and Cole. Were we friends? Or was it just infatuation?

I felt Sofia lay her head on my back and then sigh. She must've looked sad, because her father looked sad, too. He said, "Only marry your best friend, Sofia. That's my dad advice."

I said, "I thought you were supposed to chase her dates away with a shotgun. I thought *that* was dad advice."

"Maybe *your* dad," Paolo said. "He shoots lots of things, joy included."

Both he and I laughed, sharp and surprised and guilty. I sat up, shoving Sofia off, and rearranged so that my shoulder was against hers. I held out a hand for a root beer. For the first time

in a week, I didn't feel awful. I might be okay. I might survive this.

I thought about returning Virtual Cole tonight. The options
of putting it in Cole's hand myself or leaving it on his car.

Then I thought of a third idea.

I pulled out Virtual Cole and then my phone. I checked to
make sure I had Baby's phone number programmed in to it.

"I have to make a call. Do you mind?" I gestured to Virtual
Cole. "This is actually Baby's phone. I'm going to return it
tonight."

As I stood, Sofia started to pat my shoulder before realizing
that I wouldn't tolerate it now that I wasn't crying. She tapped
the neck of her root beer against mine instead. We were learning each other.

As I dialed Baby, I wondered if I was really doing this.

This was life. This is what it looked like. This was
happening.

CHAPTER FIFTY-THREE

· COLE ·

The last track took forever, and I was sure it was making pretty shitty television. I'd saved it for last because it was the most difficult — I wasn't good at slow stuff that was supposed to be pretty. It was easy to hide a lack of songwriting with some thrashing drums or a flailing tempo. People would forgive all kinds of deficiencies as long as they could dance to it.

But "Lovers (Killers)" wasn't a dance tune. It was going to be the outro, the last one on the album, the last sound in the listener's ear. I couldn't cheat.

We were seven hours into the recording process. I thought both Leyla and Jeremy wanted to kill me, but were too evolved to say it out loud. I was making Leyla record her drum part for the ninth — tenth? maybe tenth — time. I sat in the big recording room on the vinyl couch, the room headphones on my head, listening to Leyla playing her kit in the isolation booth. Jeremy looked asleep or at peace on the opposite end of the couch.

On the other side of the soulless studio, T and Joan looked

as if they were hoping for sleep, too. This hadn't been the most riveting episode so far. I kept waiting for Baby to spring something on me, but it seemed like she, too, was tired of playing the game.

Leyla picked her way through the track again. Unlike the rest of us, she improved as the hours stretched, like she unwound into a different version of herself. If she was this much better after ten times, I probably ought to make her do it three or four more times and see what happened. It was a little bit of a shame that it had taken six weeks to learn how to work with her, and now it was about to be over.

Over.

A lot of my brain was on the Mustang parked outside. Before I'd come over here, I had packed everything I'd brought from Minnesota back into my backpack, and put it in the tiny backseat. Tonight I was staying at Jeremy's, and in the morning I was doing some wrap-up stuff with Baby and a couple of interviews with some magazines. And then —

I didn't even know.

I didn't want to go back to Minnesota. But I couldn't stay here. I saw *her* everywhere, in everything. Maybe one day I could come back, but not now, not like this. I couldn't spend every day looking at L.A. but not feeling it inside me.

I dropped my head into my hands, listening. There was no reason to have Leyla redo her drums. She was fine. It was my vocal track that needed work. I sounded like I'd been anesthetized.

Standing, I made a chopping motion across my neck to the sound engineer in the mixing room. I had tried and failed to remember his name, and now, at this late point in the game, it seemed pointless to try again. "She's fine. It's good. I need to get back in there, though."

Everyone in the room heaved a collected sigh, except for Jeremy. He just said, "Eventually, it'll have to be over, Cole."

"It's over when I say it's over." I headed into the tiny, glass-walled isolation booth.

In the booth, I slid the headphones on again, and as the engineer adjusted the levels and got ready to record another vocal track, I tried to think of how I'd improve on my previous attempt. Maybe I should just add another layer of harmonies this time around.

Or maybe I should stop sounding like I was heartbroken.

I fidgeted. I was well aware that the cameras could see me through the walls of the booth. It was a goldfish bowl.

"Okay," the engineer said. "You're good. Go for it."

I heard the now endlessly familiar synthesizer loop that began "Lovers (Killers)" and then Leyla's tapped-in drum, and then Jeremy's tripping, gentle bass line. My voice sang in my ears, a Cole who was weary and heartbroken and homesick for a home he hadn't left yet but was about to. I kept waiting for a place that begged for me to put down another layer, but nothing stood out.

I closed my eyes and just listened to my sung miserable confession.

I didn't want to go.

Because of the headphones, I felt more than heard the door open. A rush of cooler air entered the booth.

I opened my eyes.

Isabel stood in the door, cool and elegant as a handgun.

Behind her, through the glass, I saw the cameras pointed at us, and Baby standing in the double doors that had been opened to the night. In the parking lot beyond, several hundred people were gathered, craning their necks to see inside.

I didn't understand.

Isabel stepped into the booth. Reaching up, she pulled off the headphones, setting them carefully down onto the stool beside me. I couldn't tell from her face what she was thinking.

Baby's smile was so giant and the camera angles so favorably pointed at Isabel that I knew that, impossibly, Isabel must have agreed to be filmed. Agreed to be on the Cole St. Clair show. Dozens of faces crowded closer through the door, trying to get a better look at whatever was happening. They looked . . . anticipatory.

"Isabel —" I started. But I didn't know what was happening, so I couldn't finish it.

"Ta-da," Isabel said. The big microphone in front of me picked up her voice and played it through the headphones sitting on the stool. A smile was threatening on her face. A real one.

"Culpeper, maybe I don't like ta-das," I said, even though there was nothing in the world I liked better.

She knew it, so she just put her arms tightly around me. It was the first time I'd felt her hold me before I held her first. The first time I felt her hold me like she wanted to hold me more than anything.

She said, loud enough for the microphone to pick it up again, "Stay."

But I *had* been staying. She had always been the one going. "How do I know you'll stay, too?"

In my ear, she whispered, "I love you."

She rested her face on my shoulder, and I pressed mine into hers, and we just held each other. Like something solid, for once. I thought of all those times standing on a ledge, real or not, looking for something real or not, never finding what I needed.

I felt it now. This was what I needed.

The heart was pumping sunlight.

I didn't want to think about the cameras, but now that I could breathe again, it was hard not to. And it was hard not to realize that Isabel had framed an absolutely perfect ending episode to this show, because she was a diabolical genius and she knew me. How that crowd must be dying inside right now.

I felt Isabel shaking, and it took me a moment to realize she was laughing soundlessly and witheringly.

"Fine," she whispered into my collarbone. "Just do it. I know you're thinking it, so just do it."

She lifted her head. I looked at her. She asked, just loud enough for the microphone to pick up, "Why did you even come here, Cole?"

I touched her chin. This place, this beautiful place, this girl, this beautiful girl, this music, this life. "I came here for you."

And her mouth quirked, because she knew it was no less real for saying it in front of a crowd.

Then we kissed the perfect kiss. The people in the studio went absolutely insane.

I'd known how to pull off the way just fine when I was just Cole St. Clair.

But we did it better together.

Epilogue

· COLE ·

F♮ LIVE: *Today on the wire we have young Cole St. Clair, lead singer of NARKOTIKA, giving his first interview since* Heart (Attack) *released. Cole, most bands tour after their release. Instead, you've opened a recording studio. Let's discuss. Actually, let me go deeper. Since you moved to L.A., you've survived a stint on reality TV, recorded two pretty damn hot albums, opened a recording studio, produced Skidfield's hugely successful debut album, and digitally released a new song every month this year, culminating in* Heart (Attack). *All the while, you've refused the advances of every major label. Please tell me you've also finally gotten a dog.*

COLE ST. CLAIR: *No dog. But we've decided to keep Leyla on as our drummer, and she's pretty hairy.*

F♮ LIVE: *Do you think of yourself as a label? Is that happening?*

COLE ST. CLAIR: *Whoa, whoa, Martin. Keep your shorts on. "Label" sounds a lot like commitment. It's more like,* sometimes friends come over to the studio and we throw some stuff together.

F♮ LIVE: *Friends like Skidfield?*

COLE ST. CLAIR: *Yeah.*

F♮ LIVE: *That thing you "threw together" with them sold over a million copies.*

COLE ST. CLAIR: *Yeah, well, they're good friends.*

F♮ LIVE: *I'll bet the — What's that noise?*

COLE ST. CLAIR: *Los Angeles. Leon, can't you make these people move? Martin, possibly you remember my fearless driver. Say hello.*

LEON: *Hello.*

F♮ LIVE: *Leon! Where are you taking our fearless hero today? To record another indie hit? To take over Broadway?*

LEON: *Can I tell him?*

F♮ LIVE: *Tell me what? Is that Cole shouting? What did he say?*

LEON: *He said, "Now I don't have to work anymore!" His girlfriend is graduating from medical school today.*

F♮ LIVE: *Wait — this is Isabel, right? The girl from the show. Put Cole back on.*

COLE ST. CLAIR: *Of course it's the girl from the show. Who else is there? Congratulate me. I always wanted to date a doctor.*

F♮ LIVE: *Congratulations. After th —*

COLE ST. CLAIR: *You know what — yes. Yeah, I'm just going to get out of the car here.*

F♮ LIVE: *Wait! Where are you? Are you on the freeway?*

COLE ST. CLAIR: *Yep. You know what, Martin, that's what I'm going to do. I'm hopping out here. You should go ahead and play that track I sent you, and I'll call you back to see how the world liked it.*

F♮ LIVE: *Look both ways, Cole! Look both ways!*

COLE ST. CLAIR: *Always. All right, I'm out. Leon, you coming with?*

F♮ LIVE: *Is he?*

F♮ LIVE: *Cole?*

F♮ LIVE: *Leon? Is anyone still in that car? Well.*

F♮ LIVE: *Ladies and gentlemen, that was Cole St. Clair of NARKOTIKA.*

MAGGIE STIEFVATER

is the #1 *New York Times* bestselling author of
the novels *Shiver*, *Linger*, and *Forever*. Her
novel *The Scorpio Races* was awarded a Printz
Honor, and the first three novels in The Raven
Cycle, *The Raven Boys*, *The Dream Thieves*, and
Blue Lily, Lily Blue, each received five starred
reviews and were named to numerous best-of-
the-year lists. She is also the author of *Lament:
The Faerie Queen's Deception* and *Ballad: A
Gathering of Faerie*. She lives in Virginia with
her husband and their two children. You can visit
her online at www.maggiestiefvater.com.